Book Two, La Patron's Sword Series

Sword of Mercy

Mercy wasn't in his nature until she came along

Sydney Addae

Sword of Mercy – Book Two, La Patron's Sword Series
Sydney Addae
Copyright 2014 by Addae, Sydney
ISBN: 978-1-937334-65-9
First Edition Electronic December 2014
Print January 2016
Published by Sitting Bull Publications, LLC

Sword of Mercy

BOOKTWO OF LA PATRON'S SWORD SERIES

Scrambling to stay one step ahead of the Liege, Asia and Hawke discover more than they had bargained for.

Hawke discovers his Alpha was also his father and that he had been given to the Liege as part of an experiment gone bad. Mercy has no place in his heart for the treachery he discovers. It takes his mate's loving hand and cool head to keep him from destroying those La Patron entrusts him to protect.

Asia isn't big on family, but she understands the basics. Family is important, to a point. But her mate's family delivers a bag of surprises that she isn't prepared for. It takes Jasmine and Silas to help steer the newly mated pair through the halls of family drama and come out on top in Sword of Mercy.

<<◇>>

This book may be read alone, however, it is a continuation of the La Patron, Alphas Alpha series. To understand the depth of the relationships between Jasmine, Silas, Asia, Angus and Hawke, I suggest you read the following books. BirthRight, book one is a free read and sets the tone for the series.

Book one is BirthRight,
Book two is BirthControl
Book three is BirthMark
Book four is BirthStone
Book five is BirthDate
Book six is BirthSign
Sword of Inquest

Thanks to all my Den-mates and admins, Michelle and Vicky, you are all the best at keeping me laughing with new creative ideas. I heart you much.

A special shout out to Sally R., Karen M., and Kelly, I could not have presented this story without your help.

Thanks

Sydney

Chapter 1

The plane landed in a small private landing field fifty miles from Bucharest in Romania. Boris Lancaster gazed out the window at the dreary landscape and felt a connection to the old country. Animals grazed nearby and barely glanced in the direction of the plane as they taxied. There were no overt signs of prosperity. If crops had been planted in the fields opposite the small landing strip, nothing showed above ground. From his vantage point inside, everything appeared frozen in time.

Had it been a century ago, he had bartered his soul for a position of power with Lord Konstantin? Or longer? His father had been certain the stately older man had the answers to all life's problems and all but worshipped Konstantin. Those had been the days, the government sat back and allowed men to rule men without interference. He sighed and shifted in his seat waiting for the plane to come to a complete stop, and longed for the comfort of his Colorado condo. The weather was cold, crisp and perfect this time of year.

Roderick, the leader of the Liege, sent him to oversee Hawke's downfall and to capture his mate, Angus. Time confused Roderick, made him forget critical elements of the Black Wolf's nature. Once a black wolf tasted freedom, they would die rather than return to captivity. The chances of Roderick "unwrapping" Angus were slim to none. But since Roderick had allowed him to bring the crown prince of project LOBO, Damian, he kept those facts quiet. Especially with the last insult, they had asked for his resignation as lead on LOBO, Boris was not inclined to remind any of the ingrates of many things, like the covenant, or the limitations of their products or that Damian lacked a proper tracking computer chip. Next time they won't be so hasty to undermine him.

Damian, seed of Hawke, his prize protégé, had been born and raised within the Liege compounds and was one hundred percent loyal to them. He had no idea of pack, or family or memories that needed altering. The pup had been refitted with metal arms and legs when he reached his teens. Damian passed every test they had, and scored higher than everyone, except Asia and Hawke, while maintaining control of his beast. He and Roderick agreed field testing for the young Alpha would help prepare the wolf for future jobs. Several countries requested services similar to the ones Asia had performed and they wanted to send Damian after testing. Gordon, another Liege, requested they spend additional funds on surgeries for the pup and insisted they invest the same money and time on Damian as they had on his sire, Hawke, or at the very least, Asia. Dealing with Gordon would tax his patience, but he would complete his version of this assignment and return to LOBO by the end of next week, or sooner.

The door to the plane opened and Councilman Jeddick stood at the bottom of the stairs. Damian walked out first, scenting the air as he buttoned his sports coat and scanned the area. He took a few steps looking around and then looked over his shoulder and nodded. Boris stepped onto the ladder, holding his satchel filled with documents that needed work. Hawke made a mess of the files and some would never be recovered, which set them back on the projects he'd been working on. The tranquilizer formula for one thing had been erased and a team of scientists had been trying to recreate it in the lab but hadn't gotten it exact. Which put a dent in their financial and marketing plan since they had to cancel pending and incoming orders.

"Welcome home, Lord Lancaster," Councilman Jeddick said bowing low. Boris walked past him without acknowledging the greeting. Instead, he headed to the car and slid into the back seat while Damian rode up front with the driver leaving Jeddick on the tarmac.

There had been too many losses and he needed to rectify that as quickly as possible. Jeddick would be eager to get on his good side and would make a decent sacrifice to the cause. Pity they'd lost Councilman Connall, he had been a quick thinker and kept the Liege current on things they needed to know. Jeddick made it known to them that he welcomed a closer alliance with the Liege, but refused the surgical implant, which would allow them to monitor his movements and see through his eyes. The kill chip had been the deal breaker in the end stopping negotiations.

Boris opened his bag and pulled out two pictures. Hawke and then his mate, Angus Black Wolf. Of all the rotten luck, Hawke and Angus, those two would be difficult to destroy, but that was his mission and he refused to fail again. His phone beeped with an incoming message. He shook his head.

"I knew you'd be pissed," he murmured reading the message from Lord Gordon. Boris glanced at his watch and then shoved his phone into his pocket as they turned onto the main highway leading to Odessa. Gordon would be a problem. The man thought of Damian as a son of sorts and objected to him being on the continent without a full vote of the board. With Lord Phinneas' recent filling of Griffith's spot, and Roderick approving Damian's trip, Gordon would have been out-voted but that wouldn't stop the hard headed man. Even though the man had not mentioned his arrival, Boris expected Gordon to arrive within days.

When the car pulled in front of the luxury hotel, Damian got out, checked the area and then opened the door. Boris walked into the lobby without looking right or left, expecting the hotel manager to meet him and escort them to the floor he'd reserved for his use. The manager, a short, stout Midwestern man stood in the middle of the lobby and personally ushered them to their space.

Once alone, Boris placed a laptop on the table and motioned to Damian, who stood near the kitchen area, to boot it up. Boris pulled out a sheaf of papers and made plans to bring Hawke to his knees. After all the surgeries Hawke endured, killing him would be near impossible. Plus, who knew what a mated Hawke could do at this point. The only way to get to Hawke would be through his mate. Angus's age, over three hundred, and his connection to La Patron, made taking him down hard and risky. The challenge of defeating these two powerful Alphas caused his heartbeat to race with excitement.

He glanced at Damian. The young wolf favored his sire, but lacked the mental sharpness and strong will of

Hawke. Boris couldn't think of a more fitting end, Hawke destroyed by his son's hand.

He pulled out a private cell phone and placed the call. "I'm here. Pick up the package so we can finish this. No failure, no excuses, no second chances."

Chapter 2

Dark clouds rolled into the room like an impending storm. Cold blocks of concrete made up the walls in the dank, dingy room. A lone window near the ceiling allowed slivers of moonlight to brighten the space. A scratching sound against the cobblestone floor grabbed his attention. A lone black pup cowered in the corner, shaking and shrinking as far back as it could in the shadows. A large masculine hand grabbed its front paws, lifted it and without mercy threw it back on the ground. The pup's side rose and fell in slow, deep movements to breathe.

The hand placed a leash around the pup's neck, causing the pup to bark and struggle to break free. The leash tightened and pulled the pup along the dirty floor without waiting for the pup to stand.

Painful whimpering from the pup speared Hawke's gut. He reached forward to remove the leash. The pup increased to the size of an adult wolf and snapped at his hand. He jumped back, confused by the waves of hate rolling off the wolf.

A nearby sound caught his attention. A large Black Wolf walked in front of him and sat a few feet away. The lone black pup had returned to the size of a pup and sat shaking while watching the large black wolf. In time the pup inched forward until it reached the Black Wolf and rested against him. The Black Wolf looked over his shoulder at Hawke, his green gaze penetrated his mind.

"W*rongs must be righted, soon you will understand.*"

Hawke jackknifed in the bed. Sweat poured from his forehead wetting his chest and the bed. Asia's hand fell from his chest as he gulped down air. What the hell? Dust from his dream hit the back of his tongue, the scraping sound of the pup rang in his ears and the fierce green gaze of the majestic black wolf seared his mind. Had it been a dream? It seemed so real.

"What's wrong?"

Sleep filled fuzziness filtered through their link as he gazed down at her. "I'm not sure. This dream… I don't know what it means, but I think I should." Her hand rubbed up and down his chest as she sent warm comforting waves of peace through him. When his breathing stabilized, he pulled her close and kissed the top of her head. The green gaze remained front and center in his mind while he tried to relax. Hawke's heartbeat refused to slow down and his thoughts continued flying at a rapid pace. Something happened, something that would impact him in some way. Over the past three and a half decades living beneath Liege rule, he needed a break before dealing with cosmic drama and puzzles.

"Tell me about it," Asia said after placing the side of her face on his chest and rubbing the middle of his ribcage with her index finger.

He looked around the room they had been sharing as Chacal's guests for the past month and exhaled. How to explain the unexplainable? Fortunately the Goddess had blessed him with a mate who understood his past and everything he had gone through living with the Liege. Without fanfare, he told her of his dream and waited for her to explain it to him.

"Could mean a lot of things," she said when he finished. "We've been tracking down leads to find the missing black pups since the castle fell. It shouldn't be a surprise you're dreaming of one."

She had a point, but he couldn't let it go. "Except this had a personal feel to it, like it was a personal message from Alpha Black Wolf. A wrong being righted. And the pup, first small and then when I tried to help free it, it was full sized and then small again."

Her head moved against his chest and he ran his palm up and down her arm. "You're right. That does sound personal. Have you ever seen a room like that? Maybe we can find the location, maybe the pup wants you to find him."

"Or her." He placed a kiss on her soft, fragrant hair.

Her head lifted and she looked at him. "Her?"

He shrugged. "Just saying the pup could've been a bitch. I don't know. I didn't get a sense of gender at all. Which was strange now that I think about it. What if there are two pups? One full grown and the other still a pup? The adult wolf hated me for some reason." The hate disturbed him on a visceral level he couldn't explain. Hawke was certain he'd never seen the pup or the wolf before and yet they disliked him. Was the Liege involved in some way? He didn't see a connection but that didn't mean much. That group specialized in remaining in the shadows until they wanted to be seen.

"Two pups would be stretching it, don't you think? Maybe the adult wolf had been the pup and sought comfort from the Black Alpha?" Asia said, returning to her spot on his chest and placed a kiss near his nipple, derailing his thoughts for a moment.

"Could be. I don't know what any of it means, the Black Alpha says I will understand soon." He rolled over on top of her and slanted his lips over her mouth, taking a kiss. "No need worrying about it now when we could be doing this." He placed kisses all over her face and then kissed her long and hard again.

Her hands wrapped around his neck, holding him close. He reveled in her scent. No one on the planet smelled as mouth-wateringly good as his mate. He rested between her legs and held her close. "Have I told you today how much I love you?" he whispered against her ear delighting in the shiver that ran through her.

"Yes." She cleared her throat and burrowed her head into his shoulder. "But I don't mind hearing you say it again."

Hawke chuckled at her hesitant admission. A month ago, he wondered if they would ever get to this place of easy camaraderie. Asia was a warrior through and through with sharp edges who didn't believe in softer emotions or second chances. What did her Mistress call him? Asia's do-over. He liked the sound of that. Their mating had been fast and with trust issues. Both of them had enough emotional luggage to fill a dump truck yet they'd waded through the muck of past failures and evil deeds to find joy in each other's embrace. For that he thanked the Goddess every moment of the day.

"*I am in love with you, Asia,*" he said through their link releasing his feeling so she understood what words could never express. The warmth of his love touched off a firestorm of need and he took her lips again.

"*I love you too.*" The words flowed through their link in slow motion, wrapping around him and holding on tight. His mate didn't use those words often and whenever she spoke them he treasured the gift of their offering. This time she released her tightly held chest of emotions, linking them with his. Heart racing, he shuddered beneath the onslaught of pride, love and appreciation twisting around him as bright colored ribbons.

"Asia," he murmured before taking another kiss, softer, gentler this time.

"I never thought this would happen to me," she murmured holding him tight against her. "But I'm glad you're mine, and in my life. Thanks for loving and believing in me."

He nibbled on her bottom lip and then kissed it when she tried to push him away. Just as he pressed against her, there was a knock on the door.

"Angus," Asia said as if he didn't recognize the man's scent. Hawke rolled over and took a deep breath to calm his raging libido.

"Something's happened," Angus said and walked off.

Asia patted his chest, rose on her elbow and kissed him. "Later, I promise."

Nodding, he prolonged the kiss a little longer, tormenting himself in the process. "I'll remind you." Hearing the same words from Angus that he'd thought seconds ago cooled his ardor. Remnants from the dream re-emerged and he wondered at the warning and the timing.

She grinned, stood and strode toward the bathroom. "I'm sure. Whatever's happened must be serious otherwise he would've waited."

Still thinking of the green-eyed Alpha, Hawke agreed and pulled on a pair of pants and tee shirt. Asia walked out, looked at him and shook her head. "What?"

"Why didn't I think to put on the clothes I wore yesterday instead of showering and brushing my teeth," she called as he headed to the bathroom for a quick hygiene routine.

"Don't know. It's an early unplanned meeting, this is as good as he gets," Hawke said. A few moments later they met Angus and Chacal in the den. To see an expression on Chacal's face was a surprise, let alone one of concern.

"What happened?" Asia asked, taking a seat facing Angus. Hawke sat next to her.

"Another pup was taken from inside a den. No scent, no alarm, nothing."

"Which pack?"

"Ulric's," Angus said and Hawke heard the pain in his voice.

"I've noticed the disappearances are centralized in certain areas. In northern Egypt and on pack lands in the Ukraine, Romania and Russia. Have the packs considered moving?" Asia asked.

"The land in Egypt has belonged to the Black Clan for centuries, I doubt they would leave now, but I will discuss it with Ulric as a temporary measure. Moving alone won't solve the problem. Those pups need to be returned to their dens. They are too young for this separation."

"That brings the count to three in the past two weeks. It seems they are escalating," Chacal said in a thoughtful tone.

Hawke thought of his dream and wondered if he should share it.

"Yes, I agree," Angus said, looking at Hawke. "We have searched three of the locations you've given us of former Liege compounds and labs for clues. All of them have been vacated and empty for years. We plan to head out to another one later today, have you remembered any others that may help us understand what's going on? Some place recent? My Alpha grows more concerned each day I don't have answers."

"I've written down all the locations I could recall. And it's possible I was never given access to information regarding the pups. I've never seen another black wolf until you."

"Not even to mate with?" Asia asked frowning.

"The first time I mated was on my tenth anniversary date and as far back as I remember I never mated with a black bitch."

"Tenth? You were ten?" Asia asked,

Hawke shrugged. "No one knew the exact date of my birth. That was the tenth year with the Liege, so I was older than ten. There was a celebration and they brought a bitch in heat to my room. After that, a bitch came once a month for the next five years and then every week."

"They wanted to breed you. I remember hearing them mention you impregnating the wolves. Something about you having a pup and them wanting more."

"The black wolf gene is dominant, I could produce black pups with any bitch. As far as I know my seed never took root. Lancaster said I was sterile and useless in that area." He looked at her. *"But with you it will be different,"* he said through their link.

"Or half-breed," Asia murmured.

Angus looked at her.

"What?" Hawke asked.

She shook her head. "Just trying to wrap my mind around motive and opportunity. I don't understand how they are accessing the den without detection." Asia looked at Hawke. "Were you working on a cloaking device or something? Maybe like the chameleon, but different?"

Hawke searched his memory. "No. I remember being ticked when I figured out you had access to new technology I hadn't heard of. Whatever or however they are doing this never came across my desk or I would've made notes in my personal files. Angus? You created the bracelets is there a chance the Liege could have modified what you've done?"

"No. Plus the thefts happened long before I created the bracelets. Like Chacal said, they're speeding up for some reason. It's like they know we are aware of what's happening and they're not trying to hide or be subtle anymore."

"Or they've ramped up their time-table," Chacal said in an ominous tone.

No one spoke for a few moments and then Angus threw the glass in his hand across the room into the fireplace. It shattered on impact and fell into the flames. "Damn-it, we've got to shut this down. Where are they taking the pups? Even when they disappear they have to hide them somewhere." Angus stood and paced in jerky movements.

"You've been eating the root I gave you?" Hawke said watching Angus.

"Yeah, nasty shit."

Hawke nodded. "Yes, but once it is in your system your tolerance for the drugs in the tranquilizer will increase and it will not have the same impact as it once had." Neutralizing the drug that incapacitated Angus during their conflict against the bluebirds and Liege had risen to the top of Hawke's to-do list after the castle fell. They couldn't afford to fall to the side in the middle of a battle. After studying the components in the drug, he realized a root that grew in the wild would solve their problems. He and Asia ate a healthy dose daily and had spread the word to the local packs. Irritability and jerky movements were initial side effects that went away after a short period.

"Good to know I'm not eating this shit for nothing," Angus muttered.

Asia smiled and winked at Hawke. "If you run into a bluebird again, you'll be happy you ate that shit."

Angus looked over his shoulder at her and growled. "True, but I have a sword with those bastard's name on it." He tapped the sharp blade sheathed and worn on his side. "In the chest below where a human heart would be, right?" He looked at Hawke who nodded.

"Yes, that's their soft spot. Hit them there and they drop like a fly, or cut off their heads. Both will kill them dead." He met the Angus' gaze and then glanced at Chacal who sat listening without offering anything to the conversation.

"Glad you finally had access to your files, it's been a lot of help." Angus nodded and turned away. "Ulric is here and wants to meet with us, Chacal."

The other man nodded, but didn't move.

Angus looked at Asia and then Hawke. "After we meet with him we are heading to the next place on the list you gave us. How's your search coming with Alpha Radoff?"

"Slow. The people he's introduced us to were hesitant to share information. Later today, he's taking us to an area northwest of here on the corner of pack lands. He says he's come across some new information. Sounded excited about it last night." In fact excited was not the right word, levitating with joy and doing flips had been more accurate. Despite his insistence they come to the address he gave them, the Alpha refused to discuss anything over the phone. He and Asia had spent some time guessing what had the man floating with joy before they fell asleep last night.

"Let's hope it pushes us one step closer to solving this mystery. I hate not having anything to report to Silas and Jasmine," Angus said meeting Asia's gaze. "They are really concerned."

She nodded and after a moment stood. "Ready?"

Hawke glanced out the window, streaks from the rising sun peaked across the sky. He stood, and slapped his palms against his pant leg. "Can I have breakfast first?"

Asia looked past him to the brightening sky and then met his gaze. "Make it fast."

Chapter 3

Angus and Chacal left the house and walked toward the forest to meet Ulric, Alpha of the Black Wolf Clan. Ulric shifted from a large black wolf into his human form which wasn't much different in Angus' opinion. A few black wolves stood near the tree line while Ulric walked forward to meet them.

All three of them, Angus, Chacal and Ulric, were similar in height and size, although Chacal was the smallest. Angus and Ulric's black hair, green eyes and deep tans were signature traits of the Black clan. Chacal's blackish-brown hair and gold eyes identified him as a hybrid of wolf and jackal.

"I hope there is a good reason you called for this meeting," Angus said instead of a customary greeting. He delayed his report to Silas just in case he learned something worthwhile from Ulric, but he needed to rectify that within an hour or Silas would contact him. Lately, his litter-mate had become more concerned over the threat the Liege presented to the wolf nation and seemed to be willing to take the fight wherever it took them, pack protocol be damned.

"Another pup was taken earlier today," Ulric said through clenched teeth.

"I am aware of that. From your beta's den I understand," Angus said with sympathy. A wolf's den was sacred; no one should've been able to penetrate his safeguards.

Ulric slapped his ball fist into his palm and walked back and forth a few times. "How can I lead if I cannot protect them? I flounder like a pup seeking a teat. Those bastards are winning. How? How are they doing it? They appear and disappear like ghosts. How's that possible?"

Angus' heart clenched at the despair in the man's voice, but he had no idea how to explain what happened. Baffled, he met Ulric's gaze and remained silent.

"What… what would your Alpha do?" With a look of defeat he stared at Angus.

The idea of anyone breaking into Silas' compound and surviving long enough to get to the nursery, was daunting. But if they made it that far, and neutralized the security detail that remained on duty twenty-four hours, that person would deal with either Jasmine, Victoria, Rose or one of the nurses who were trained security bitches as well. A battle of epic proportions would break out, and that's before Silas arrived. Jasmine would be a force to reckon with if anyone came near her babies.

Rather than explain the bloodbath that would follow such an attempt, he cleared his throat and kept his face neutral. "I cannot imagine what he would not do if one of his pups were taken. I can only say life as we know it would change in a nanosecond."

"Would he hunt down the Liege? Destroy them in their beds? Start a war with the humans? How far? How far would he go to find his pups? To protect his den?"

Angus swallowed and blinked back the image of an out of control Silas. "There is nothing he would not do. The Liege would pray for death by the time his mate found them and she would. La Patron and his mate would not rest until they found their pups."

"And the parties responsible for taking their pups?" Ulric pressed. "What happens to them?"

Angus released a breath. "They'd die." He didn't bother to add, they'd die horribly without mercy. Ulric understood.

Ulric nodded and stepped back. "Lancaster arrived near Bucharest four days past. He stayed in the hotel at first, but has moved. I will find and kill him. Perhaps we should've killed them from the beginning before they made monsters of our young."

Angus stilled. Thinking of Tyrese and Hawke he frowned at the comment. "Monsters? What are you talking about?" Both young wolves had no control over what happened to them and were valued assets to the wolf nation.

Ulric looked around before clearing his throat. "Those two men, Hawke and the other, his mate I suppose. They aren't normal, they've been altered by the Liege. Their minds and their bodies are twisted. I don't want my pups turned into a machine, with metal legs and arms," he spat as if he smelled something distasteful. "They've put computer chips in their minds and cameras in their heads." He tapped his forehead and then shook it. "We cannot allow that to happen to our pups, not if we plan to survive."

Anger raced through Angus at the biased slight. "The Liege has been stealing pups for decades. Now that your pups are in danger of being changed, you stand here and criticize those who were victims while you did nothing to save them?"

"That is not what I meant –"

"Then what else could you mean? Hawke was taken, probably given away by his own pack to the Liege and he had no fucking choice. Have you seen his body? It's a roadmap of cuts and scars from all the surgeries he underwent while you and your pack remained safe on the continent. He's a fucking black wolf and no one, not you or his pack rescued him. He was with Lancaster for over thirty damn years and you.... You stand here and criticize him for surviving?"

"I meant they will destroy all of us!" Ulric yelled and then wiped his face with the back of his hand. "None of my wolves can defeat Hawke or the other who walks with him. They change into these, these huge beasts and our hybrids cannot win against them. What if he changes loyalty? What happens then?"

"The Liege has hybrids that shift to the same sizes. Hybrid full-bloods they control one hundred percent. How would you defeat them?" Angus crossed his arms over his chest and stared into the widening eyes of his friend.

"What?" Ulric looked gut punched.

Angus chuckled and shook his head at the man's audacity. This limited foresight had been one of the main reasons he hadn't been able to remain in the pack with this Alpha. "You're going after Lancaster and don't know anything about his army of hybrids? That's why Hawke and other wolves can shift to larger sizes, the Liege experimented on full bloods. So far, only the black wolf can maintain his humanity and handle the extras, like steel limbs, and electronics. The others become machine-like or die."

"He travels with one other," Ulric murmured, and then met Angus' gaze. "Lancaster does not travel with an army, but with one."

"Then believe me that one is capable of doing what an army can do. He will morph to large sizes and fight to the death to complete his mission. If that is to destroy you, the Alpha of the Black Clan, he will never stop until you are dead." Angus reiterated the threat of the hybrid in case Ulric retreated behind his veil of invincibility.

"Do you know how to destroy it?" Ulric watched him closely.

Angus shrugged. "If it were a hybrid, I'd say hit it in the left eye and pull out the computer chip that makes it run. Or if it were a bluebird, take a sharp object and pierce it here." He pointed to the spot on his chest. "But this may be something new, so I cannot say."

Ulric frowned. "Bluebird? Hybrid?"

"Yeah. They are wolves who've been changed by the Liege. Bluebirds are hyper-fast, but you'll hear them coming. Make sure you eat a lot of that root I told you about because the tips of their talons are poison and will knock you out if you don't." He ignored the look of horrified distaste on Ulric's face. They were in a war and attempting to change the tides of the battle and didn't have time to deal with anyone's sensibilities. Losing was not an option.

Ulric nodded. "We are including it into our daily diet." He paused. "And the hybrid?"

Pleased with Ulric's level of concern, Angus tempered his tone. "You won't hear them coming. Just be ready to fight for your life, they cannot stop until their mission is completed."

"A severed head stops them both," Chacal said in a dry tone standing with his hands behind his back while staring over Ulric's head.

Grinning, Angus patted his sword. "Yeah, that's right."

Ulric's gaze followed his hand movements. "Have you talked to your Alpha? Will he send more assistance to defeat this threat?"

"He is aware of what is going on." Angus couldn't share Silas' plans with Ulric even though they were both Alphas, they did not operate the same. Plus Silas was the Goddess' emissary with abilities no other Alpha shared.

"Is he coming to defeat the Liege? He is in danger just as we are," Ulric said, sounding desperate.

"He is not the Goddess, Ulric. He cannot fix your problems. The bulk of the takings has occurred on pack lands here or in Egypt. The question is why? There are packs all over the world, but the Liege's success is limited to these areas. Find the answer to that question and follow the trail."

Ulric jerked back at Angus' remark. "I'm aware no pups have been taken from your Alpha's lands. That does not mean they will not make an attempt," Ulric said watching Angus.

"You're missing the point," Angus said, shaking his head. "Instead of asking what La Patron is doing about the problem, ask what is it about these lands that allow the Liege access to come and go at will."

Ulric stared at him and nodded slowly. "Good point, I will research the history of the lands to discover if there is a link. I shall delay going after Lancaster until I know more of his security."

Angus nodded. "Good idea, if I hear anything, I'll let you know."

Jaw clenched, he raised and pointed his finger. "And so you know, I am aware La Patron is not the Goddess, but he has a close relationship with her. Pity she favors him to the point she does not respond to the rest of her servants." He shifted and walked into the forest with his pack following.

Chapter 4

"I cannot believe how big they've grown," Renee, Jasmine's sister, said watching David and Adam run after each other around the large nursery.

Jasmine smiled with pride and placed her fingertips to her temple. A low, dull throb behind her eyes robbed her of energy, she needed to lay down. "They are a hand full, no doubt. Some days I get tired just from watching them."

"Auntie Nay, Auntie, look." Renee walked over and handed her aunt a picture she had been drawing. Not to be ignored, Jackie followed and lifted a puzzle she'd just finished to show Renee as well. Both girls stood next to Renee, their eyes lit with adoration as they stared up at their relative. Jackie's long black ponytail had escaped the band and fell down her back in a messy fall. Wrinkled jeans and a tee shirt were her favorite outfits. Jackie was laid back and comfortable.

Renee, Jasmine's diva in training stood with a perfect ponytail as if she'd painted every strand in place. Despite her use of paint, not one drip or splotch landed on her clothes. With Renee everything matched and remained in place.

"Oh my, this is beautiful, Renee, you are a great artist. And Jackie you did such a great job on this, I'm so proud of both of you." Renee dropped to her knees and hugged them both causing the girls to squeal as their faces lit with pleasure.

"Me too," Adam yelled changing directions as he ran into Renee's outstretched arms. Jasmine watched David walk slowly toward the group, stretch forth his arms and offer his aunt a hug. Renee grabbed him close and placed several kisses on his face, which he wiped off as soon as she released him. Jasmine and Renee laughed at his actions.

Victoria walked into the nursery and a chorus of "Nana" rose from the children. Pleased by their response to her entry, Victoria ushered the four close for hugs and kisses. Renee returned to Jasmine's side with a huge smile of satisfaction. This visit had been delayed a month because of the mating ceremony and both sisters were happy to see each other. It had been too long.

"I'm jealous, they are so cute and smart and loving. Don't know how you keep having such great kids, but I'm glad you do." Renee hugged her with one arm while watching the scene with Victoria.

"Rose is pregnant." Jasmine dropped that bomb and waited for her sister's reaction which didn't take long.

Renee screamed and tightened her hold. "She is? That's so awesome. I'm going to be a grand-aunt. No drop the grand, aunt sounds a whole lot better and more me. And you? A nana?" Renee laughed.

"Not funny, but I'm excited for them. Rone's so happy he's driving Rose crazy with all his hovering. She begged Silas to give him something to do outside the building so she could get her work done."

"Did he do it? I mean I can't see Silas changing things around for someone," Renee said.

Jasmine waved off her comment, she'd heard similar ones whenever they talked on the phone and wouldn't tolerate them in person. "Get over the Christening thing, you know that was a serious situation. In the end he was right, so stop coloring him with that event."

"I know. It still stings how he just shut me out. Anyway, did he do it for Rose?"

"Yeah. Rone is working with the new security trainees on the opposite side of the compound. He manages to come by once a day for lunch, which is way better than before. Rose doesn't need any additional stress, she's scared enough."

"Scared? Why?"

Jasmine remembered Renee didn't know her son and his wife were products of breeders with different concerns. "She had some spotting early on, the doctor said it was nothing. But she's a first time mom." Which had scared Rone to the point he demanded Rose remain in bed for the duration of the pregnancy even though the doctor told them it wasn't necessary.

"Hmm, can't help with that. I've never been preggo. But I'm happy for them too. What about Rese and Dannielle? They trying?"

Jasmine laughed at the idea of her controlling son and his independent mate having pups anytime soon. Those two spent a week deciding where to live, another week on how to decorate their space and another arguing over Danielle returning home alone to pack her belongings. They were oil and water, two hard-heads in love and lust who kept everyone entertained with their lively debates.

"Trying? I don't know, but nothing yet. They're taking time to know each other first, children will come later. At least I hope. Cam and Lilly don't seem to be interested in starting a family either, so I'm glad Rose and Rone are getting started." Her voice dropped to a low whisper as the pain in her head increased.

"You okay?" Renee asked, touching Jasmine's forehead.

"No, my head hurts like someone's having drum practice." She rested her face in her palms to close out the light.

Renee draped her arm around Jasmine's shoulders. "Take a pill and lay down a while. Mom and I'll stay here with the kids. Go on, take a break, we got this."

Jasmine watched her mom on the floor with the girls lying on each side doing their own thing while David and Adam played some kind of game with a ball and agreed.

"Silas, my head is hurting, I'm going to the room to lay down for a few minutes. Mom and Renee are here with the kids."

"I felt your pain earlier and tried to siphon it off so you could enjoy your visit with your sister. It still pains you. Go rest, Sweet bitch."

Jasmine smiled at the hint of playfulness in his words. The man still aroused her with a few simple sentences, she suspected that would always be the case. "Mom, my head's bothering me, I'm going to lay down."

Victoria nodded. "Feel better, we'll be here for a while. Jacques is in the lab and says he'll be there the rest of the day helping Matt."

Renee squeezed her shoulder before she walked over to the boys, bent low and started talking. Seconds later she had the ball and the game was on. Pleased everything seemed in order Jasmine left the nursery and headed for the suite she shared with her mate, Silas.

The fragrance of gardenias washed over her the moment she entered the living area curing the throb in her head instantly. Fatigue took its place, her legs grew heavy as she moved toward the bedroom. By the time she reached the doorway placing one foot in front of the other became a struggle. Blurry eyed, she made it to the bed in the middle of the room, exhaled and fell face down. The moment her head hit the mattress the lethargy lifted. Energized, she pushed up on the bed, looked down and gasped at her face reflected in a pool of water. Unbound, her hair caressed the sides of her face, making her eyes appear larger and her lips fuller. Struggling to stand, she noticed her black trousers and multi-colored blouse were replaced with a sleeveless long white gown that brushed against her bare feet. Jasmine wiggled her toes against the cool grass and looked around the forest surrounding the small pool.

Green leafy trees offered shade. A small creek wound through the middle of the land and fed the pool. Fragrant grass and flowers of various colors gave the setting a surreal feel. The temperature seemed a perfect lukewarm blend for comfort. This had to be a dream or something, she'd never smelled or seen anything like the sights in front of her, plus she didn't own anything like the gown she wore. And she would never be without feet coverings in a strange place.

"What is going on?" she whispered and jumped when she heard the echo of her words.

"Jasmine, mate of Silas Knight, the Patron, welcome."

Jasmine tried to move, to see the face with the sweet sounding voice, but couldn't. No matter how many times she commanded her legs to move, or her head to turn neither responded.

"Thank you. Where am I?" Her gaze flitted around the limited area of the forest.

"I am the Goddess of La Patron and all wolves, you are with me. I must speak with you on important issues, therefore you will not be allowed to interrupt. Afterward, you will return to your mate to discuss the matters I share with you."

Jasmine nodded.

"Positive, nurturing energy flow through females, as such you will be my emissary for this next, critical mission. Asia must secure her mate's loyalty to the nation immediately. The two must merge completely and become a Sword in truth, otherwise victory is not certain. Asia must lead in this. You must lead in this. Be merciful, your nose will lead to understanding. This is a time of testing. Taste the truth and embrace it, reject the lies, and ride the wave of change. Change is on the wind."

Jasmine blinked as the words vibrated in her head and grew louder and louder until she wanted to scream. She closed her eyes and repeated the Goddess' words until they imprinted beneath her lids. A whirlwind of power swept around her, lifting her hair, her gown and sending tingles across her skin and then stopped.

Gasping for breath, she flopped over on the bed. Chest heaving, she sought Silas through their link. *"Wolfie?"*

"What's wrong?"

"I just had a meeting with the Goddess and it was fucking fantastic."

"I'm on my way."

Chapter 5

"I'll be back in a few minutes, continue without me. When I return I expect a full update," Silas said to Matt and Dr. Passen, the two were working on decoding some information Hawke had sent last week. Silas believed it would help them locate the next Liege stronghold in the states and wanted that information posthaste. But his mate meeting with the Goddess trumped everything, he needed to be with her to process whatever riddle the Goddess left behind.

"Yes, Sir," Matt, Davian –Jasmine's ex-husband's mate, said turning back to the computer as Silas left the lab. Anxious over his mate's condition, Silas kept their link open and scanned his mate for any abnormalities. He'd been summoned by the Goddess numerous times through the years and knew how her visits upset his biology. Being human, he hoped Jasmine recovered soon with no permanent damage. He moved quickly down the halls and took the lift to their floor. Moments later he entered their suite.

"Jasmine?" The smell of gardenias hit hard and he took a step back to block the strong aroma. "Jasmine?" he called again, worried she'd been overtaken by the smell.

"In here."

Covering his nose with his arm, Silas headed toward their bedroom and opened the door. Jasmine lie on her back, staring at the ceiling. Worried the event with the Goddess harmed her in some way, he hurried to her side and placed his palms on her cheeks so he could look in her eyes and assess the damage.

"Wolfie." She giggled and ran her fingernail down his cheek.

Silas frowned. "I thought you met with the Goddess." Instead of being half-fried she appeared drunk.

"I did. Told you I did. Didn't see her though. She didn't let me talk." She paused, looking up at him with a slight frown. "That's a lot of dids, isn't it?"

Silas sat back watching her closely. "How do you feel?"

"Great. Headache's gone, everything's better." She leaned up on her elbows, the tips of her breast brushed against his chest. "I'm her emissary, did you know that?"

Surprised, Silas sat back. "No. I didn't know that. When did that happen?" He didn't understand what happened, but the Goddess' visit impacted Jasmine a lot differently than him. The tension eased from his shoulders as he watched his mate pull her thoughts together.

She repeated her conversation with the Goddess.

"She told me those same words when I first met you. I assumed you, the twins and the pups were the change she meant. Obviously there is more going on. You always said Asia was special, that the Goddess would use her."

Jasmine nodded. "After all the poor girl went through, there had to be a greater plan for her life."

Silas agreed but wondered at the larger picture. "Hawke and Asia are important in changing things. Okay. You'll talk with her about that, help her understand what needs to be done. But how does this play into the pups missing? She must've addressed that." He stood from the bed and looked out the window. "So far one attempt was made to take a pup. The pieces of the sucker who tried will never be found. But it was sloppy, more of a human kidnapping than a pup-snatch in Angus' reports. Still, the very idea that someone could take a pup from any den or the compound doesn't sit right with me."

"There's been no cases stateside," Jasmine said, rising from the bed and then falling back onto the mattress.

"That doesn't matter. If it happens to one, it happens to all," he snapped.

"Check the attitude and the tone at the door. I didn't say it was right, I made an observation. Maybe there's a reason it's happening over there. Maybe they did something. Maybe there's a curse or a secret stone with powers. We don't know."

He looked over his shoulder at her. "A secret stone?"

She grinned. "Hey, I watch movies. Things happen for all kinds of reasons, there could be a kernel of truth in those old Indiana Jones movies. Don't knock 'em."

Silas withheld a sigh and took a seat in front of the bed. "I'm going to lock down the compound. Keep the kids inside, no traveling into town or the forest. Not until I'm satisfied no one can enter my den."

"Silas."

"A pup was stolen from inside a den Jasmine. Another while his father was within a few feet." Jaw tight he stood. "I'm shutting this down."

"Renee is not going to believe this."

Silas shrugged. "I know she promised to take the kids to the circus in town tomorrow. That's canceled."

"How do I explain you canceled something you approved? What if we take additional security? Each of us will have a child on our lap. Will that work?"

Silas hated to see the look of disappointment in her eyes and stood. "If one of our children was taken, what would you do?"

He watched her straighten and her eyes cloud over. "I cannot imagine that, Silas. But I would be very angry."

"So would I. Jasmine, we cannot afford to get *that* angry. I would rather your sister hate me for all eternity than the combined destruction we would unleash on the population searching for one of our pups. The Goddess would not be pleased and would punish us. Chances are we would not see our pups again, even after they were returned."

She glanced at him and rolled off the bed. "Combined destruction, unleashed... really Silas? Dramatic much?"

"You mock me, but I remember your actions when Tyrese was taken and he is a seasoned warrior, capable of taking care of himself. I would not be much better. Let's not bring in the twins or Cameron. Let alone all fifty Alphas." He rubbed his forehead just thinking of the fallout. His sons and godson would wreak havoc on anyone they thought harmed one of the pups. His children had wormed their way into the hearts of his closest associates who would leave no stone unturned in their search.

Jasmine touched his arm and he wrapped his arm around her waist. For a few moments they remained close, their links open as they battled their unspoken fears for the safety of their den and all the pups in the nation. He meant it earlier when he said if it happened to one, it happened to all.

"I'll explain it to mom and she can help me come up with something to tell Renee." She placed a kiss on his chest. "We'll take care of it and find something else in the compound to do."

He placed a kiss on her forehead and inhaled. "Thank you for not fighting me on this. But I'm worried. Something is wrong and I think it's closer to home than we think. The Liege has too many operations on this continent not to be interested in my pack. We must be prepared."

"That's defense, which is good. But who do you have tracking the bastards down for elimination?"

Silas met her gaze. He hadn't sent anyone to track them down and destroy them, but it wasn't a bad idea. Asia and Angus were his best trackers, but he needed them to continue where they were. Leon and Brix had been assigned to watch the pups but he could reassign Jarcee from the Alpha training team to watch the pups.

Pleased with his choices, he squeezed Jasmine around the waist and kissed her long and hard. "The Goddess chose the best emissary a Patron could have. Thank you, I will send Leon and his mate Brix to track down the Liege in this country to send a message they are not welcome on my turf."

"Will you clear it with the Pentagon? Just in case there is some backlash?"

Silas thought of his previous dealings with the Joint Chiefs during his mating ceremony. They betrayed his trust, and even though the President apologized, Silas was not ready to deal with them again. "No. I don't need them."

Her brow rose.

"Not for this. No one will see Leon or Brix coming, they both wear Chameleon bracelets. If a Liege Lord is in the states, these two will find and terminate them." The more he thought of it, the more he wondered why he hadn't done it before. Was he becoming soft? Three years ago, he would have ordered the death of a human enemy without having all the facts. Yet, he hadn't ordered the demise of these heinous criminals. Ironically, his human mate suggested the termination.

"Good. I don't want them anywhere near our packs," she said pleasing him more.

Chapter 6

Another urgent summons to meet Alpha Radoff came right after they started breakfast. Asia and Hawke left Chacal's compound in a new black Hummer, courtesy of Alpha Ulric, and headed west towards the foothills in Romania. She'd used the chameleon bracelet Angus had given her to change her appearance into the white male everyone considered Hawke's mate. The Liege had an eight million dollar bounty on her head and would love to recapture her. The bracelet had saved her life on numerous occasions and helped her free her mate. She would do everything within her power to keep Angus' secret and the bracelet safe.

Radoff had been excited by something he and his pack uncovered, and for some reason he did not want Angus or Chacal to know, not yet. Something about muddying the waters. Eager for new information regarding the missing pups, Asia agreed to hold the information close for now, but explained she would tell her Mistress anything she deemed important.

The man agreed and told them to hurry.

After a few hours they arrived in a small town that looked as if it were taken from a page of a medieval novel. Half fallen towers, large blocks of stone littered the ground from where the walls crumbled over time and an air of abandonment rested over the large building.

Hawke parked the Hummer out front and they walked into what must have been the keep at one time. Overgrown grass, and twisted vines greeted them. Birds took flight and insects stopped chirping long enough to give them a quick inspection. Asia placed her hand on the hilt of her sword and kept her senses open.

The sudden quiet disturbed her. Where was Radoff?

Hawke stopped and looked around. *"Someone's coming."*

Asia nodded and then relaxed her guard. *"It's Radoff."* They both turned to watch the shorter Alpha stride across the grounds with a sparkle in his otherwise dull brown eyes and a spring in his step. The man vibrated with excitement.

"He's pleased about something," Hawke said, inching closer to Asia.

Rather than respond, her gaze flicked over Radoff, and noticed in the streaks of dirt on his face, the dust and cobwebs in his hair and something dark on his hands he tried wiping off on his pants. She'd guess he'd found an underground lair or something. Based on what she knew about the man, the idea of him on his knees crawling below ground seemed unlikely. So, what had he been doing?

"Alpha Radoff, you wanted to see us?" Asia asked when he approached.

"Yes… yes. I think I've found it." He stuffed his hands into his pocket, she suspected to keep from clapping or waving them about.

Asia's heart raced. She glanced at the old, drafty castle and then back at him. "This is where they bring the pups?" she asked in surprise. The building looked abandoned and lacked heat to keep the pups warm. None of that mattered, they'd be moving the pups to a better location anyway.

Radoff frowned. "Pups? No. Why? Did you see something?" He turned and looked behind him and then faced her again.

Asia withheld a growl of disappointment. "What did you find then?"

He met her gaze and the sparkle returned to his eyes. "This is Lord Konstantin's castle." He spoke with an air of pride and amazement.

Asia had no idea who Konstantin was and crossed her arms over her chest waiting for an explanation. They had driven hours to reach this place and she hoped Konstantin knew something about the missing pups or she'd be pissed at the delay. Mistress and La Patron were counting on her to shut the Liege down.

Radoff seemed confused by her lack of excitement. "Lord Konstantin." He leaned forward and waited a beat. "The Lord who started the Roundtable of Lords back in the late 1800's." He looked behind him and then at them again. "This place isn't in the official records of his land holdings. He had a special place where he met with the Roundtable and the Fekete Farkas, or Black wolf clan."

Asia sensed Hawke's surprise through their link. She took another look at the crumbling estate. "Roundtable of Lords?"

Radoff's grin widened as he nodded. "That was the original name of the group, it changed in the 1900's to Liege Lords, more modern I suppose." He shrugged and looked at the building as if it were an early Christmas present. She prayed there were answers to their current problem behind those walls.

"Why is this important?" Hawke asked, gazing at the building.

Radoff took on the look of a professor intent on a lecture. She recalled his warning that she slow down and learn more before rushing ahead and prepared to listen.

"Lord Konstantin was Hungarian and part of the aristocracy back in the 1800's. They ruled what we know as Romania with an iron fist. Didn't matter that they were the minority, they kept the majority poor and ignorant. Konstantin shied away from politics and invested in land. He owned thousands of acres across this area, Egypt, Moldova and Russia. The man was ahead of his time when it came to agriculture and making the land productive."

He glanced at Asia and waved his hand. "But that's for another day. Konstantin had an affinity for the land and animals. Liked them better than people actually. Most of the public conservation areas in this country were his ideas and he set aside private places for wildlife. The man had a soft spot for wolves. Black wolves in particular. Rumor has it he was attacked and robbed by rebels on his way to his estate and left along the road with his guards for dead."

He paused, gauging their attention and continued. "Alpha Nikolas of the Fekete Farkas Clan saved his life, took him into the forest and did something. Whatever the Alpha did to Konstantin, made him stronger than he had been before. He maintained lands here for years until there was murmuring about his failing to age and then he moved to

Egypt. Over the course of his life he moved all over the continent deeding pack lands to various clans. Most Alphas refuse to have anything to do with human authorities, so the Roundtable was set up to ensure packs would always own their land and thrive. Years later Alpha Nikolas died in a pack battle and was put to rest, Konstantin died a month later. They were tied in some way no one has ever understood."

Asia wondered if Konstantin and Nikolas were mates. Stranger things happened.

"And we are here because?" Hawke asked.

"Because this is where it all begun. Pacts were made. Strategies how to go forward were created. I'm hoping we can find records of some sort that would give insight on why the Liege is taking the pups."

"And you think the answer is in this building?" Asia asked, taking another look at the fallen stones littering the courtyard.

"There are documents hidden inside, I've seen them. But I cannot translate them. Hawke can." He looked at Hawke, who held his gaze and then nodded.

"*How do you know you can translate these pages without knowing what language they're written in?*" Asia asked through their link.

"*I'm fluent in most languages and can make out the rest. Chances are I'll figure it out.*" He followed her as she followed Radoff into the castle. Radoff turned on a flashlight and it became obvious his pack had cleared most of the cobwebs and tidied the place.

"Do you have pack members staying here?" she asked.

"Yes, I purchased the land. I thought it was important to secure the location until we had an opportunity to go through everything. Some areas cannot be accessed, but for the most part the building has held up well over time." He moved down a dim corridor and turned left. Fire lit wall sconces provided the only light as they ventured further into the castle. Both the interior and exterior walls were made of heavy stone. Uneven floors, high ceilings, and large candelabras with mounds of melted wax hung from the rafters.

Radoff stopped in front of a large blackened fireplace and looked over his shoulders at her and then frowned at Hawke. "Stoop low." He pressed the mantle above the fireplace, and the wall opened with a grinding sound. Radoff's grin showed his pleasure at his discovery.

Once inside the small room, Asia understood Radoff's happiness. On the wall was a tapestry in mint condition of a large black, green eyed wolf and a pale man sitting on the ground as if having a conversation. The image of the black wolf struck a chord in her, he seemed familiar.

"Here's a book we found tucked away." Radoff handed the leather bound book to Hawke with all the reverence of a man in the presence of a great treasure. Hawke stared at it for a moment, sat and then opened it with equal care. The pages stuck together, until he gently pried them apart.

Intrigued, Asia sat next to him while Radoff stood slightly behind him at his shoulder. Quiet, Hawke stared at the page without turning for so long, Asia thought he couldn't translate it.

Hawke sighed and shook his head. "This is the notes of one of the meetings of the Roundtable Lords." He dropped his head into the palm of his hand and continued staring at the page.

"What does it say?" Asia asked, glancing at Radoff. The man had stepped closer and stood directly at Hawke's elbow peering over his shoulder.

"It does not translate too well into English, so I will paraphrase. The Lord is reminding the men of their commitment to protect and serve the wolf-shifter in all its forms. They were the custodians of Konstantin's wealth which was set aside for shifters." Hawked shook his head. "Hard to believe this is the same group." He turned the page.

Asia glanced around the room. "Were all of these things here when you found the place?" she asked Radoff pointing to the small statues of wolves and artwork.

He nodded and moved toward a bookcase with several black wolf figures the size of large chess pieces. His index fingertip traced the body of one piece before he spoke. "Imagine what he dreamed for us. He set aside all of his wealth and gave away his land so that we could co-exist in harmony with man." He turned to face her. "But greed is a terrible thing."

Hawke released a bark of laughter grabbing their attention. "What?" she asked, looking at the letters and symbols on the page and then back at him.

"Seems Konstantin expected greed and prepared for it. None of the land can be taken from the packs by humans, the packs can sell it or give it away if they chose. Plus, there is a curse on any member of the Roundtable if they misuse the money left for anything other than research to assist shifters, to make their lives better."

"Well, that's open for interpretation, don't you think?" Asia said, pushing away from the table and taking a closer look at another piece of art. "Lancaster and the others may have met the legal interpretation of the stipulations but not the spirit. Wonder what Konstantin would say if he saw how the Liege operated now?"

"His son died." Hawke looked up at her and then continued reading.

"What?" She spun around.

"Konstantin had a son who took his place on the roundtable after his death. He thought his father foolish to leave so much to animals and redirected funds to his personal pursuits. Within three months he died from some type of disease." Hawked met her gaze. "Whoever wrote this spent a lot of time describing how bad the disease was and how it crippled the young man. I don't know if this person was a sadistic bastard delighting in the other's misery or wanted it explicit to serve as a warning to the others."

"Could be a combination of both," Asia murmured, looking at the spine of a book on the shelf. She pulled it out and looked at the pages. The small, neat handwriting hid secrets. Looking at another page she frowned.

"Have you seen this before?" She showed Radoff.

He took the book and stared at the small design. "No. It looks like a crest and something else. I can just make out Konstantin's initials, badly smeared but they are there." He pointed at the design.

"Okay, I see that now, but what is the rest of it? I've seen this before." She continued to stare at it a bit longer and then snapped her finger.

"*What?*" Hawke asked, watching her.

"*One sec.*" She looked at Radoff. "This has Konstantin's initials and what else? Can you make it out?"

"Looks like an upside down wolf, look here." He pointed to the design. "That looks like a snout and a paw. Considering all he did for the Black Wolf Clan, I'm not surprised he made some type of brand or seal for them." He turned and looked at the other books. "Let's see if we find another one that might be clear enough to make out. He handed her a book and took one for himself. They looked through the pages and in each book found a similar symbol, which resembled the birthmarks she had seen on La Patron's pups.

Chapter 7

Night fell and Hawke continued to read through the books, gaining more insight into the purpose of the Liege and Konstantin's fascination with full-bloods. If it had been within the Lord's power he would've become a wolf. Asia had asked about the connection between Konstantin and the Alpha Nikolas, Hawke had not ruled out the possibility of the Alpha biting the Lord. During his time with Lancaster, the Liege played with the idea of full-bloods biting humans and as far as he knew nothing had ever come of it. Perhaps there a link had been formed between the Lord and the Alpha back in the 1800's that caused the lifelong bond. It was something to think on as he continued searching the records.

He asked Radoff to check the dates of the other books to help find answers. These journals were of the Roundtable and took place years after the initial meeting of the black wolf and noble Hungarian.

"Asia?"

Jasmine stood and walked toward the corner of the room. She would've preferred to walk outside for fresh air, but Hawke would insist on accompanying her which would delay the translations of the journals. Stubborn man.

"*Yes, Mistress.*" There were a few things she wanted to share and questions that needed answers regarding the birthmark.

"*I had a meeting with the Goddess –*"

Asia straightened, and her thoughts scattered at the announcement. "*She contacted you?*"

Hawke looked over his shoulder at her. "*What's wrong?*"

She waved him down and listened harder.

"*Yes, earlier today. I had a mutiny on my hands otherwise I would've contacted you sooner.*"

"*Mutiny? With who?*" Asia couldn't imagine anyone crazy enough to confront her Mistress.

"*From Silas' pups, that's who.*"

Asia smiled at the frustration she heard in Jasmine's voice and relaxed. "*What happened?*"

"*Silas is concerned over the missing pups, so am I, but he took things to DefCon 6 or something and shut down the compound the day before the kids were supposed to go to the circus. Which wouldn't have been so bad if we hadn't been pumping up the damn thing up for the past week. The nursery was filled with circus toys, books and puzzles.*"

"*Uh, oh.*" La Patron's pups were just a stubborn as he was and would not be happy with that type of change.

"*You got that right. Those demons gave me so much attitude with the screaming and hollering I told Silas to deal with it.*" Jasmine chuckled. "*He thought I put them up to it, but when he realized they were angry with both of us, he stopped trying to explain and went all Alpha on them.*"

Asia covered her mouth to stop the laugh that spilled over into their link anyway.

Jasmine chuckled. *"You're right, it was funny. They didn't pay daddy any attention and continued falling out. I swear if I ever see Renee paint another picture of a clown with her daddy's face in the middle I'm going to lose it."*

"No, she didn't."

"Yes, she did. Adam wasn't much better throwing things around. He tore apart the clown and all the circus books. Jackie joined him, the room looked like a tornado ran through it. A well coordinated tornado, seems like these four can link when they want to."

Asia had to ask. *"What did David do?"* He had been the runt of the bunch at birth and now seemed to be the unspoken leader of the group.

"He said one word, 'why?' While the others were all emotional he asked me why they couldn't go to the circus. I explained the danger and I swear that little boy weighed my words before he nodded and walked to the other side of the room, sat and ignored everyone else."

Asia wasn't surprised. In her opinion, David would be the one to watch, he shared Jasmine's intuitiveness and La Patron's natural leadership abilities. *"That's funny. Wonder what he would've done if he didn't like your explanation?"*

"Am I the only one who sees a problem explaining myself to my kids who aren't two years old yet?"

"They are operating on wolf biology so they are more like four or five. David might be more like eight or nine. You could have them tested so you'll have a better understanding of how their biology works."

"That was a rhetorical question, Asia. I know they aren't fully human, but I don't recall the twins moving this fast. They were smart and developed faster than others…

maybe they did and I didn't pay attention." Jasmine sighed and it tugged at Asia's heart. Her mistress had to adapt to so many new things in their culture it had to be overwhelming at times.

"*The twins didn't have La Patron as their sire. That is a major difference. He's older and the ruler of our pack. It comes as no surprise his pups accelerate in knowledge,*" Asia said in a pacifying tone.

"*Humph, that's no excuse for bad behavior. I'm not having it, next time they'll think twice before having a hissy fit against me.*" It was the chuckle at the end of the statement that made Asia ask.

"*What did you do?*"

Jasmine snorted. "*I'm making them clean the entire room by themselves and threatened to spank them again if they ever yell at me like I'm their playmate. None of my children will ever talk to me that way. I'm not having it. Not from the first two or from these four rascals.*"

Asia covered her mouth at the rant. "*You spanked them?*" She couldn't imagine the sophisticated woman she knew raising her hand to anyone. Jasmine could wiggle her fingers and lift you from the floor, or rob your voice with a command. Those things she understood, but spanking? Asia couldn't see it.

"*I swatted each one of those butts for spouting off to me. It's one thing to be angry. Silas told them they could go and then changed his mind. So I understand the disappointment. But they made it personal and talked trash to me, like I'm a servant or something. Oh no, that makes it a different party. They will never make that mistake again.*"

"*Wow.*" Asia had nothing else to say. Behind the anger and sorrow rolling through their link whatever the pups said, it hurt Jasmine to discipline them. Better to bend the branch now while it was flexible, than later.

"Yeah, now they have these long faces, but they're cleaning up that mess and I'm standing here watching. Rone came in and fussed at them for disrespecting me. I don't think they expected that."

"They apologized?"

"Oh yeah. Before Rone came in, I told them why I popped them on their butt and they apologized and hugged my neck. David then told them to get to work cleaning up their mess." Jasmine chuckled. *"He is a bossy one. So much like Silas, it's scary."*

"He has a lot of you as well, Mistress."

"True, sometimes I wonder what will happen with these four. Silas wants more kids, but these four keep me on my toes, I'm not ready to have more. Maybe later, much later." She paused. *Oops, sorry I got sidetracked. The Goddess summoned me, which was really cool by the way, and she told me I am her representative for the mission you and Hawke are on."*

"She mentioned me?" Asia's heart raced in fear and excitement, she couldn't believe the Goddess paid her the least attention.

"Yes, and Hawke," Jasmine said in a soft voice. *"I told you, Asia. You are special. There is something going on and you and your Mate are the keys for the success of turning the war."*

"Keys? War?" Separately, she understood a key and she had told La Patron they were in a war. But those two words in a sentence together didn't make much sense to her.

"When she talks, it's in riddles, let me see if I can remember what she said exactly." Asia listened as Jasmine repeated her conversation with the Goddess.

Closing her eyes, Asia went over in her mind what Jasmine said. *"He's loyal already, what more does he need to do?"*

"Who is his Alpha?"

Asia bit her lip before answering. *"He doesn't have one. We want to belong to the same pack, so we're waiting to come home and then he'll pledge to La Patron."* Since they hadn't actually discussed this she assumed this was her mate's mindset.

"Let me talk with Silas. That needs to be done right away, maybe Angus can help but for her to say it was important to happen immediately it must be."

"Yes, Ma'am. As soon as La Patron knows what he wants to do let us know. Now, as far as merging, I thought we did that when we mated. Is there more? Something we haven't done?"

"I don't know and I don't know how to contact her for answers."

Asia wasn't surprised. The Goddess was big on allowing her followers find their own path with a gentle push. *"Okay, we'll deal with that later. But this one... becoming a Sword in truth, please tell me you know what she meant by that?"* Based on everything Jasmine said, Sword in truth seemed to crystallize the message.

"I assume that once the two of you completely merge, you both will be La Patron's sword. It makes more sense when you back into it," Jasmine said.

"So Hawke needs to pledge his service to La Patron, which should help us merge closer and La Patron will deem us both as his Sword? Is that it?" Asia tried to make sense of what she'd been told.

"Sounds about right. I asked Silas about the pledging thing and he'll use Angus to do it. Is he around?"

"No. We're in Romania at an old castle." Thoughts continued to roll through her mind over what the Goddess expected of her. How could she and Hawke be responsible for victory in the war? The Liege had decades of a head-start and were committed to a cause grossly twisted over the years.

"Asia? Asia?"

"Yes, Ma'am?" She hadn't been paying attention.

"What are you doing in Romania?"

"Another Alpha had information regarding the Liege and needed Hawke to translate some books." She paused and then gasped. *"I saw the birthmark or one very close to David's."*

"What? When? One second, let me get Silas and you can tell us both the same time."

Asia looked over at Hawke, who met her glance with a frown.

"What's going on?"

She told him about the conversation with the Goddess and watched his brow rise. *"Really? Swords? That's interesting. I'd like to listen."*

Asia merged the links so they could all be in the discussion.

"Silas is here with me. Now what's this about the birthmark? We've had Maheegan, the pack historian, searching everywhere to find information about it and she hasn't had any luck."

"Mistress, Hawke, my mate is on the link as well. He has been translating old texts from the Lords Roundtable."

"Roundtable?" Jasmine asked.

"That was the name of the original Liege Lords," Asia said and went on to explain what Radoff told them.

"This Hungarian fellow set up the Liege to help the full-bloods?" Jasmine asked in a doubtful tone.

"Yes," Hawke said. *"He was emphatic, almost evangelistic over the cause. He set aside his entire considerable fortune to ensure shifters never died out. It's impressive actually, he had little use for humans other than to use them to help carry out his agenda."*

"Was he a shifter?" Jasmine asked.

Asia sensed Hawke's surprise. She hadn't thought of that. But it was possible.

"I don't know, but something happened between him and Alpha Nikolas. Perhaps there is some truth to the rumors of shifters making other shifters through the bite," Hawke said and then explained the Liege's initial interest in the bite.

"That is one theory," La Patron said without saying more. Asia wanted to push, but years of conditioning stopped her. As her Alpha he would decide how much to tell her.

"What would be another theory?' Hawke asked.

"That he was under Alpha Nikolas' control, fed off his life force and was linked to him in some way."

"Like a minion?" Jasmine asked.

"That might be a word for it," La Patron said.

"Is that possible?" Hawke asked.

"Under a certain set of circumstances, it could be. I was born in the 1700's, this happened in the 1800's. To my knowledge Angus, my litter mate, has abilities no other person has. Some would say the things he does with items from nature is magic. During that time the Goddess gave gifts to men to perform certain tasks, that's why I say it is possible Nikolas turned the Hungarian into a shifter through the bite or turned him into a minion, extending his life force through the bite. It would also explain why the Hungarian

died not long after the Alpha. The Alpha sustained his prolonged life force."

"Okay, if Konstantin was part wolf why are his initials in this mark?" Asia asked to get the conversation back on track. Radoff had given them both a disappointed sigh when Hawke told him they were on what amounted to a conference call with La Patron. *"Why not Alpha Nikolas initials?"*

"Or Black Clan?" Jasmine asked.

"You say there is a semblance of a snout and paw?" Silas asked.

"They seem to have been drawn by a few different people over the years, there are some variations. Sometimes the initials are clear, other times they aren't. Different body parts as well. Sometimes a paw, others a snout, ears, one had teeth."

"I don't know the answers to those questions, but I will have someone do some additional research. Any chance of sending a book here for review?"

"I can ask Alpha Radoff but he's holding them close, won't even allow us to leave out the room with one," Asia said.

"Will he allow my pack historian to come there to complete her research? She knows the birthmark and could shed some light on the issue," Silas said.

"This may not be the best time," Asia said, looking at Hawke, who was speaking to Alpha Radoff.

"Perhaps, but all of this is connected and I want answers," Silas said in a hard voice.

"No, he won't allow the books to leave and yes, she may come to see them here. He's pleased you think they may be of some value. Most of the journals are meeting notes and deal with member infractions," Hawke said stifling a yawn.

"We will leave shortly to find a hotel and return in the morning."

"I will contact her and get her flight plans to you and Angus. If anyone can make sense of those notes, Maheegan can. It's her gift." La Patron sounded confident which eased Asia's concerns of having one more person to watch over.

"When should we expect her?" Asia asked, thinking Chacal would have another visitor.

"She is en-route to my compound. I will change her plans so that she will arrive within a day or two. It depends on what she needs to leave the country."

"The Goddess wants Hawke's loyalty to you locked down," Jasmine said breaking the silence.

"So I heard," La Patron said and Asia assumed he didn't appreciate his mate bringing it up at the moment.

"How do you suggest we do that?" Hawke asked, surprising her. She thought they'd have more time to discuss it, but it didn't seem that way.

"Normally, there'd be a blood exchange, but that's not going to happen right now. Are you and Angus linked?"

"No."

"Why not?" Silas asked.

"He's not linked to my mate and I met him through her."

"I see. I'm not linked to your mate either, my mate is linked to her."

"I'm aware of that. But the Goddess has vouched for you when she made a decree that my loyalty to you be secured. I trust her and my mate. Both agree that you are a worthy Alpha," Hawke said without pretense.

"Good to know."

One moment Hawke sat in the chair the next he fell sideways and just barely stopped himself from hitting the cobblestone floor. His chest rose and fell as he breathed in deep gulps of air. He pulled the fabric over his head so the air would ease the fire rolling through his veins.

Asia touched his face. "Are you alright?"

"What happened?" Radoff asked.

A burning sensation raced through his body and slammed into his chest. A sharp pain scraped his right side, burning from the inside as if someone took a pencil and drew lines. Gritting his teeth, he tensed as the sensation continued to run through his body on a loop, and then slumped forward when it stopped.

"*What happened to Hawke?*" Asia asked Jasmine. Hawke wanted to ask the same question, but couldn't talk.

"*Silas marked him. Took a lot of energy from both of us, I'm going to go rest and will contact you when Maheegan's on her way.*" She sounded winded as if she needed to catch her breath.

"*Hawke?*"

"*One second. It's cooling.*" He exhaled as cool tingles surrounded the area. A few moments later he sat up and rested his forehead in his palm without speaking.

Asia gasped.

Radoff moved to face him, both stared at his chest. The pain eased a bit and he looked down. A miniature sword was carved in his flesh like a tattoo. Amazed that it didn't disappear like most of his wounds, he continued to stare.

"Well, that's one way to do it," Asia said and sat in the chair next to him.

Chapter 8

Angus parked the truck in front of the building and sighed. It looked abandoned, just as the others had. Chacal stepped out the passenger side and closed the door. Angus rechecked his notes, looked at the building and joined Chacal.

"This one's not as old as the others," Chacal said looking around. "Someone has been here recently."

Angus nodded and tried to identify the scent. "Human, maybe lab workers or custodians. Maybe we can get a clue what's been going on, or if we are lucky there will be someone we can talk to, let's check it out." He walked down the overgrown path toward what appeared to be the entrance. Once he cleared the large columns, he noticed a large piece of wood covered the opening.

"*Wonder who put that there?*" he asked Chacal through their link.

"*Humans. The Liege don't bother closing a building after they leave.*"

Angus nodded and walked around the building. If this was, like the other abandoned former work-sites, everything that would connect the Liege would be erased.

A small village lay beyond the hill which was highly unusual. "Let's go talk to the people in that place. This is the first Liege stronghold this close to a town. I'd like to hear what they have to say." He looked at the building again in disappointment, so far they'd all been the same, abandoned with no clues. Hopefully they'd learn something of value from the locals.

Chacal nodded and they returned to their vehicle and pulled off. "It's not like the Liege to change the way they operate and have a lab this close to people. Something's strange about this," Angus said as he drove down the dirt road and parked near the pub.

"True. Maybe that place dealt with their legitimate businesses, if that had any. Or was an administration only site," Chacal said.

After taking a deep breath, he looked at his friend. "I don't smell anything but humans inside this place, you?"

"That is true. But we will soon discover what type of humans." Chacal stepped out the truck and headed toward the door of the small establishment without waiting for Angus.

By the time Angus entered the bar, Chacal had his hands wrapped around the throat of a tall, burly man whose face grew redder by the second. No one interfered, so Angus took a seat at the bar and ordered a beer.

The bartender wiped the glass with a half-clean rag, filled it and placed it in front of him. "You with him?" He tipped his chin toward Chacal.

Without turning Angus nodded and picked up his glass.

"The first one's on the house." The bartender grinned, showing a wide gap between his front teeth.

Sensing a story, Angus stared at the man. "Why?"

"He's a regular pain in the arse, that one." He looked over Angus' shoulder with a smirk. "He had it coming, the thief."

"Thief? What does he steal?" Angus glanced over his shoulder, although Chacal had already told him everything was okay.

"Anything not tied down," he spat and watched Chacal walk the much larger man out the building with his hand still on his neck.

"I'm going to question him," Chacal said through their link.

"He tried to rob my friend? That was a big mistake," Angus said in a low voice and gauged the atmosphere of the place.

A chair scraped the floor in the main area. A young male in his late teens sat on the stool next to Angus and nodded at the bartender. "What're you and your friend looking for?" His breath smelled sour, like stale beer and meat. Thin shouldered, acne marks on his narrow face and a short pug nose, he glanced at Angus and then looked away.

Angus turned aside and looked at him in the mirror behind the bar. "What makes you think I'm looking for anything?"

"He came in here looking for a fight, Harwg's stupid enough to give him one. But I saw the gleam in his eye, he wanted information. I might be able to help you if the price is right."

Angus inhaled, filtered out the bad hygiene and searched for the tart scent of deception. He smelled none.

The male leaned close to his ear and whispered. "You want information 'bout LOBO don't cha?"

Angus frowned. "What?" The name meant nothing to him.

The male seemed surprised and looked at the bartender who chuckled. "Well, if you didn't come looking for information 'bout that large building up there, what were you snooping around there for?"

"It's for sale, we were looking to buy it. But what are you talking about? What's a LOBO?" Angus sensed both men wanted to talk but wanted to make money if they could.

"I told ya," the bartender said in a righteous tone. "No one has heard of this thing you keep prattling about. It is all in your mind." He tapped his forehead and walked off.

Angus took a sip of the beer and waited.

"It's not in my mind. I was there. I saw them." He looked behind him and lowered his voice. "That building you thinking of buying did a lot of things to animals. Small dogs or foxes I suppose. Anyway they called it LOBO. Can't recall what the first two letters stood for but the last two were big fancy words. Behavior optimization, don't think I'll ever forget that." He snorted and took a long sip of his beer.

Angus watched the guy out the corner of his eye, sensing movement in the back of the club he angled in his seat to catch a glimpse of the man seated behind them. "Did they mess up the building with the animals, because I don't want to buy it if it's torn apart?"

"No...no. If it's messed up now, it's because of the gypsies who live there different times of the year. They have no respect for law or property. The building owners cleaned everything out when they left. If I hadn't..." he glanced at Angus and then looked into his beer.

"What?" Angus sensed the guy was about to say something important.

"Nothing, well it is something. Look, how much would you pay to find out what was going on in that building? You need to know before you buy it right?"

Angus rubbed his chin and stared at the young man. "It depends on how valuable I think it is. Are you saying something is wrong? That I'm being suckered into a bad deal?" His voice rose a little at the end.

"Shhhh, keep it down. These guys are powerful and there are ears everywhere. That's why I want to get rid of this." He dropped his forehead into the palm of his hand and closed his eyes. Angus sensed his genuine distress and decided to push.

"Fifty US dollars."

The guy looked at him wide-eyed.

"That's how much I'll pay you to tell me or show me what you have that's wrong or right with that building." Angus tipped his chin to the right.

The guy licked his lips and then glanced around the almost empty room. "Okay, follow me to the loo, I'll give it to you then."

"No. Follow me outside and then we walk towards the building and you give it to me on the way. I have no use for blank pages or useless prattle."

Chacal walked inside at that moment and took a seat at the table near the door. *Loudmouth, poor hygiene, but he knew nothing. They didn't hire locals, and had nothing to do with the villagers. Seems they stayed in that building for two years and then moved.*

"Tell your friend it's okay to bring the pages, so we can go," Angus said softly taking a guess at the identity of the male seated nearby.

"Fifty you say?"

Angus nodded but didn't speak. Instead, he told Chacal the gist of the conversation with the young man through their link.

"LOBO, an acronym? How original."

Angus watched the young guy lean back, and toss a coin onto the bar. "Come on then," he said, standing and motioning to his friend who sat in the back of the bar.

"I'm going to see what this kid has in the briefcase, monitor the bartender just in case he wants to get involved," Angus told Chacal who stared at the barkeep.

"Got it. Watch your back, I don't smell deceit, but you never know."

Angus followed the guy out the bar until they reached his car. He leaned against it and waited. It took some time for the other guy to arrive and when he did, he handed a roll of leaves to the other guy and walked off.

In a few moments the leaves were removed and Angus looked down at a stack of documents. L.O.B.O was stamped across the front page.

"Fifty American dollars."

Angus reached into his pocket and pulled out three twenties. "Keep the change," he said, taking the papers. The young guy walked around the car and headed in the opposite direction of his friend. Within seconds he disappeared into the woods.

"We need to leave and verify this information."

"On my way. The barkeep's nervous, he keeps looking around like he's expecting company."

"You make him nervous. What'd you do to the big guy?" Angus unlocked the truck and stepped inside.

"He's sleeping."

Angus shook his head and read the first page of the report. Liege Organized Behavior Optimization. "What the hell?" he leaned forward and read through what appeared to be a chapter of a training manual. He looked up when Chacal slid into the passenger seat.

"Read this." He slid the pages to his friend, started the truck and pulled out with a u-turn. They needed to research this immediately, which meant getting back to Chacal's compound, an hour and a half away.

By the time they reached the main highway, Chacal had read through several pages without saying anything.

"Is it as bad as I think?" Angus didn't care for what the name suggested and could imagine what the Liege would call optimized behavior. On the other hand, this might be the break they needed to find the bastards.

"Probably worse. On paper, it sounds benevolent, as though the Liege is a large charity taking in homeless strays and making their lives better. When the reality is they train these pups to blindly obey their will, and deny their wolf. And this is just one chapter. Imagine what the rest of it is like."

"Damn." Angus slammed his palm against the steering wheel and pulled onto the shoulder. "I need to read that and make a report." They exchanged seats and within moments were back on the road. The more Angus read, the angrier he became.

"*Silas?*"

A few moments later Silas responded. "*Yeah? You found something?*"

Angus explained what they'd discovered and then listened as Silas called the Liege every foul and disgusting name in the book.

"They are all those things and more, but now we have a name and their objectives. They are taking pups faster now, taking larger risks."

"That type project is not happening in Russia, Europe or Africa, they are bringing them here and training them here in the states somewhere. That's why the places you're checking are closed and have been closed for a while. They're doing this bullshit on my turf. I'll have Jacques begin a search for any group or organization bringing in wolf pups into this country. Now would be a good time to test the sincerity of the Oval office, he said they'd work with me, and this is a top priority."

"I agree." Angus looked out the window, listening to Silas' rant over the Liege and their operations. *"Excuse me, what?"* He missed something.

"I said, the Goddess spoke to Jasmine about Asia and Hawke. They're important in winning this thing. I marked him earlier."

"Marked him?" Angus straightened in his seat. *"What do you mean?"*

"He agreed to serve and I marked him with a sword on his chest."

"You drew it?" He frowned, trying to understand.

"No. Well, in a way. What's important is I can link with him and stay in the loop. He and Asia are in Romania with another Alpha. They found something interesting." Silas told Angus what the two had discovered.

"What? Un-fucking-believable. I've heard stories about the Alpha Black Wolf for decades but I've never heard of this Alpha Nikola one. Hard to swallow, we started as friends with the Liege, but it makes sense in a weird way. The tone of this section comes off as a benevolent act to the pups."

"Hawke's translating the journals to see if there is anything we can use to beat the bastards. I hope he finds something. I shut the compound down and started a war."

"With Jasmine?" Angus couldn't imagine his sister-in-law pissed at not being able to leave if it was dangerous.

"No, my pups took exception." He told Angus about the circus and everything they'd done to prep the kids to go.

"Even David?" Angus couldn't imagine that one getting upset over anything.

"No, he stared at me for a few minutes and then gave me his back." Silas laughed. Angus didn't blame him.

"He's going to be a force when he's older."

"Yes, I believe you are right. I sent Leon and Brix to track down and eliminate any Liege Lord they find in this country. They are not welcome on this continent."

Angus' brow rose. *"Continent? You claiming all of it now?"*

"Where the safety of my pups and every pup in my pack is concerned, yes. For what they have done, their days are numbered."

"Understood. We are headed to Chacal's to do some research on LOBO and will keep you updated."

"Send copies of what you have so I can see it. I need to talk with my alphas, we need to plan and prepare."

"Okay, will do." Angus disconnected and stared at the page.

Project LOBO: Liege Organized Behavior Optimization. What the hell did that involve?

 *Chapter 9*

Silas strode from the lab and headed to his office. He'd put it off as long as he could. Rose sat behind the desk, her extended belly made it impossible for her to get any closer.

"You doing okay today?" he asked as he did every day.

"Yes, we're doing good. I left a stack of messages on your desk, mostly Alphas requesting call-backs."

He nodded. "I'm about to do a conference call. Set it up. Have Rone and Rese meet me in five minutes."

She nodded and got busy.

"*How are things?*" He asked Jasmine once he settled in his chair. He'd left her to deal with the pups and knew she'd be pissed. But he couldn't take the tears on Renee and Jackie's faces. He had almost changed his mind and offered to take them himself. Which may become his last option.

"*Hmmm, feeling guilty?*"

He closed his eyes and swallowed a grimace at the bite in her voice. *"No. Yes. Just a little. I didn't expect them to react like that. Goddess, did you see David turn his back on me? Unbelievable."*

"No. The unbelievable part was looking for you to stand up to your children and not finding you anywhere. You created this mess and didn't stick around to clean it up."

Silas rubbed his forehead with his fingers. *"I know, you're right. My princesses, Renee and Jackie got to me, I couldn't take it. What are they doing now? Still crying?"*

"Go check."

He released a long sigh. *"I have a meeting with my Alphas in a few minutes, otherwise I would."*

"What happened," she asked in a no-nonsense tone.

"Angus came across some papers about a Project LOBO that the Liege have for pups."

"What?"

Silas told her what he'd been told, Tyrone and Tyrese knocked and entered. *"The twins are here, we need to get ready to brief the Alphas on what's happening. I'm sorry I left you in the midst of battle and will do better next time."*

"Hope so."

Silas exhaled and left his office. Rone and Rese stood nearby talking. "How's Danielle," Silas asked about Rese' mate.

"She's fine and on her way back with Maheegan. They should arrive in an hour."

"Okay, come with me. You'll need to leave to pick them up, but I want you to hear most of this."

Tyrese nodded. "Yes, Sir."

"Maheegan will be leaving soon, I need her to do some research in Romania. She got the message just as she was boarding. Did your mate tell you?" Silas asked as he closed the door to the conference room. The large screen on the wall filled with Alphas logging online.

"Dani said you were sending her nana somewhere, but didn't say much more than that."

"Good, as long as she knows. I forgot to tell Angus, but Asia knows. I'll tell him later." He looked at the monitor and the number forty-three flashing beneath it, after seven more Alphas checked in he would start. "Have a seat," he said to the twins who took a chair on each side of him. One day all six of his pups would share this table with him. His chest expanded with that thought.

First, he needed to insure every pup in the pack was safe from the Liege's grasp and optimizing project. The need for retribution burned deep inside, too many of his kind lost their lives and mates in those experiments for him to ever allow the Liege to get off lightly. Each one would pay dearly for what they had done. He'd make sure of it.

When the counter beneath the screen reached fifty, Silas spoke. "I have important news to share with you concerning the Liege and the threat they represent to our pack." For the next two hours, Silas answered questions, eased fears and concerns, and stopped a lynching party packed and ready to head to Romania.

Chapter 10

Beams of the morning sun filtered through the curtains of the hotel room. Asia rolled on her side and rested her leg on top of her mate's thigh. His palm cupped her ass and squeezed. She hadn't loved him when they mated. Fond of him? Yes. Interested? Yes. But this gut-wrenching need to be joined with him at all times? No. This was new. And now she understood the often misused and misunderstood term, falling in love.

"Morning," he said against her forehead. The warmth of his words slid down her back and nestled in her core. After the many times he'd taken her and she'd taken him last night, the press of his hardness against his belly soothed her.

"I'm sore." She snuggled closer.

"Me too." He rubbed his cock against her.

"Seriously, you wore me out last night. I might not be able to walk today." She bit his nipple causing him to moan.

"I'll carry you wherever you need to go. You can always count on me to fix anything I break, with you that is."

He chuckled and she enjoyed the movement of his chest against hers.

She rolled on top of him and looked into his face. Her fingertip traced the scar near his mouth and then his lips. He drew her finger into his mouth and sucked on it for a bit sending giddy tingles through her body. His hazel eyes glowed with sexual intent.

"I know what you're thinking," she said, tapping the tip of his narrow nose.

Hawke placed his hands beneath his head, leaving himself to her mercy. "No you don't."

His long black hair spilled on the white pillowcase providing a striking contrast, not only with colors, but hard and soft as well. She picked up a few silky strands and played with them while watching him.

"You want to get started translating those journals so we can finish and leave this place," she teased when he frowned and then laughed.

"That was not on my mind." He paused until he captured her gaze. "Kiss me."

Her heart fluttered at the softly uttered command. Her wolf went wild and pushed her forward. Asia placed her palms on the mattress next to each of his ears, leaned forward and brushed her lips against his. Firm, yet pliable, she slid her tongue along the seam of his mouth asking for access and he complied. Kissing Hawke had become her favorite pastime. The man didn't just invite her into the kiss. When they kissed, he opened himself to her emotionally and everything he felt for her resonated in the simple touching of mouth and tongue. Their kisses always left her panting and breathless, wanting more. Her core clenched in need as he rolled her to the side, deepening their kiss. Heart soaring, she embraced his commitment to love and cherish her forever.

He called her his sun. She named him her moon. The two dependent on each other for balance.

Instead of giving her words of love, he showed her how much she meant to him and how empty he was until she came into his life. She accepted his love and returned it on the wings of an equal pledge to love and honor him with her life. He colored her world and completed her in ways she never imagined.

"You are my today and all of my tomorrows," she gasped when they broke apart. He pulled her tight and held her close. Sunlight and roses burst through the link warming her as he rolled her onto her back.

"My everything," he whispered and plunged into her. Her nails dug into his arms as he thrust repeatedly into her, taking her higher.

"Merge with me," she whispered and met him in the halls of their link. Bright, and strong, his energy rolled forward meeting hers, twisting and intertwining them together as he continued driving into her snug warmth.

"My everything," he said again, this time their energies changed and became one color, a bright white that spilled over and out of their link. Asia held onto his arms as he sped up and lifted her higher until the brightness surrounded them. She couldn't breathe, couldn't stop. More she wanted more of him.

"Hawke," she called and rose on her toes beneath him and then flew apart. Her body shook as waves of pleasure rolled through her. Thoughts couldn't land. She couldn't speak. Small tremors continued shooting through her as she tried to breathe.

After a few more strokes, he roared and held her hips so tight, she winced in pain. When his breathing normalized, he sent warm energy through her system easing her aches.

His thoughtfulness tugged at her heart and she melted into his embrace.

"I only have two more journals to translate," he spoke into the silence.

Too wiped to speak, she nodded.

"There are a few outbuildings around the castle. I'd like to look through them before we head back."

She nodded and rubbed her hand across his chest, flicking his nipple.

"Still hungry?" He growled against her forehead.

"Always, but we need to get moving. At some point we should check in with Angus and Chacal to see if they found anything and to tell him about the journals." She rolled to the side. He stopped her before she left the bed.

"Those things can wait. I need to hold you a little longer. Most days we don't have a chance to spend time alone like this. We're newly mated. Everyone will understand if we don't show up first thing."

"Are you sure you want to look inside this building?" Asia asked Hawke while looking at the dilapidated structure.

"Yes… I cannot explain it, but it seems familiar." He looked at her and then back at the building where Alpha Radoff and his Beta packed the now translated journals into boxes for safe keeping. They would be leaving shortly to lock the books in a vault. The Alpha had allowed Hawke to keep a digital copy of the translations which Hawke stored in his cloud.

"Alright," she said, taking his offered hand.

He understood her concern and hesitation and would have turned around if he didn't sense the importance of going inside.

"Stay behind me." He didn't give her time to argue and stepped through the opening into the dim room. Someone had broken the furniture and ripped out the windows allowing nature to move indoors. Grass and small twigs sprouted in the walls and between the stone pavers on the floor.

Closing his eyes, Hawke tried to pinpoint the source of his unease. Moving on instinct he walked further into the building and stopped when he reached the stairs. He opened his eyes and frowned. "This shouldn't be here. There's… he stomped on the bottom stair, then the one above it, and then the one above that. A grinding sound came from behind them. Asia had her sword in her hand and faced the dark entrance.

"I don't like this."

"I understand." Driven by a sense of urgency he couldn't explain, he walked toward the opening.

"But you are going down there anyway?"

"Yes, Sexy."

"Sexy?" She looked at him with a gleam of amusement in her eye. Listening to his thoughts through their link she smiled. Considering she looked like an older white male in need of a tan and visit to the gym, most would think him insane for thinking she was sexy as wildfire.

"My Sexy Bitch. If it were you, you'd go. So let's just do this." He read the resignation in her gaze before she nodded and stepped aside.

Pleased, she remembered his request to allow him to lead in these type situations he walked down the staircase. *"Let me go all the way down to test the stairs. No need in both of us falling through the boards."*

"No need in going down there period."

He grinned at her sour response and continued down the stairs, pulling down cobwebs as he went. The wood was in surprisingly good condition. At the bottom he found a light switch, flipped it and was surprised when the room illuminated. This room had been used recently. He inhaled. "Full bloods use this basement."

Asia came down the stairs and looked around. "Radoff doesn't know about this. I don't smell him. These scents are different, wonder who's using his land as a hideout?"

Hawke walked down the hall a bit and looked into each room. Some were empty. A few had twin sized beds, a chair and table. "These are sleeping chambers," he called over his shoulder while continuing his search. A sense of familiarity nagged at him, but he couldn't recall ever being in this part of the country, not working for the Liege or on his own. So why was he down here searching for... something? He didn't know.

She came up behind him. "Yeah, someone probably lives here." She picked up an ashtray with old cigarette buds and returned it to the table. They moved further down the hall and came to a large room with benches and a dais with high back chairs.

"What the hell?" Asia said, looking at the wall.

Hawke followed her gaze and closed his eyes as blinding pain ripped through him. He fell to his knees as knives cut into his brain, sawing and tearing him apart.

"Hawke?!"

Her voice echoed in the chamber of his mind giving it an unreal quality. His wolf snapped and pushed for him to rise. Time crawled as he attempted and failed to stand several times. Something was wrong. *"Asia?"* he called through their link.

"Busy right now." Blood ran down the side of her face while she fought five full-bloods.

His wolf snapped again at the idea of their mate in danger. Sobered, he shifted into battle mode and charged into the fray. His wolf leapt onto the back of the closest beast and ripped his throat out. Turning, he attacked the next closest wolf and within minutes that one left the living. Hawke slammed into the other wolf and went for his neck. The wily beast pivoted and Hawke missed. Meanwhile, he caught a glance at his mate standing to the side breathing heavily. Pleased, she was okay, he focused on his enemy.

No one attacked his mate and lived.

Hawke extended his claws and swiped the wolf across his belly. Blood and organs poured out from the wound. Next he swiped the beast across the neck to decapitate him. The wolf flew back against the wall and lay motionless. Hawke shifted to human and ran to Asia, checking her over. The blood had stopped and she assured him she was fine. He glanced at the men on the floor and shook his head.

"Why would five full-bloods attack us?"

"I don't know," she said. *"What the hell?"* She pointed to the last wolf who'd landed against the wall. Both of his wounds were healing and he sat staring at them. Hawke strode forward as the wolf reverted to his human form.

"Stop," the man gasped.

Hawke grabbed him by the neck, lifted him off his feet and shook him like a rag doll.

"Hawke, put him down," Asia said, standing behind him. *"You can't kill him."*

The man grabbed at his hands to gain release. *"I can kill him. I'll rip his head from his body this time."* He shook the man again.

"No, you can't kill him. Breathe. Inhale. His scent is familiar to me."

Hawke looked over his shoulder at her. *"What? What do you mean it's familiar?"* He inhaled and frowned. Slowly he turned and looked at the man.

"Who the hell are you?" He eased up on the hold without letting go.

"Niall." The name meant nothing to Hawke. He glanced at Asia for an answer.

"He smells like you," she said sending a caress through their link.

Hawke opened his hand and stepped back. Niall dropped to the ground gasping for air and rubbing his throat. "You didn't have to do that," he complained.

Hawke looked at the others they'd killed and then turned back to Niall. "Why did you attack my mate?" If Asia picked up the similar scents, Niall should have known she was his mate.

"What? We did not attack him." He pointed at Asia. "We were using this old tunnel as a shortcut and walked into this room. You were on the floor and he attacked without asking questions."

"It's true. I could not allow them to come near you while you were in that condition," Asia said. Hawke sensed her shame at the needless killing. He strode to her, place his finger beneath her chin and kissed her.

"Never be ashamed for protecting your mate. I would've done the same thing. We are newly mated and things we do now, we may not do later. But we live in the now. I am proud of you, my Precious."

He turned toward Niall. "Who are you?"

"I told you–" Niall stood and faced him.

Hawke waved down his words. "My mate says you smell familiar, who are you to me?"

"Your litter-mate. That's why my life was spared. Litter-mates cannot kill each other."

"Is that true?"

"Yes, several times Angus told the story of his meeting with La Patron. It's true."

"Who is that?" Niall pointed at Asia.

"Timber, my mate." Hawke glanced at Asia to see her reaction to the name he'd won on a bet with her. She didn't like it then or now.

Niall nodded at Asia and took a step back.

"Is this your home?" Hawke asked, looking everywhere except the dais.

"No. We use it as a short cut from time to time. I heard you had been released and wondered if you'd pay a visit."

Hawke scowled. "Released? Visit? Why would I visit you? I didn't know of your existence until a few moments ago. And would've killed you without a thought." He looked at the bodies on the ground and then at Niall.

"I see. I thought you came to assist… but no I suppose you have no idea. You killed the men I hired to retrieve me mam. She was taken a week ago by another Alpha north of here. We were on our way to get her back."

Hawke frowned. "What?"

"Your mother, Hawke. Someone kidnapped your mother. They were on their way to rescue her, but we, I killed them."

He looked at Asia and read the regret in her gaze. "Who is the Alpha?" he asked, knowing for her sake he'd get involved.

"Verrick," Niall spat his name.

"*Verrick, the one we met before?*" Asia asked.

"In the Ukraine?" He asked Niall.

"Yes, you know him?"

"No." The blasted man had tried to have his mate arrested for releasing the test wolves from Lancaster's Castle. Some of the wolves had no restraint and attacked humans, putting them all at risk. Asia had done what any of them should have done, but Verrick hadn't seen things that way.

Niall looked at the dead men on the ground and then at Hawke. "Did you have to kill them?"

Hawke rubbed the back of his neck and met Asia's gaze. "*What do you want to do? Our mission is clear, shut down the Liege, stop them from stealing pups. This is a detour.*"

"*One that I caused.*"

"*If it comes to placing blame, I caused it. You were protecting me.*"

"*What happened? I felt your pain and then you snapped out of it.*"

"*I'm not sure. Something about the dais, looking at it ripped me apart. Does it look familiar to you?*"

"Well, I need you to help me rescue my mam, since you killed these guys," Niall said, rocking on the balls of his feet.

Asia looked at Niall and then Hawke. "*No, it doesn't. Maybe this is why you needed to return, to see this place. Maybe something happened to you here.*"

He nodded and looked at Niall. "What do you know about this place? The history of it?"

Niall shrugged. "Nothing, just an old tunnel that cuts through pack lands. Mam would know any and everything about this place. She's the pack historian. Can we go get her now?"

"We need to do this, make it right," Asia said. *"Plus, she's your mom. You can ask her questions, get answers, find closure. Don't you want to know what happened? How you wound up with the Liege?"*

He nodded and searched his emotions. "I *don't know her and have no feelings for this woman. But it's important to you, so we will leave and reach Verrick in a few hours before nightfall. Perhaps he will release her and we can return to Chacal's before midnight. I want to rest in your arms again."*

Asia nodded and looked at Niall. *"He looks like you a little. Smaller, but there is a resemblance."*

"Let's go, woman."

"Woman?" Niall asked, staring at Asia who looked like a man. Neither Hawke nor Asia explained as they turned and walked back the way they came. They needed to inform Radoff of this space and the four bodies on his land.

Chapter 11

The three of them walked toward Radoff and a few of his pack members standing near their vehicle. Radoff frowned at Niall, looked at the building they'd just left and looked at them again.

"Who is this?"

"Niall, my litter mate," Hawke answered not bothering to explain the new connection.

"Hello," Niall said, looking at the other men.

"Where'd he come from?"

"There is a tunnel beneath that building and four bodies," Hawke said.

Radoff stared at him and then looked at Niall. "Okay, I'll take care of it. But someone needs to tell me what is going on." He waved his hand toward the house and three of his men jogged in the direction Asia and Hawke had just left.

"*Mistress?*" Asia called while Hawke and Niall spoke to Radoff.

"Asia? Good, I meant to contact you, Maheegan should be arriving in an hour at a small airport in Suceava, that's the closest one to the co-ordinates Silas picked up from Hawke."

"Okay...let me write that down." Asia pulled out a small pad from her pant pocket and wrote the information down. She'd forgotten about Maheegan. With the trip to Verrick how would they work this out?

"So what else is going on?"

"Ma'am?"

"You called me, what happened?"

Asia turned from Hawke's gaze, inhaled and told Jasmine what happened in the basement. *"Okay. I understand you need to fix that. But pick up Maheegan first so she can get started. That Alpha said she could go through the journals, right?"*

"Yes, Ma'am," she said, relieved Jasmine wasn't too angry. *"Hawke has the translated copies as well."*

"But not the images of the marks?"

"No, Ma'am, he doesn't."

"That's a big part of the reason she's coming so she'll need access to the physical journals."

"Yes, Ma'am. I'll let Alpha Radoff know she's coming."

"Good. Good. Be careful with that Verrick guy. He knew more than he let on before. Alpha's have the ability to mask their scents so you won't know if he's telling the truth or not. Good luck finding your mother-in-law."

"What? Who?"

Jasmine's laughter filled their link. *"Technically, that's the title for his mom. But I'm not going to push, you've got a lot of things going on right now. At least you've had a break from those blue things."*

Asia nodded. *"Yes. The castle fell. Lancaster is on this continent, so the peace will not last."*

"True. But he doesn't know you and Hawke are mated. Nor does he know you are in his back yard."

"That's a good thing. I will keep you informed of our progress."

Chapter 12

Maheegan and Alpha Radoff headed back to the castle to look at the journals. Hawke suspected something happened between those two at the airport, but Niall had pushed for them to get on the road to Alpha Verrick's and he didn't have time to ask questions. But Radoff had looked stunned when Maheegan greeted Asia and then the woman's face reddened when she inhaled and met Radoff's gaze. After that, Hawke doubted either Radoff or Maheegan heard a word he or Asia said since they never took their eyes from each other. After securing the older woman's luggage the two waved goodbye and walked away holding hands with broad smiles.

Hawke looked in the rear view mirror at his litter-mate and then back at the road. He had what Asia called family. Impossible to believe after all this time. Where had Niall been all his life? Niall's scarred face, black hair and hazel eyes tied them physically even though Hawke stood a foot over his brother's shorter and thinner frame.

Remembering the brief fight in the basement, Hawke would say Niall did not spend a lot of time practicing self-defense.

"What do you do?" Hawke asked and glanced at the startled expression on Niall's face.

"I was a chemical engineer for a large company near Chisinau."

An odd note in the tone of his voice struck Hawke. "Was?"

Niall nodded, but didn't say anything else.

"*What happened to him?*" He asked Asia who sat in the passenger seat.

"*I don't know. Ask him.*"

"*Is that customary?*"

He felt her gaze, but kept his eyes on the road.

"*You're asking me? How would I know? I don't have any litter-mates or experiences with any.*"

"*But you've spent time with your Mistress' pups. Would they ask personal questions when the other person doesn't volunteer the information?*" He had no idea what was proper in this situation.

"*Hmm, Rone and Rese would ask. At least I think they would. You could ask through his link.*"

The car swerved as Hawke jerked and then looked at her.

"Hey, watch it. I want to get to Verrick's in one piece," Niall said, straightening in the back seat.

"*You should be able to link with him,*" Asia said without looking at him.

"*No.*"

She shrugged and continued looking out the window.

Hawke glanced in the rear view mirror at his litter-mate again. "How did you hear I left the castle?"

Niall shrugged. "I saw the news. The castle fell, explosives, something like that. Figured you'd made it out, didn't feel like you were gone."

That confused Hawke. "Feel like what?"

Niall turned and met his gaze in the rear view mirror. "Are you telling me you don't know anything about litters? How they work?"

Hawke glanced at Asia for help. She continued looking out the window. "Would I have tried to kill you if I knew I could not?"

Niall shrugged again, but didn't speak.

"Feel. Like. What.? Hawke asked again, a low growl slipped through on the last word. Niall met his gaze in the mirror.

"Litter mates can tell when one of their mates dies. There… I said it. Happy?" He turned to the window and stared with a mulish expression.

"*I don't know what he's talking about,*" Hawke told Asia, confused with the conversation.

"*Maybe one of your litter mates died and he felt their death. For answers you have to talk to him.*"

"*He doesn't want to talk to me; he acts as if I've done something wrong.*"

"*Ask him.*"

Hawke sensed no animosity or sarcasm from her. "*Why do you want me to talk to him? Is there something we need to know?*"

Asia spun to face him with nostrils flared. "*I would give anything for the opportunity to talk to someone about my past, my family, my litter-mates. You have this chance to find out who you are, to fill in the blanks of your past, to discover your heritage and you're asking me questions.*" She closed her eyes and exhaled.

The heat of her frustration scorched him. How could he have forgotten the reason she showed up to the castle where he'd been a prisoner for over thirty years? She had been on a quest to free her former mentor to ask the same questions she posed to him.

"Talk to your brother, talk to your mother, question them until every blank in your mind is filled and every block is colored. History can help uncover destiny. For some reason the Goddess has favored us with a huge task. Maybe something happened when you were a child, there was a reason the Liege took you and not Niall or any of the others in the litter."

Hawke stared straight ahead as each word she spoke created pictures in his mind. His mate was right, there were too many blank lines and uncolored images for him to make sense of anything. He pulled the car over to the side of the road.

"Hey," Niall said, frowning. "Why'd you pull over?"

"How many were in our litter?" Hawke demanded.

Niall's eyes widened and then he looked away.

"How many?" Hawke said in a low tone. Asia touched his arm.

"Six."

Hawke's jaw dropped and then he closed it. "How many still live?"

"Three."

"Who is the other?"

"Pia."

Hawke ground his teeth in frustration at Niall's short answers. "Where is he?"

"She is in Egypt with her mate."

"Our sire?"

"Dead."

"When?"

"Ten years ago."

"What happened?"

"He kept leaving, finally never came back...like you."

Hawke ground his teeth at the comparison. "I did not leave, I was taken."

Niall turned slowly and met his gaze in the mirror. "Taken? By who?"

"The Liege. I have been a prisoner in Lancaster Castle since I was a pup. I have no recollection of anything before that time. Believe me, I did not run away or leave on my own."

Niall continued staring and then nodded slowly. "Well, that might explain your ignorance on pack protocol and biology."

"You thought I ran away? Left the pack on my own?" Hawke couldn't wrap his mind around such nonsense. No pup would do that, would they?"

"After you left...disappeared. We were forbidden to discuss anything about you. We called you Omari meaning first born. Hawke suits you better. Over time I stopped asking and life went on."

"*Omari, I like it,*" Asia said.

"You said you felt the deaths of the other litter mates, tell me about that." Through the years he experienced many things, but had no point of reference, maybe this explanation could clear up a few things.

"There is a tearing, or searing pain that accompanies their crossing and the length of time you feel it depends on the way they died, the amount of pain they endure. Afterward, there's emptiness in that place. Pia says when I mate that space fills, everything heals because of the completeness of being mated, but I don't know if that is true. She is a romantic bitch."

With all the beatings he endured, the surgeries he begged for, and the computer chip that controlled him, Hawke couldn't recall anything close to what Niall spoke of. He glanced at Asia and she squeezed his arm in understanding. Hawke started the car and pulled onto the road.

"What is the name of our pack?" he asked.

"Fekete Farkas Clan, that's the legal name anyway. It's been shortened to Farkas over the years."

Asia met Hawke's surprised gaze. They had seen that clan in the journals. Nikolas had been Alpha of that clan when he met Konstantin. "That's Hungarian, what's the history behind that?" Hawke asked, glancing at Niall in the mirror. "We a Hungarian pack?"

"Not that I know of. I've never been to Hungary. Unlike most packs, we didn't get a lot of pack history lessons, just the names of a few former Alphas. The pack's been around since the late 1800's so it's older than most."

"You left and went to college?"

Niall glanced at him and then stared out the window. "Yes. I have no interest in clan politics, and as the runt of the litter, I opted to use my mind instead of my fists." His tone indicated he thought Hawke mastered the second option.

Rather than debate intellect, Hawke asked pointed questions about pack life. "Who is your Alpha?"

Niall's brow rose. "Don't you mean our Alpha?"

"No. I have an Alpha, La Patron. Who is yours?"

Niall's eyes widened, and then he leaned back against the seat and laughed. Tears rolled down his cheek from laughing so hard. Asia glanced over her shoulder and then shrugged.

"*I guess he thinks it's funny.*"

"*I suppose. But it makes me more curious.*"

Asia nodded.

"What is funny?" Hawke asked after a few moments when the laughter didn't stop.

"They… no, he thinks you are returning to challenge him for Alpha. It was one of the reasons he wouldn't help me go after mam. He would love for us to just disappear."

That made no sense. "Why would I return to a pack that gave me away, or serve an Alpha who had a part in that?"

Niall shook his head. "No, our sire, Hiram, was Alpha and the last direct descendant of Nikolas the Alpha who started the clan, when you disappeared. Not that interloper, Muzik, who runs the clan now. He challenged Jirek on the return from a battle knowing Jirek had fought the previous five hours and won."

"Jirek?"

"Litter-mate number three, and previous Alpha after, Lorenzo, litter-mate number two and first Alpha after our sire's death. Lorenzo died in battle protecting the clan."

"After Hiram died, Lorenzo became Alpha, and he died. Then Jirek became Alpha, he was challenged and killed by the current Alpha? Did I get that right?" Hawke said.

"Yes. Muzik thinks you are returning to take the Alpha spot which belongs to you."

"Why did you say it like that?" Hawke glanced at Niall in the rear view mirror and caught a flicker of emotion he couldn't identify.

"Like what?"

"That it belongs to me? Why do you say that? I've been gone for over thirty years, have no idea how to run a pack or clan or whatever you call it. Plus, I have no allegiance to anyone in your clan."

"Well, he doesn't know that and there's this thing. Someone in Nikolas' line will always be Alpha. Nikolas did some heroic deed and received a promise that his line would never die out, or something like that. That leaves me, you or Pia. As you have probably noticed I am not Alpha material. I would rather read or work with numbers than deal with a bunch of hot-heads. I am no threat to Muzik, he knows this and leaves me alone for the most part."

"Most part?" Hawke growled, his wolf stirred at the idea of someone picking on Niall.

"Yeah, well. I stay out of his way, out of everyone's way. It's just easier all around."

Asia rubbed his arm. He looked down, his fingernails had extended into claws. Hawke inhaled to calm his wolf and willed the nails to return to normal.

"This Muzik going to be a problem?" Asia asked without turning.

"Could be, depends on how mam reacts when she returns. He wanted to mate with Pia but she refused. Then he made mam an offer, she refused and moved to the edge of pack lands. That's how Verrick got her."

"We're on Verrick's land now, should see his place soon. Don't expect a friendly welcome, I've met him before. I'm sure he knows we are here and the only reason no one has stopped us is because he's curious."

"You're friends with that pig?" Niall spat.

"Friends? No. I met him not too long ago in an interesting situation." Hawke glanced at Asia but she looked out the window.

Several rows of small houses became visible as they turned a corner. No one spoke. They were in the middle of

Verrick's pack and sound carried. At the end of the road, one house stood larger than all the others. Hawke parked and waited.

Niall touched the door handle.

"Do not open that door," Asia growled. "We are uninvited guests and need to wait for an invitation to step on his land. Anything else is considered an insult."

"Oh, okay. Got it." Niall leaned back against the seat.

Hawke listened and inhaled. Verrick was coming. Good. He'd been afraid the Alpha would send a minion to deliver some obscure message, demanding they leave without a conversation.

The door to the large house opened and Verrick, still bald and brawny, stepped down the stairs and stood watching them for a few moments.

"Why do you court death?"

"I'd like to talk to you." Hawke glanced over his shoulder, Niall's face lost its color and fear rolled off him in waves.

"Niall?"

His litter-mate's head snapped around and stared at him. *"Hawke? You opened our link?"*

"Yes. I smell your fear, which means Verrick smells it. It'll make him harder to deal with. Can you bring it down a notch?"

"I'm… I'm not doing it on purpose."

"I know. Instead of looking at him and the wolves standing next to him, look at me, or my mate. That should help keep you calm."

"Can you promise nothing will happen to me?"

"No. I cannot. But I will try to keep anything from happening to you."

"Talk? Are you sure? Why is the little one so afraid if all you want is talk?" He pointed toward Niall who stared at Hawke.

"Yes, Verrick I'm sure. Will you give me ten minutes of your time?" Hawke said in a calm tone.

No one spoke.

"Ten minutes? You may meet me here to talk, but only you. This one caused many problems not too long ago. I do not trust." He pointed at Asia who remained still in her seat.

"*Pig,*" Asia said.

Hawke winked at her and opened his door. "*Indeed, he is. I will ask for... what is her name?*"

"*Who? Your mam?*" Asia asked.

"*Yes, I don't know her name, isn't that odd?*"

"*Not really. Ask Niall.*"

Hawke stepped out and around the car to face Verrick. "*What is your mam's name?*" he asked his litter-mate.

"*Mam's name is Granira.*"

"Thank you for allowing me on your lands. I am returning south when I came upon my litter-mate. He was on his way here to seek his mam, Granira. Is she here?"

Hawke noticed Verrick tensed at the name.

"The witch is your mam?"

Witch? Hawke had no idea.

"You label her a witch?"

"No. She labels herself a witch. She is your mam?"

"That is what I've been told."

Verrick threw his head back and laughed. The deep, husky sound raked across Hawke's skin. "Who told you this, that lovesick whelp in the back-seat?"

"What the hell is going on?" Hawke asked Niall. *"Is Granira your mam or not? Do not lie to me or I will give you to him."*

"What did he tell you?" Verrick pointed at Niall. "Did he say she was kidnapped? He's come to rescue her?" Verrick took a step toward the car. "I told you to leave her alone. She told you to leave her alone."

Hawke had the feeling he had stepped into a bad comedy. "So the woman you took from the pack lands is not his mam? But someone else?"

Verrick ran his large palm over his shiny head and shrugged. "Ask her. You can have the witch, she is of no value to me. She may talk to you." He pointed at Hawke. "But I know she wants no parts of him and told him so the last time my men caught him trespassing."

Hawke sighed long and hard through his link. *"I'm going to kick your ass,"* he told Niall.

"No. Please help her. She wants to leave, but they won't allow it. Please Hawke, she's my mate. I know it. She just needs a little time to... settle into the idea."

Hawke nodded and watched the smile creep onto Verrick's face. This couldn't be good.

"If I release her to you, you'll owe me, is that understood?"

"I must clear it with my Alpha, first."

Verrick looked surprised. "Muzik?"

"No. La Patron." Hawked noticed the surprised look on Verrick's face before he wiped it clear.

"La Patron?" Hawke stood with his legs braced and waited a few seconds.

"Yes?"

"I am at Alpha Verrick's keep and he is attempting to secure a favor from me." Hawke told Silas everything that happened to that point.

"My mate would say he is your brother, not litter-mate, which means he is family. Family has an odd way of changing plans. Even so, I cannot allow you to grant him a favor. The Goddess has stated you and Asia have specific roles in this war, but we don't know what those are yet."

"I understand. However, what if the favor he requires is a part of the overall plan? It is just a thought because we don't know. I will abide by your decision."

"For now, I'm saying no. This does not feel right. Keep me informed."

"Yes, Sir."

"Alpha Verrick, I thank you for your time. However, my Alpha says I cannot be in your debt." He nodded and returned to the car.

"What are you doing?" Niall yelled when Hawke started the engine. "We cannot leave her. She is my mate! Don't you understand?"

Hawke backed up and turned around. Verrick remained on the steps, watching them.

"I can't leave her," Niall yelled.

"If she's your mate, call her to you. Mates cannot be separated from each other for long periods of time, it's impossible. She would've come outside or called you through the link if she was your mate," Hawke said and drove down the driveway.

"You're lying," Niall yelled.

"No, he's not. If this woman is your mate, her wolf would be calling you right now, she would be in physical pain and you would feel it," Asia said looking out the window.

"I don't feel pain. Just my heart, it's sick because I'm abandoning my mate."

"She's not your mate, that's why she sent you away the last time," Hawke said, pissed at being duped.

"That was a misunderstanding."

"Shut up," Hawke yelled while watching for an ambush. They were still on Verrick's land and could be stopped.

When they reached the main road, leaving the pack lands behind, Hawke pressed the accelerator and shot down the highway toward Chacal's. Asia placed her hand on his arm, calming him slightly, but the anger that rolled through him at Niall's games wouldn't settle. The fool lied to him, wooed him away from a serious mission to go on a fool's errand as if he were some boy.

Hawke noticed a small store on the side of the road and pulled in. He stepped out the car, jerked open the back door and pulled Niall out by his shirt collar lifting him off his feet. Hawke drew Niall's face close to his and shifted slightly into his hybrid. His long fingernails dug into his brother's skin, causing his face to scrunch in pain.

"You lied to me." He shook him.

"You killed the men I hired to get her."

"You lied to me." Hawke shook him harder this time; his fingernails dug deeper drawing blood.

"Hawke."

"No, Asia. I can't kill him, but I'm going to kick his ass so hard, he'll remember not to play with me like this again."

"We didn't smell a lie."

That stopped him. *"What?"*

"Only Alphas can lie without being detected and he's no Alpha. We didn't smell him lying. Why is that?" She

leaned on the side of the car with her arms crossed staring at him. "*Ask him who is the woman?*"

Conflicted, Hawke leashed his anger. "Who is the woman you went to save?"

"Mam."

"Who is mam?"

"She's the pack… she's an older pack bitch."

"Why are you trying to take her from Verrick? He says she doesn't want to leave."

"Could you put me down? Please?"

Hawke allowed his feet to touch the ground but kept a hold on his shirt. "Last chance or I kick your ass and leave you here."

Niall looked around as if considering and then straightened. "I apologize for not telling you everything. Granira is not the bitch who birthed us, our mam died before our sire. Granira helped raise us and is the pack healer. Some call her a witch because she works with herbs and can do things. She also heals."

"Not everyone." Hawke corrected thinking of his two dead litter mates.

"No. The last Alpha challenge, she couldn't save Jirek and it did something to her. She moved away to the edge of our land, that's when Verrick's men stole her. But she is a stubborn full-blood and he cannot break her spirit."

"Still, she refused to leave with you."

"She didn't know who I was. I think she was drugged or something."

"Stop making things up, she wants no part of you." Hawke yanked Niall closer and snarled in his face. "Worse, you dragged me into that bullshit when you knew I wanted no part of it. That's over. Do whatever you want to do." He released him.

Niall stumbled back a few feet and touched a pole behind him to steady himself. "I will."

Hawke turned and headed toward the driver's seat. Asia looked at Niall, shrugged, turned and slid into the passenger's seat. Hawke started the engine.

"*I'm sorry*," Asia said. "*I pushed you to go there, I didn't smell deceit then or now, if he's lying it's on an Alpha level because I cannot tell.*"

Hawke took her hand and kissed the back of it. "*Let's leave the family matters alone until we finish this assignment, we wasted a lot of time and went out of the way for this. Let's agree to focus on the finding the Liege and stopping them from stealing pups.*"

She smiled. "*Agreed.*"

The back door opened and a tall, dark woman with hazel eyes slid in the back-seat. Hawke spun around and met the woman's too sure gaze.

"Thanks for waiting, it would've taken too long to track you down," she said moving over as Niall slid in beside her.

"Let me guess," Hawke said. "You're his mam."

She smiled. "Is that what you told him?" She looked at Niall who returned her smile. "I'm Granira, a simple healer."

"*There is nothing simple about her*," Asia said. "*She's lying.*"

"*I know.*"

"Get out," Asia said without turning around. "You're lying and we don't have time to deal with your lies."

"No, I suppose not. You've got to find who's stealing pups and stop them. If you take us to Strith, it's on your way, I promise to give you information that will help you."

"*That wasn't a lie*," Asia said.

Chapter 13

"What do you know about the missing pups?" Asia asked as Hawke pulled onto the highway.

"Stealing or taking a pup is not new, it goes back decades." Granari paused. "Even before Omari or Hawke as he's called now, was given away. There is an old agreement in place that the Liege has twisted over time and used to their advantage. For the most part, full-bloods see things in black and white. Hungry, we eat. Tired, we sleep. The Liege understands this and operates in gray areas, so that they do not violate the letter of the agreement but the spirit."

Asia glanced at Hawke. *"Why am I not surprised she knows the Liege and speaks of them with ease and disgust?"*

"She is old. Can you sense it? No doubt she has seen much," Asia said.

"Her ability to lie at will, and hide the deception fascinates me. Perhaps she is a witch."

"Perhaps. Is she lying? I smell no deception. Not even when she said I was given away."

"We will deal with that issue later, remember? Right now we focus on the missing pups. I think she's hiding something," Hawke reminded her.

"Who did the Liege have an agreement with?" Asia asked.

"The pack. A century past, packs worked together, the high council had honor and convinced everyone the agreement would work. For a season it worked well and we all lived in peace. If Konstantin could have cloned himself through the years, it would have been successful. He had a heart and passion for packs. But humans are greedy and full-bloods prefer to keep life simple."

Asia glanced at Hawke. *"She sounds as if she knew him personally. It's possible, La Patron is over three hundred, so is Angus."*

"Could be."

"The Liege twisted an old agreement in their favor and is taking pups. How do we stop them?" Hawke asked.

"You can't. Not without closing a few loopholes first. In his desire to protect the wolves Konstantin installed safety measures which would allow the Roundtable, sorry, Liege members to access pack lands to save them from outsiders. The Liege use that agreement to steal pups and train them," she said, her voice low and sad.

"Can't is not acceptable," Asia said. "What are the loopholes?"

"Why are those full-bloods following us?" Hawke asked.

Asia turned to see a large number of motorcycles gaining on them. She glanced at Granira and then Niall. Neither spoke. "What did you take?"

Granira's gaze met hers and for a long moment she stared into Asia's eyes. "Angus is here, good. I heard he had returned, but hadn't seen him."

Undeterred, Asia glanced at the cycles who were much closer and then at Granira. "What. Did. You. Take?"

"I don't have anything."

"I will ask for the last time. What did you remove from Alpha Verrick's?"

Granira remained silent.

"Pull over, let them have them both. We don't have time for this bullshit."

Hawke drove a little further, pulled onto a side road and stopped. Within seconds the motorcycles surrounded them.

"Get out," Hawke said.

"No," Niall said when Granira moved to open the door. "They may take her again."

"Not my problem," Hawke said.

Asia watched the full-bloods get off the bikes and head toward the car. She'd hoped Verrick would be with them so they could discuss whatever was going on but didn't see him. That sucked. She opened and closed her hands in preparation.

Hawke rolled the window down. "Is there a problem?"

"My Alpha requires the pups be returned."

"What?" Hawke jerked and straightened in his seat. "He wants what?"

Asia mirrored his surprise and glanced at Granira who sat quietly in the back seat. Inhaling, Asia didn't scent pups and wondered what the woman had done with them.

"The pups went missing when this one left." He pointed toward the back seat.

Hawke opened the door and stood next to the full-blood. "The reason I'm surprised by your request is I don't smell any pups, do you?" For the next few moments, every full-blood inhaled and filtered scents including Hawke.

"Do you smell any pups?"

"No. But that does not change my orders. She must return the pups."

Asia could hear the confusion in the man's voice and smiled. Hawke would attempt to handle this logically, first. But if logic didn't work, they'd fight.

"Contact your Alpha, tell him I would turn the woman over if there's proof she has the pups. You can check the car, the pups are not here."

The male nodded and looked away for a few moments.

"*How do you know the pups are not in the car?*" Asia asked.

"*I asked Niall, promised to leave the both of them with these men if he lied. He swears the pups are not here. But she did remove them from Verrick's.*"

"*Really? I didn't realize Verrick was a player in this game.*"

"*Based on Niall's ramblings, I don't think he's a player, more like a suck up. Lancaster has arrived in the country and you can bet Verrick has already told him about our visit.*"

"*Shit.*"

"My Alpha says I should search the car and if the pups are not here, you may leave. Have them step out the car."

Hawke waved everyone out the car. "*Take everything you need, chances are Chacal is going to be out another car. I hope you don't mind riding a bike.*"

Asia chuckled through their link while gathering all her things. She noticed Niall helped Granira do the same. Their glances met and the older woman nodded, but continued pushing things into her bag.

"No, I love them. I have my eye on the big red and black one near the road. Are we expecting bluebirds, hybrids or something new?"

"I don't know what new toys Lancaster has brought to field test. We'll know in a few moments. I'm surprised she told Niall about Lancaster and not us." Hawke waved Asia and the others closer to him before standing in front. Asia stood behind Niall and Granira to watch Hawke's back.

"The last few weeks were too quiet I suppose," Hawke said. The full-bloods moved closer, and surrounded the car. No one opened the door or hood to start searching. In an unsurprising move, the full-bloods went into frenzy and tore the car apart. The wolf who'd spoken to Hawke stood away from the others watching Hawke with a smirk.

Asia rotated her neck and then her arms. Granira looked at her with a concerned gaze. "How well do you ride motorcycles?" Asia asked, causing a few of the full-bloods to stop mid-destruction and look at her.

Granira's face lit with understanding. "Quite well, thank you." The male who'd been smiling at Hawke frowned as Hawke bulked to his hybrid and attacked. He picked up two full-bloods and slammed them together like cymbals. The sound of breaking bones filled the air as he ripped off their heads and through them at the Beta's feet. The man jumped back in surprise and shifted.

Asia bulked and stood in front of Niall and Granira, sending a message to their rivals. A few full-bloods thought she'd be easier than Hawke and ran at her. Before they could blink, she pulled out her sword and the whistle from her swing was followed by the sound of three heads hitting the ground. Some shifted and sprung forward. Asia used her sword with precision to decapitate the beasts. She jumped up to avoid a wolf and kicked him beneath his jaw, sending him flying and impaling on a jagged piece of metal on the car. Hawke's lethal claws cut through flesh and bone, separating heads from bodies.

"Pull back!" the beta who'd spoken to Hawke yelled to the remaining full-bloods. Asia dropped-kicked a four legged beast so hard he hit a tree and broke his neck.

"Bluebirds or Hybrid or other?" Chest heaving, Asia asked.

"I'm not sure, but that was a nice appetizer. They left plenty of bikes to choose from. Nice of them." Hawke said as the remaining full-bloods took off on their cycles and parked a short distance down the road. *"Should we take the bikes or wait a few minutes for the main course."*

"Let's wait. Whatever he sends, Lancaster is somewhere watching. Asshole's probably recording a marketing video. It'd be nice to disable the cameras first. Any ideas?" Asia asked.

"Hybrids, heads off. Bluebirds, heads off. If there is something new? Heads off."

"Your consistency is sexy." She hefted her sword, rested it by her side and settled into her mental quiet spot in preparation.

"Niall just asked why we were waiting. If he pisses in his pants, it's because of the answer I gave him. It was pretty graphic. I told him to stay out of the way."

"Good. I don't think you need to worry about Granira, she's tough." Tingles raced down Asia's back. *"Incoming."* She jumped, twisted in the air and swung, her sword cut through the cords of the hybrid's neck, sending it

flying toward the road while the remainder of the body fell in front of Niall and Granira. Asia turned to attack the next hybrid and noticed the older woman held Niall close covering his mouth.

The bloody fight took longer than Asia anticipated. The Liege had made some improvements to the hybrids, their movements weren't as predictable as before. Her fist no longer penetrated their eye sockets with ease. Hawke cut through the hybrids without bulking to his super size or using his sword. Instead, he ripped off heads or sliced them with his razor sharp nails. Breathing hard, she looked around at the pile of bodies littered around the wrecked car.

"*Who's that?*" she asked Hawke. Across the street a full-blood sat on a motorcycle watching them. He wore sunglasses and remained cool while surveying the carnage.

Hawke looked at the guy and shrugged. "*A full-blood. Probably Lancaster's eyes and ears for this bullshit.*" Hawke picked up a bike sat on it and then got off. He glanced over his shoulder at the young wolf, grabbed the bike and threw it. The full-blood jumped out of the way with lightening reflexes and laughed as the bike slammed into a tree on the other side of the road. He looked at the bike, then at Hawke and then he clapped.

"Well done, old man. Well done. Thanks for the show. Lord Lancaster sends his regards and will see you soon."

Before Hawke or Asia could catch the next breath, the full-blood took off down the road leaving dust in his wake.

"*Well,*" Asia said a few moments later. "*Seems like the new Hawke model just made an appearance.*"

"*Yeah.*" He looked at her as she helped Granira stand. "*Did he seem familiar to you?*"

Asia paused and thought of the fleeting glimpses of the young full blood. *"No, but I didn't really look that hard, your brother ... well he didn't handle this well. I hope he can sit on a bike. We have a ways to go to get to Chacal's."*

"Hmm, okay. I suppose we take them with us. Granira needs to explain what happened to the pups and how she masks scents so well."

Asia nodded and strode to the red and black bike she'd picked out earlier. They rode out a few minutes later, leaving a blazing fire on the side of the road.

Chapter 14

Hawke, Asia and their two guests rode into Chacal's compound and parked. Hawke waited for Chacal to open the door and ask questions about Granira and Niall or his car. Asia parked her bike, got off and headed to the door.

"*Chacal's inside, why hasn't he come to the door to check out these two?*" Hawke asked as he dismounted.

"*Maybe he trusts us… on some level at least.*" She opened the door and walked in. Hawke brought up the rear.

"Where are we?" Niall asked, looking around the foyer at all the artwork.

"You'll see," Hawke said, pushing him forward.

Granira remained silent and walked steadily ahead. She stopped, smiled and increased her pace.

"Nira? What are you doing here?" Angus said, walking into the hall and lifting the older woman off her feet. "Not that I'm complaining, it's always good to feel you."

"Who is this?" Niall asked, staring at Angus. "Why are you calling her Nira? That's not her name."

"I'm Angus, who are you?" He looked over his shoulder at Niall without releasing Granira who seemed glued to his side. The woman looked quite content to remain in Angus' arms.

"Niall. I… we just rescued Granira from Alpha Verrick." He pointed and then his arm dropped while he stared at the two.

Angus looked at Hawke and then Asia before walking to a sofa holding Granira's hand. "This is our host Chacal. Chacal, this is Niall and Granira, I'm sure I've mentioned her over the years. She's in the Farkas clan quite a distance from here." The comment held a question. Hawke wondered if Angus would be more specific or would Granira give him an answer.

Chacal nodded and remained quiet.

Angus sat, and pulled her with him. "What happened? Why were you at Verrick's? And no tricks, Nira. I can smell through that dampener you wear and will know if you are lying."

"*Dampener?*" Hawke took Asia's hand and sat across from Angus. Chacal remained quiet and seated in his usual chair while Niall sat perched on the arm of the sofa near Granira.

"*We knew something was off. She must have given Niall some as well because he lied.*"

The older woman wet her lips and met Angus' gaze. "A lot has happened since you left, Angus. There are so few strong black wolves left to fight the darkness, we needed you here."

"I'm here now, Nira. What's going on?"

"Before you left, the Roundtable or Liege Lords so they call themselves now, were taking pups claiming to improve the lives of the full-blood."

"I know," Angus said, watching the woman intently.

"Did you know the high council gave them permission to do that?"

"No." Angus' voiced dropped an octave as he faced her fully. Hawke sensed Chacal became more alert as well.

She exhaled. "There's an old agreement that states the Roundtable will always seek ways to enhance the life of the wolf. Which grants them rights to pack lands, and packs."

"Have you read the agreement?" Hawke asked, curious of her recollection.

"Yes. A long time ago, we were all in agreement because of the Hungarian's constant good deeds to our people." Her shoulders slumped and her gaze lowered. "At that time, food was scarce, we were hunted and lost many of our kind before Konstantin purchased lands for us and set up safe havens for our non-shifting brethren. We trusted him and did not think beyond the century. Our short-sightedness on human behavior set this dark twist in motion."

No one spoke as the words settled.

"What exactly are you saying?" Angus asked in a low growl. "That we, full-bloods, gave the Liege permission to do what they are doing to our young? That we agreed to the deaths of thousands of our kin? Or their usage in experimentation?" The heat of anger from his words brushed against Hawke.

Granira took Angus' hand. He shook her off. She sighed and held her head down for a moment before speaking. "The permission to enter pack lands at will, yes, that was given in this agreement. When I tried to remind a few of the newer Alphas of this, they didn't believe me, called me a witch, rather than try to understand the history of our pack. None of the Alphas and leaders who agreed the original agreement are alive. Mistakes were made and we now suffer because of that."

"Were they killed?" Asia asked.

"What?" Granira said, frowning.

"Those who agreed to allow this bullshit; did the Liege kill them over time to keep the rest of the full-bloods ignorant while they destroyed lives?" Asia asked what Hawke had been thinking. Neither Radoff nor Ulric had knowledge of any type agreement in place.

"They... they died. Some were killed in challenges or in battle, but they are all gone."

"My mentor, Gunnolf, did he agree with this?" Asia asked. Hawke rubbed his thumb across the back of her hand to ease the distress this question caused her.

"Gunnolf? Yes... yes, he was in agreement, but things were different then. No one saw this gross abuse of power these men wield now. The millions of dollars Konstantin left were never to destroy wolf life, but to make things better."

"Do you have a copy of the contract?" Chacal asked into the sudden silence.

"Yes, I keep it locked away. Niall also scanned it for me so that it's in an electronic place that cannot be destroyed." She looked up at the young man and patted his cheek.

Hawke didn't understand what was going on with his litter-mate and the older woman, right now he needed to focus on the conversation, but he planned to have a long talk with Niall soon.

"I would like to look at it," Chacal said, looking at Niall and then Granira.

She looked at Angus, who nodded and then at Niall. "Download it for him, please and print Hawke a copy. He should read it as well."

Surprised, but pleased Hawke met her gaze and nodded. "I'd like that, thanks." She continued staring at him.

"You are the product of that agreement, it's only right you understand what happened and why. Although after that display on the side of the road today, I'm not as convinced as I was before that everything the Liege has done is evil. You saved our lives today. Those altered full-bloods would have killed us in seconds." Her gaze flicked to Asia and then back to him. "Both of you have been altered by the Liege and fight as well as any large pack." She looked at Angus for a few seconds. "Do you shift into a larger hybrid as well?"

"I have another form, yes. Most black wolves do."

She shook her head. "No, they don't. Only a few the Goddess smiled on. And they came through a specific line. The Black Alpha's line. Nikolas was a descendant and I believe your sire was as well."

Angus nodded, but didn't speak.

"Watching Hawke today, I understand why they're targeting black pups who are direct descendants. He is phenomenal and so is his mate. The ones who were not black pups and were changed by the Liege… they were machines. I looked into the eyes of those monsters and saw nothing. Blank slates with written instructions obeyed blindly without thought. Those beasts are no longer full-bloods, no longer our brethren, and the line crossed by the Liege." Her face brightened and she smiled.

Angus frowned.

"They broke the agreement, we can cancel it and keep them out of our lands." Her eyes glowed with righteous fervor.

"They broke the agreement a long time ago, Nira. What's new about that?" Angus asked.

"First off you had no idea there was an agreement. Second, I only knew pups were missing, I never saw what the Liege did with them until today. They modified them in a way I never suspected. With Hawke they amped his existing qualities. But the others, they stripped them of their identity, which, among other things the Liege is sworn to protect."

"I wish they hadn't. If someone had asked I would never have participated in that hell for thirty plus years. No one should go through what I went through. No one," Hawke spat.

"I'm sorry. You're right, of course," Granira said looking down.

"What did you do with the pups you took?" Asia asked.

"What?" Granira looked at her.

Asia repeated her question.

"I released them to their parents."

Angus exhaled and grabbed her arm. "What did you do with the pups? Tell the truth."

She snatched her arm from his grasp. "I released them, sent them on their way."

Hawke sat back and stared at her. "How old were the pups?"

"Six and seven with well developed senses. They told me their father lived nearby and took off."

"Verrick's stealing pups?" Hawke asked. He didn't see it, but stranger things were happening. Like that arrogant pup on the road earlier. Hawke hadn't been able to get the pup out of his mind.

"I don't think so. From what I heard he picked those two up as a peace offering for Lancaster. All the remaining Alphas are bending over backwards to get into his good graces while he's here. So far he's ignored them all. Some say he blames them indirectly for the fall of his castle." She glanced at Hawke and smiled.

"Which brings me full circle," Angus said. "What were you doing in Verrick's holdings? Don't bother telling me that kidnapping stuff either, I know better. Few hunt or fight better than you. If you were taken it was by your own design. What are you up too?"

"They're getting bolder and sloppier. I heard Verrick had some type serum the Liege used on full-bloods to change them. I wanted to see it. We've got to get in front of them and stop this or they'll destroy our future."

"Did you find the serum?" Angus asked, watching her closely.

"Yes. It took a bit of doing, but I exchanged a sample this morning. Niall is the only other person I trusted to get me out of there. He came once before, but I hadn't secured the sample yet, so I sent him away and called for him once I knew I was close to retrieving it. I saw the pups by accident yesterday and couldn't leave them behind."

"Did Verrick harm them?" Angus growled.

She patted his arm and rested it there. "No. They were scared and treated well, but still prisoners."

"Is that the same serum the Liege used against Tyrese." Asia asked Angus.

"Probably." He turned to Granira. "Let Hawke take a look at the serum, it's unstable and does more harm than good."

Granira nodded. "I'll need to dig it out of my bag and give it to you later."

Hawke didn't have anything to test the serum and wondered why Angus wanted him to look at it. "Sounds good."

Angus glanced at him. *"I'm testing her to make sure she's honest. Chances are she has it."*

Between Angus, Asia and Hawke's questions they got a clearer idea on the state of things. It didn't look good. Not as long as the Liege had access.

"What if the packs moved until we fix this?" Asia asked the question they'd discussed before. "Explain the prior agreement to Ulric, let him see the document so he'll understand the pups in his pack are targeted. I'm not saying move forever, just move for a short period of time."

"If you can fix the problem in ninety days they can move," Chacal said returning to the room holding papers. "Any longer than that and the Liege can claim it as abandoned and reassign the land to another pack. Which we know they'll give it to Alphas, they control like Verrick." Chacal sat in his chair and continued reading. Niall walked in eating a sandwich.

Hawke's stomach growled in anticipation.

"After what I saw today, I'm sure my brother and his mate can have this fixed within three months." He looked at Hawke with a large smile. "Right, bro?"

Hawke growled, took Niall's sandwich and popped it in his mouth.

"Hey!" Niall yelled. "That's rude."

Asia chuckled and left the room.

"So is lying, yet you continue to do it so well." Hawke swiped his lips with his tongue.

Niall left the room, muttering as Asia returned with a tray of meat and sandwiches. "Here, eat this," she said and left again. He'd finished one sandwich when she returned with a liter of water.

"*Thanks baby.*"

She nodded and chuckled. "*You know Granira is wondering what you see in this short, average looking man.*"

Hawke grabbed her lapel and pulled her closer. His lips brushed against hers and tasted like ambrosia to him. He would never grow tired of her taste. "*I don't give a damn what anyone says about you. I love you in every form.*"

"Seems like the Liege took the suggestion of helping shifters to a whole new level with LOBO." Chacal said flipping the page of the documents.

"LOBO? What's that?" Asia asked in between bites of food.

"Liege Organized–"

"Behavioral Optimization," Hawke finished with a sinking feeling in the pit of his stomach. He glanced at the document in Chacal's hand and then at Asia.

"*What?*" she asked into the cool silence in their link.

"*I created that plan or large portions of it. But it was to help adult wolves grow stronger, better. Not pups. Pups cannot survive the things I put into that manual. Oh shit... what the hell was I thinking?*"

"*You weren't. The computer chip, programmed by the Liege, did all the thinking for you,*" Asia stressed.

"*But if a pup survives training in LOBO, they'll be little more than machines when they leave. It calls for numerous surgeries, including all metal limbs, metallic layered skins, sharpened fangs, everything.*"

"*In other words, they'll be like you?*" She looked at him and touched his hand. "*From where I'm sitting that's not a bad thing. Once they find their mates the Liege's influence dies over them and they can help the pack."*

He shook his head and looked at his hands in disgust. *"The Goddess sent you to me, it could be decades before they find their mates and until then they'll destroy whoever the Liege tells them to destroy. It never entered my mind to resist, not until you came along."*

"How'd you know that, Hawke?" Angus asked. "Have you seen it before?"

Hawke looked at Angus. "Something similar, behavioral optimization is code for absolute obedience. In the mind of Lancaster and his cronies, that is the golden standard."

"Were you obedient?" Granira asked.

"How do you know about LOBO?" Asia asked Angus, ignoring Granira.

"Yesterday we checked out two locations," Angus said. "One was a lab from Hawkes' list. That's where we found the pages on LOBO and another smaller building not far from here." Angus explained the bar, their impressions of the surrounding area and the building. He paused and stared at Asia.

"There was another location purchased by the same corporation the Liege used for other transactions within thirty minutes from here." He met Hawke's gaze. "It wasn't on your list. Once we got there we understood why. The charred remains of animals, including wolves, filled a large incinerator, filthy, stacked cages lined three rooms. Based on the smell of things, the deaths were fairly recent, the place stank. We didn't check all the rooms, but the ones we saw were bad."

Granira gasped and covered her mouth.

A bitter taste hit the back of Hawke's tongue as if he were in that room with Angus. His nose itched from the imagined smell. This could not continue. Whatever role he needed to play to correct the damage he'd unwittingly created, he would.

"Let's just say, it was bad enough that Chacal changed his mind about remaining on the sidelines," Angus said in a low voice.

"The things they are doing... it's inhumane and not allowed per this agreement. If they feel they are operating in the gray areas, they're wrong. They have violated everything these pages stand for." Chacal placed the papers on the table next to his chair.

"What I saw in the camp wasn't science, or behavioral modifications. It was murder, bordering on genocide of our people. No one should stand on the sidelines and allow outsiders to destroy them. I certainly cannot," Chacal said with more heat and emotion than Hawke had seen in the month they'd stayed in the man's home. Hawke glanced at Asia's stunned expression and touched her arm.

"Well, damn, someone found the button to his conscience."

Hawke shrugged. *"Yeah, I guess so."* Once everyone discovered he wrote most of the LOBO manual that animosity would be turned toward him. He and Asia could move to the hotel in town or to Alpha Radoff's pack lands to finish this job. He exhaled beneath the heavy weight of shame. Not once had he ever considered the experiments wrong. Quite the opposite, learning new things, perfecting his body, stretching his abilities had been the nourishment that kept him going. Now, sitting on this side of the fence, he saw, understood why the test wolves hated him and thought of him as a butcher and a quack.

"*Hawke, don't do this,*" Asia said, lacing her fingers through his. "*There is always another side to consider.*"

"*Don't you understand? The reason they're stealing the pups is because of me. I gave them that damn manual.*"

"*What I understand is you're the only person who knows what those assholes are doing and how. I understand that you have the blueprint for their weaknesses as well as strengths in that incredible brain of yours. Where you see failure, baby, I see success and that's what the Goddess is talking about. You know those bastards and can guess what they'll do next. We need you to guide us into the dark paths of their minds and game plans. So don't be upset by the things you've done, I'm not. We'll use your knowledge about them, against them and destroy them.*"

Hawke stared at her and checked their link. She was serious. Interesting. He did know how the Liege thought, or at least how they thought when he'd been under their domination. Most of the plans he worked on were stored in his personal cloud. Even if they made changes, he still had the core. Could that be what the Goddess meant? Between him and Asia, they knew enough about the Liege to shake that organization, and possibly bring it to its knees.

He smiled and squeezed his mate's hand. "*Thank you. As usual, you are right. The image of Lancaster on his knees feels good.*"

Chapter 15

The transmission of the fight wasn't as good as those transmitted through the cams embedded in the eye, but since Damian lacked that device, the one mounted in his sunglasses had to suffice. Boris Lancaster watched the screen until it went blank. Inwardly he battled pride, sadness, loss and anger at the scene he'd just seen. Hawke looked good. His pet protégé appeared to be thriving outside the castle. Boris had hoped to see a weakened and confused Hawke which would spell disaster for their research, but would have soothed the ache of loss in his chest.

The bleep on the monitor pulled him from those ridiculous thoughts. Even without the computer chip in his brain, Hawke operated with clear thoughts and excellent movement of his limbs. Throwing the motorcycle had been over the top, but it allowed Boris to see the quality of their work. *Superb.* He saved the video to the cloud and sent a copy to Lord Roderick. They'd share a glass of champagne later over the successful implementation of their technology.

He'd have Lord Phineas, Griffin's former assistant, cut segments of this tape for a promotional piece for potential clients. There were a few bugs that would need to be worked out and information to be omitted, such as what happened if the product came into the proximity of its mate. But overall, LOBO proved successful.

Rubbing his hands together, he re-watched the footage and stopped on the image of the other shifter. Angus, Hawke's mate. Zooming onto the face he looked for signs of the black wolf. After long, frustrating moments, he admitted failure. Roderick might be onto something with that chameleon bracelet.

He tapped his fingertips on the desk while staring at the monitor. The power they could wield by taking over the bodies of men and women in high places. It tickled his imagination to think of sitting in Buckingham Palace or the White House. Oh... to be able to show all those people who teased and taunted him when he was a young lad with speech problems. His chest expanded with imagined pride. For a moment he basked in the glory of being the leader of the world.

They could control or topple kingdoms and do things that left a mark in history without a hint of identity theft. The more he thought of the possibilities, the more he wanted that bracelet. Then, they could leave the wolves behind without fear of retribution from that damn contract. He'd be the first to admit over the past two decades, they had been skating on thin ice, and there had been times he'd been certain Konstantin would blast them from wherever he rested in eternal bliss with the damn curse, but so far luck favored them.

But if he could discover the secret of the bracelet he could change his fortunes and destiny. Roderick hadn't said much about the bracelet other than Angus Black Wolf was the key. Lancaster rubbed his chin and stared at the face on the monitor. Perhaps he could seek more answers while bringing Hawke down. Catching one would bring the other and before he turned Angus over to Roderick he would set about securing his fortune. It was something to consider after watching Hawke.

The door opened and Damian walked in. Boris turned off the monitor and faced his new protégé.

"Report."

"I watched the confrontation. The hybrids are still slower than the black wolf. I timed his blows and they were always faster and more precise than the hybrid. The addition of the metal around the face to protect the chips seemed effective. However, the steel rings around the neck did not prevent decapitation. The sword severed the head from the body and did nothing to stop the twisting of the head. Since there is no regeneration after decapitation, I suggest researching that area."

Lancaster nodded. They'd spent millions already on research. Hawke's report had been clear and concise. Unless you placed body armor around the neck there was no way to protect it. But the armor would prevent the wearer from fluid movement and cause their death against an opponent.

"What did you think of Hawke?"

Damian frowned. "Hawke?" His face cleared. "The one who threw the cycle?"

Lancaster noted the sparkle in his eyes as he mentioned the bike. "Yes."

"He is very fast, strong and level-headed. Even when angered he didn't bother to charge instead he acted in a manner that would give him information about an unknown.

No matter if the bike hit me or not he would've learned something of my nature. I applaud his thinking."

"Good. I am sure the two of you will meet again." Lancaster watched to see if there were any signs of recognition and was pleased with what he saw.

When Hawke and Damian met it would be the first time father and son battled. Damian had passed every in-house test and a few staged events. In order to determine his effectiveness in combat, he had to fight Hawke, at least that was how he pitched this confrontation to the board. The test wasn't a matter of strength or cunning.

Hawke had been around much longer and studied everything under the sun. The wolf was a walking encyclopedia who would eventually win against any competitor. They needed to see the reaction between the two. How would Damian respond to his sire and how would Hawke respond to his pup. The idea of Hawke's downfall by the hands of his seed had been too hard to resist.

Boris knew better than most what Hawke was capable of, one on one, Damian would be destroyed if Hawke could do it. Boris' end game was the mental torture Hawke would receive knowing his son had been raised by the same hands he now despised. The anger might trip him up long enough for Boris to destroy him.

"Have you heard from Lord Gordon?" Damian asked on his way out the room.

"Yes. He will be here soon. His flight landed a couple hours ago. Make sure his room is ready." Lancaster waved him out rather than see the delighted grin covering his face. For some reason Gordon had taken an immediate liking to the pup and over the years had shown blatant favoritism to Hawke's pup. When he pulled Damian for this assignment, he knew it would piss Gordon off, that's why he didn't bother informing the Liege Lord of the trip. Pup testing was the only reason Gordon hadn't dropped everything and flown over the first day.

Boris glanced at his watch, stood and grabbed a cup of coffee. Damian returned to the room, glanced at him and then looked at the entry door as if that would bring Gordon faster. Lancaster couldn't imagine anyone had ever done that for him, couldn't imagine how he'd feel if they had either. Gordon had been from the same wealthy social class as Roderick. Both men had married and lost their families through the years. Gordon said Damian reminded him of his youngest son and spent a lot of time with the pup. Lancaster had warned the Lords against tying themselves with the product. One day those pups would go on dangerous assignments and may not return.

Gordon always argued on the side of loyalty being nurtured rather than cold brutality. After Hawke's betrayal, Boris agreed with him... to a point. But this didn't bode well. Gordon should not rush to Damian's side. The wolf hadn't met his sire and that would be the battle of battles.

Damian moved so quickly, Boris couldn't track him. The door stood open and Gordon walked in. Damian knelt and bowed his head. Gordon stopped and stroked the top of the pup's hair.

Boris rolled his eyes as the two talked in hushed tones. He tossed back the rest of the dark brew and turned to face the two. Gordon walked toward him with an outstretched hand, which Boris shook. When had they started the handshaking instead of the cordial nod?

"Good to see you, Gordon."

Gordon's brow rose. They both knew that was a lie. "If I had known you were coming I would've traveled with you."

Lancaster shrugged. "The castle fell. Hawke's on the loose, Roderick wanted this handled with a small footprint after the castle deal. So I grabbed Damian and came over."

"Small footprint? What do you call what happened on the side of the highway. It made the news." Gordon handed Damian his bag as he took a seat near Lancaster.

"That wasn't us. Damian stood across the road watching with his special lens, taking notes. Verrick sent his men after Hawke and that was the result."

"Verrick doesn't own any hybrids. And in his arrogance would've lost all of his men before calling them off in the middle of a fight. That's not how wolves fight, your fingerprint is all over this," Gordon said.

Boris gritted his teeth and counted to five. The bastard came across the continent looking to be disagreeable. "I sent the hybrids, and told Verrick to detain Hawke. I needed to see what I'd be dealing with." He met Gordon's cold gaze with one of his own.

"How did it go?"

Boris' gaze flicked to Damian, who stood a distance away. "According to Damian's report and the video he recorded, Hawke is operating above our expectations. The loss of the computer chip hasn't diminished his capabilities."

Gordon smiled and nodded. They all had one thing in common, the push for excellence in everything they did. "That's great to hear. Have you scheduled the confrontation between Hawke and Damian?"

"Not yet. Roderick wants Hawke's mate, Angus. Now that I have the tape and see how they work I can begin to plan."

"If you take one the other will follow," Gordon said as if that was the easiest thing in the world to accomplish.

"How much of that footage was on the news?" he asked.

Gordon's jaw tightened. "Just the fire."

Boris nodded, stretched out his legs and hit the remote. A large screen on the opposite wall appeared and within moments displayed the fight between Hawke and the hybrids. "Take one indeed," he murmured.

Chapter 16

Hawke sat in front of the monitor sifting through his notes on LOBO. Asia completed another rep of squats while wondering what bothered her about the day. Something had been off but she couldn't put her finger on it exactly. After grabbing a bite to eat, she and Hawke left Niall, Chacal, Angus and Granari in the living area talking. Since the conversation veered from their assignment, it didn't interest her.

Her mate immediately went to his laptop while she showered and changed into a tank top and a thong. When she finished her last squat, she grabbed a bottle of water from the mini-fridge and sat on the bed.

"Mistress."

"How are you, Asia?"

"Good, thanks." She told Jasmine about their day, the fight, the pups, Granira and Niall. When she finished Jasmine released a long sigh.

"I don't like so many people getting involved. How long will they be in the house?"

Asia agreed but was surprised Jasmine felt that way about Hawke's brother given the way her Mistress felt about family. *"I'm not sure. We plan to return to Alpha Radoff's tomorrow to discuss breaking the contract and stop Liege access on pack land. We could leave them there."*

"That sounds good. I don't like the coincidences of them below ground while you were there. The lies of who she is and then the pups being released. Too many inconsistencies for me. Make sure no one learns your identity, not even Hawke's brother. He's a liar and cannot be trusted."

"I agree. We're in our bedroom and it's warded so the only ones who can enter is Hawke or myself. No one comes in here when we're gone, we clean up our own mess."

"In this instance, that's a good thing. I'll tell Silas, bring him current. The fire did make the news over here, they don't know who or what started it, but there were too many bodies to do much else I suppose."

Asia heard the question and answered. *"Yes, Ma'am. We needed to leave the area, but couldn't allow the bodies to be examined by humans. Fire was the only option."*

"By the time the police arrived there wasn't enough left to identify the bodies, so I doubt there will be an autopsy." Jasmine paused. *"Take care of Hawke, this is not his fault, although I'm sure he feels it is. Alpha men tend to take more than their shoulders can carry, that's why we step in to help. He's going to need you more than ever in the coming days as more and more of the Goddess's mission is revealed. How you handle your mate will determine how he handles all the things thrown at him. I went through that with Silas, and still do on some days. It's not easy, but it's*

what mates do for each other. Become his hiding place. A place he can rest and be himself."

Asia' heart thumped in her chest at the visual Jasmine's words produced. Her chest hurt. She blinked fast a few times and swallowed hard. *"Yes...yes, Ma'am."* She looked at Hawke as his fingers flew over the keyboard and he stared at the monitor. Earlier, during the discussion on LOBO, the heat of his disappointment in himself scorched her. Merged, the pain and disillusionment from his work threatened to pull her under the tidal wave of his misery. He struggled beneath the blame of his actions when enslaved for the Liege.

"I will definitely do that. He needs me." The sound of the words echoed, and expanded until they filled her chest, leaving no room for doubt. She would help him through this.

"Yes, he does. I can tell you see and believe it, which gives me hope. Because nothing works for our men until we are in the right head space. Our love and acceptance anchors them, keeps them tethered like a string to their purpose."

Asia saw and understood. *"Yes. That's true. Sometimes he forgets all the good he's done and wallows in the wrong. It frustrates me. And after I remind him he seems... surprised and then he gets better, on the right track again. I hadn't thought of it in the way you said, but it makes so much sense. A lot of sense."*

"That's good. You're the key in this Asia. Keep him focused, if you need me, call."

Asia continued staring at Hawke as Jasmine's words circled her mind. When had it happened? Could she recall the exact moment he ceased being her mate and became her world? The idea or thought of him in pain or accused unjustly sent her wolf into a tailspin. Jasmine vocalized what Asia experienced each day without giving it a name. Hawke, her do-over had crystallized into her everything.

"Hawke," she whispered his name in her mind as her feelings for him collided and coalesced into one bright shining light eclipsing the dark corners of her life. He looked at her, stopped typing and moved onto the bed enveloping her in his arms.

"It's going to be okay, baby. We'll beat this, just hang in there with me," he murmured stroking her back. Her tee moved down her arm exposing her shoulder. He placed a soft kiss there.

She shook her head, and realized tears fell from her eyes. Goddess help, she couldn't remember the last time she cried. Now she couldn't stop to tell him she wasn't worried about the crap happening all around them. She wanted to tell him she couldn't contain the love in her heart for him and it burst from her restraints creating this emotional overflow.

"I...I..." A few words, so simple, and she wanted to say them, but couldn't push them past her lips. They swirled in her mind trying to break free. "I'm... I..." she choked on her tears and cried harder. He held her cheeks in his palms, his forehead wrinkled in concern. His eyes darkened to the color of dull gold as he stared into her gaze.

"Asia, baby... what's wrong. Whatever it is, I promise we'll fix it. We'll work it out. Tell me, don't shut me out, please, tell me what's wrong." He placed a kiss on her forehead and held her close to his chest. His heartbeat thundered in her ears as he stroked her back. Fear from him leaked down the halls of their link. She cursed her inability to break the chains that kept her emotions superficial, making it harder to speak her heart.

Eyes closed, she tried to stop the tears from soaking his shirt, and could not. The harder she cried, the tighter he held onto her as if she'd slip away. His fear for them snaked beneath the foundation of her past and wiggled through the cracks of discontent until the walls of her prison shifted, crumbled and fell.

Inexplicable light bathed her, dissolved the burden of her shame, melted her hurt of past betrayals, and blotted out her humiliation of being used. The dark corners of her mind cleared beneath each stroke of his hand on her skin.

Calm, like the ebb and flow of the ocean on a moonlit night covered her. This… this was what Jasmine spoke of. The complete giving of oneself to another no longer terrified her. Hawke had proven worthy to hold her heart and her secrets.

"I love you so much it hurts," she whispered in a ragged voice filled with joy.

His hand stopped mid-stroke. His chest expanded, froze and then released in slow degrees.

She wiped her tear stained face against his chest. "It's a good hurt, the kind I never want to stop. The kind I'll look for every day for the rest of my life. I had no idea love could hurt this good."

Impossibly, he pulled her tighter and held her while breathing so hard she thought he'd pass out.

Emboldened by his response in a way she had never been before, she continued. "I had a mate before, at least I believe we were mated. I was told we were but… that was nothing like this. I ache for you. Not a moment passes without thinking of you, wondering if you're okay, that you have everything you need to make it through the day." She smiled at the girly comments. "If anyone had ever told me I'd want to serve a man, to utterly please him in every way,

I'd have kicked their ass. In fact, I have on several occasions." Asia paused and waited for the fear that always accompanied any type of emotional outbursts. Nothing. She reached up, placed her arms around his neck to keep him close. Happiness bubbled like a spring, she wanted to sing, which made her laugh since she sounded like a braying mule.

Instead of killing the mood and possibly damaging his eardrums she continued. "You surprised me when we first met."

"How?"

"My wolf went crazy over you, but I'd been tricked by Gunnolf and didn't trust my gut anymore. The attraction... Well, I was interested, but it happened too fast. I couldn't accept you or the mating. Plus, you tried to kill me."

His long sigh whistled above her head. "I'm never going to live that down, am I?"

Asia smiled. "Nope. But I forgive you."

He placed another kiss on her forehead. "Thank you."

"You're welcome." Giddy from the pleasure of sharing she placed kisses everywhere her lips could reach, marking him, honoring him, and treasuring him.

"Thank you for loving me," he said in a low rumble that resonated in her chest. "I have been alone for so long, the idea of having a mate and a den seemed lost forever. But my wolf never gave up hope. The day you entered the lab was the day I breathed as a man again. You, my precious bitch, saved my life."

Hawke tipped her face up and brushed his lips across hers. Her breath caught from the tenderness in his touch. Another soft caress of his fingertips on her collar bone ignited the flame in her core. "Hawke," she whispered, calling him from a place deep inside.

He lowered her to the mattress while deepening their kiss. Wrapping her arms around his shoulders, she pulled him chest to chest delighting in the pressure of his body holding her in place. Warm tendrils of pleasure curled up and around her, cocooning them in lust's hazy embrace lovers often experience but cannot fully explain.

Asia's body hummed in recognition of his gentle touch on her cheek, and his fingertips rubbed her scalp with long slow strokes. Her core tightened in anticipation. Hawke inhaled and smiled against her mouth.

"I love how wet you get for me." His hand slid down the side and rested between her legs moving the thong aside. His fingertips teased her outer lips before pressing into her tightness. "Ummm, so wet, tight, so hot for me." His fingers continued stroking her wet channel, while she pressed his mouth to her hard nipples.

"Mmmm," he murmured, pulling the taut bud into his warm mouth. Her body shivered beneath the promise in his eyes. Without removing his fingers he moved to the other nipple paying it the same tribute he paid its twin. Her hand remained on the back of his head, keeping him in place while opening her legs wider for him to rest comfortably.

Fire raced up her spine as his fingers deepened and hit her spot. This man had her sexual hotspots on speed-dial. Within moments, she stiffened, smashed his face to her breast as her back arched in response to the roaring orgasm that rolled through her. Toes tingling she remained stiff for a few seconds longer and then relaxed one limb at a time.

Hawke moved up and nibbled on her lower lip. "I love the way you come apart in my hands." His open palm rested on top of her mound, every now and then he'd slide a finger down her slit teasing her.

Asia placed her palms on the sides of his face demanding his attention. "Love me."

His eyes searched hers for a few seconds and then softened. "Every time I touch you, I love you," he said and kissed her forehead. "Whenever I do this." His lips brushed against her in a feather light touch sending fire through her veins. "I'm loving you," he said against her mouth, allowing her to taste the hunger in his words. He moved slightly. His cock bumped against her opening, but didn't enter. "This... this is a part of it, but not anywhere close to the whole." A quick move and he slid inside, stretching, filling and feeding her.

"Damn if you don't consume me, Asia," he moaned moving inside her again and again, taking her higher and higher. "Loving you is what I do, it's who I am." He filled her with slow, deep strokes rebuilding the flame.

"This is who I am," he murmured.

She tightened around him lifting from the bed to meet every delicious stroke. His fingers dug into her ass keeping them connected and in the right position. Asia wrapped her legs around his waist to remain bound to him as she flew apart. "Hawke," she screamed his name as waves of pleasure rolled through her.

"That's right, Asia. I'm your Hawke, I take care of whatever you need. Provide for you. This is who I am." He slammed into her and picked up his speed. The sound of flesh slapping flesh filled the room. The bed creaked in appreciation of his hard thrusts. Sweat dripped from his brow as he stared down, taking her with him. "This. Is. Who. I. Am. Loving. You." He punctuated each word with a deep thrust reawakening her languorous body, demanding she join him on the crest of their joining.

"With me, come with me," he said watching her closely.

Her breath caught at his primal beauty. His wolf had risen close to the surface and peeked behind his eyes. Sharp pointed teeth filled his mouth. Her wolf acknowledged the challenge and rose to play. Her long curved nails pierced his ass holding him close. Hawke howled and pushed harder, faster into her. His long black hair moved to and fro as he took her to another level.

Asia lowered her eyelids as the primal side of her took over while keeping her wolf leashed. She nipped at his chest with her teeth. Growling, he placed his forearm across her chest, holding her in place while baring his teeth.

She bucked to dislodge him. It deepened his penetration. Moaning at how good he felt inside she surrendered and together they exploded. Hawke bit her on her neck, extending the orgasm until dots floated in front of her eyes. He pulled back and placed kisses all over her face and neck while breathing hard.

Hawke rolled over and pulled her with him. "I will always love you."

Chapter 17

Verrick hung up the phone and shook his head. Would he ever be free of those leeches? He wanted no part of this brewing battle with hybrid wolves. Goddess destroy the lot of them as far as he was concerned. No one asked or cared for his opinion, but they were quick to use him and his pack to handle their bullshit as if they were disposable diapers.

He walked through the main area and looked at the men who survived Hawke's wrath. Lancaster had sent him a video and offered him a sip of the poison that would make him like the hybrids. Andrei had taken it and look what happened to him. It had taken some fancy foot-stepping to say no but he'd done it. Besides, Hawke didn't have a choice and the slew of test wolves who had lost their minds after escaping Lancaster castle remained in the forefront of Verrick's thoughts. Not all full-bloods handled the formula as well as Hawke.

"Anyone who can walk, come wit' me," he said to the men lying in various states of repair. Most had shifted to expedite the healing, but it would still take a few more hours or days to be one hundred percent.

The shuffle of feet behind him spoke of the state of his beleaguered pack. He turned and looked them over. Blood seeped from a few wounds and others could barely walk a straight line, but they answered his call. Damn the Liege.

"Those who stayed behind on the last call, with me. The rest, heal, watch the borders, keep our bitches and pups safe until I return. There's bullshit happening out there, so watch our shit." He nodded as the pack separated. Ten full-bloods followed him to the remaining motorcycles and off their pack lands.

Hawke and Asia walked into the breakfast area and grabbed a quick bite. Asia had used the chameleon bracelet to return to the non-descript boring white male she preferred to use. He longed for the day he could show off his gift from the Goddess to the world. One day at a time, he would make her world safe enough so she could be herself.

They planned to spend the next few days with Maheegan and Radoff. The Alpha sounded excited this morning when he called, but that could be Maheegan. Radoff had lit up when the bitch deplaned the other day and it seemed mutual. Stranger pairings had happened, Hawke thought. At any rate, Radoff claimed they found more information regarding the Liege and was even more excited to see a copy of the contract.

"You headed out?" Niall asked from across the room where he sat next to Granira watching them enter.

"Yes. Get your things, we'll drop you back where we found you," Hawke said without looking in his litter-mate's direction. The man's lies stood like a citadel between them. Hawke and Asia agreed to have nothing more to do with Niall or Granira until after they completed their mission.

"What? I don't need a ride, I'm staying here with Granira." He edged closer to the silent woman.

Angus walked into the dining area and looked at Niall. "Both of you are leaving, we have too much to do for houseguests."

Granira smiled, but remained silent as she looked Angus with unbridled hunger. Hawke glanced at Asia who sat at the table eating and watching everything.

"Is that how it is? We give you valuable information and you throw us out? What if Verrick comes after us?" Niall sputtered looking at Angus and then Hawke.

"You're a liar and need to go," Hawke said over his shoulder, ignoring the red flush that spread over Niall's face.

Angus looked at Granira and nodded. "There's enough bullshit to wade through without second guessing everything that comes out your mouth." Hawke wondered if anything happened between the two. She didn't appear offended at his bald comments.

"The contract–" Niall said.

"Has to be verified. A specialist will look it over," Angus said.

"The contract is a copy of the real one, but I don't blame you for being cautious," Granira said standing. "Niall be a dear and get my bags. We don't want to miss our ride, something tells me neither of these full-bloods will wait and Chacal will simply kick us off his land." Although the words were uttered smoothly, Hawke heard the bite behind them. She didn't appreciate how things played out. Had she expected more from Angus? Or had Silas told him the same thing Asia's Mistress told her. Not to trust her or Niall. Hawke didn't know or care.

Asia placed some fruit and bottles of water in her bag before hefting it over her shoulder. She stood next to him and nodded at Angus. *"I need to talk to him while you finish eating. Come outside when you're done,"* Asia said through their link. Hawke stiffened at the idea of her being outside without him. Although there were few in the world who could harm his mate that didn't stop his wolf from wanting to protect her at all times.

Instead of saying something he'd be apologizing for all day, he nodded. *"Links open."*

She nodded and walked out. Angus followed her.

A few seconds later, Hawke listened to the conversation Asia, Angus, Silas and Jasmine conducted. It still amazed and pleased him Asia could not link with anyone other than him and her Mistress.

"Someone is coming," Angus interrupted Silas in the middle of his instructions.

"Who?" Silas asked.

Hawke stood, grabbed his bag and walked out the front door. A cloud of dust rolled in from the main road. He glanced at Asia, her hand rested on the hilt of her sword. Since the fight with the bluebirds she practiced constantly until the sword became an extension of her arm.

"Chacal says Verrick is asking permission to enter his grounds," Angus said through the link. *"What do you want to do?"* He looked at Hawke.

"Call it Asia," Hawke said.

"Take it outside the bubble, can Chacal muffle the voices so Niall and Granira cannot hear our conversation?" Asia looked at Angus.

He nodded and then smiled. *"He's happy with our choice and promises to keep those two inside and ignorant of what's going on."* Angus took off running toward the main gate, Asia followed and Hawke brought up the rear. Tingles raced over him as they left the protective barrier. Angus stood a few feet in front of Verrick with his arms crossed. The links to La Patron and his mate were still open. Hawke stood next to Asia and waited for Verrick to state the reason of his visit.

"Why am I dragged into this war with you and the Liege?"

The question took Hawke by surprise. He expected anger over the loss of his pack-members or the pups, but not this.

"What do you mean?" Angus asked.

Verrick ran his palm across his bald scalp and shook his head. "They want me to come to you, to delay you so they can test you, for what?" He waved his hand as if the idea was too much to think about. "They send me tape of you." He pointed at Hawke. "Destroying my men, offer to make me like you. I want no part. I am full-blood and will die this way."

"Who told you to delay us?" Hawke asked, curious. Lancaster didn't normally deal with those who held no allegiance to the group.

"Lancaster," Verrick spat. "Now the other wants you destroyed to avoid something. These men, they have no understanding. I am wolf. Not pissy errand boy." He inhaled and breathed deep. "They watch, so I come. My pack will move north to the mountain until this is over. How long will this take?" He looked at Hawke.

"Take?"

"For you to defeat them. How long? I need idea to move my pack."

Hawke realized the man had come to get answers, not lodge a complaint or to join them. Verrick intended to leave. "We are working on it." Hawke made his response vague to see his reaction.

Verrick nodded, looked at the others and then at Hawke. "Watch your back, they want you bad enough to give me suicide mission. They come, won't be easy win. But I hope you do."

"*Is this another delay tactic?*" Angus asked through their links.

"*Could be, but I sense he is telling the truth and if he is disobeying the Liege they will show him and his pack no mercy,*" Asia said.

"*His choice,*" Silas said in a stern tone. "*Goes with the territory of being Alpha. Sometimes you need to step back and re-evaluate what's best for the pack. That's his primary responsibility, nothing else.*"

"Thank you and Goddess be with you and your pack," Hawke said into the silence.

Verrick pulled out a pair of sunglasses and pushed them up his nose. "We will need her protection, but this is best. We leave." He nodded and pulled off.

They waited until the roar of the bikes disappeared. "Hmm, I thought for sure a hybrid or that smart-ass from the side of the road would pop-up," Asia said sounding disappointed.

"*What should we do with Granira and Niall?*" Angus asked. "*I have known her for close to a century, she was pack historian for the Farkas clan and has access to a lot of information. I agree with Jasmine, the timing of their appearance is suspicious, but if she and Maheegan worked together we may find the way to shut down the Liege faster. The idea that another pup could suffer the same fate of those pups at the last lab sickens my gut. This needs to stop now."*

"Maheegan I know and trust to a degree," Silas said in a measured tone. *"Can you say the same of this woman?"*

"No, I cannot." Angus released a long sigh. *"I cannot. It's damn frustrating, like dangling a platter of meat in front of a starving man."*

"Let her help, just do not accept everything that she says. Use Jacques or Maheegan to test whatever she shares," Jasmine said. *"She may mix the truth with lies, but if there is something redeemable, use it until you no longer need her. Remember Maheegan is a master of unearthing accurate historical data and will see through false accounts. Time is a luxury we don't have, so use everything you have to stop those bastards."*

Hawke hadn't heard the Mistress speak much before, but he picked up the urgency of her summons and understood Asia's desire to serve the top bitch. *"Yes, Ma'am."*

"Hawke, can Verrick walk away from the Liege?

"Depends on the relationship. Lancaster has a long memory and will not be happy if he disobeys him."

"But he said the other... did you catch that?" Asia asked.

Hawke thought back and nodded. *"You are right. Does that mean two Liege Lords are here?"* He couldn't help but get excited at the idea of destroying two of the Lords.

"Possibly. I'll run a check to see who landed recently at the nearby airports and will get back with you. If there are two of them, I do not want them to return to the states. Is that clear?" Silas demanded.

"Crystal," Angus said with a smile.

"*Yes, Sir,*" Asia said.

"*Yes, very,*" Hawke added.

"*Good. Go look at those records Maheegan told me about and it seems she's on track to getting to the bottom of the Liege mystery. Oh, and she won't be returning stateside.*"

Angus frowned. "*Why not?*"

"*She found her mate, Alpha Radoff.*"

Chapter 18

"Thanks for the ride, brother," Niall said in a snide tone, opening and slamming the car door before Hawke stopped the car. For the past two and a half hours, Niall pleaded his case. Explained why he lied, he didn't know if he could trust Hawke, made excuses for his lies after leaving Verrick's, he had promised Granira to pick her up at the appointed time. And blamed Hawke and the situation for the lies, he would never have lied if Hawke hadn't killed the men he hired to rescue Granira. And on it went until Hawke wanted to kill the man.

The trip had been tedious. Once, Hawke stopped the vehicle demanding Niall get out and walk home. That managed to shut him up until the last mile. Asia rubbed his arm and sent tingly warm energy down their link. The feeling was one he'd never experienced and made him smile. Rather than respond to Niall, he picked up her hand and kissed the back.

"Love that, feels good."

She nodded and winked at him before opening her door.

Granira exited the car last and sent him a smile of gratitude. "Thanks for your assistance. I know he aggravates you, but he means well. After the death of your mother, a few of us helped Alpha Hiram with his young litter and Niall was the smallest of the bunch. No one expected him to survive the winter." She stopped and looked across the clearing where Niall stood talking to a couple of Radoff's pack members.

"Not only did he survive, he outsmarted a lot of them." She faced Hawke. "Lorenzo and Jirek were big, tall and fighters, like you. But they couldn't think fast on their feet and relied on Niall to help develop strategies to keep the pack safe. He should be commended." Her voice held a note of pride.

"Why didn't he fight to become Alpha?"

She waved him down. "He's not a fighter and that's what it would take." She peered up at him. "You could become Alpha. I doubt Muzik will accept a challenge from you since you're a descendant of Alpha Nikolas."

Hawke stared at her wondering at her reasoning for telling him this. "I should be Alpha and allow Niall to work by my side?" Niall was putty in this woman's hands and if he held the beta position in the pack it would give her access to power.

"It's not a bad idea, but I doubt he will remain long enough for that. He wants to return to his career in the human world."

That surprised him. "Why did he leave it before?"

Her brow rose. "To help me, of course. We're both concerned over the fate of these pups and discussed it for years. When the opportunity arose to do something, I took it and Niall helped. He's a good boy. It bothered him to lie to you, but he did what he felt was best at the time. You shouldn't be so hard on him. Niall and Pia are all that's left of your litter, you should get to know them."

Hawke had no interest in knowing either. As long as he had Asia he was content. One day they'd set up their den, and have a litter of pups. That was more than enough for him. Tired of the conversation he turned.

"My mate calls." He clicked the remote locking the vehicle and walked toward Asia who stood next to Alpha Radoff. Hawke watched Radoff straighten and his smile slip as he and Granira approached.

"Radoff, it's good to see you, again," Granira said, smiling and extending her hand.

Radoff took it and placed a kiss on the back. "Yes, nice to see you as well. I've heard of your recent exploits, and am happy to see you've returned in good health." He dropped her hand and took a step back.

"What happened? You look different," Granira asked, stepping closer.

"He's mated," Maheegan said in a neutral tone walking up to them. "I'm Maheegan, his mate."

Granira's smile slipped a notch, but remained bright for the most part as she turned to meet Maheegan. "That's great. I'm so happy for you, Radoff. Congratulations. When did this happen?" She frowned at Maheegan. "I don't think we have ever met before, where are you from?"

"Montana pack, in the states. La Patron's historian." She dropped the words with a ring of pride that couldn't be missed.

"Historian?" Granari's brow furrowed as she looked at Radoff. "You brought in another historian? I wasn't gone that long."

Bitch fights held no interest; Hawke took Asia's hand and headed to the small room where the journals were located.

"Hawke, wait," Radoff called stopping their progress. He and Asia turned. Maheegan and Granira remained in the same spot talking various techniques they'd both used in the past to catalog historical facts. Niall stood to the side, listening to the women, but remained silent.

"I need to show you something." Radoff walked ahead of them to the building where they'd met Niall. When he headed toward the basement, Asia squeezed Hawke's hand. "This is the place the journals spoke of. There is a corridor that leads to each parcel of land mentioned in the journals, except the one in Egypt of course. Alphas met down here and discussed important matters with the Roundtable, sorry, Liege. We believe this is where they initiated the pup exchanges."

"Exchange?" Hawke scoffed as he moved further into the large room. The heavy air tickled his throat as he swallowed hard. "What did the pack receive in exchange?"

Radoff waited until they reached the middle of the area and shut the outer door. "You. You are what the pack was to receive in exchange, Hawke. A smart, fast and unbeatable wolf. The Liege made a lot of promises to the Alphas back then. Remember, there was always something hindering the packs from living in peace, disease, famine, war, something always stopped the packs from thriving. The Liege reminded the Alphas of a clause or promise to aid the pack and improving the wolf's mind and body was their answer."

"LOBO you mean. That behavior optimization bullshit," Hawke said, looking everywhere except the dais or altar. Pain radiated on the edges of his mind, but he refused to give into it this time.

"True. But can you imagine how such an offer would sound to the Alphas back then? Each Alpha would present a pup and the Liege would choose one from the group. The Alphas required the Liege proved their theories with one pup first before committing to more."

Hawke tensed. His heart beat in an irregular pattern. Anger turned to fire, bubbled in his gut, and shot liquid flames through his system. "They chose me?" He slapped his chest. "My sire really gave me up to the Liege?" Asia laced her fingers with his and sent tendrils of understanding through their link.

"Your Alpha. Each Alpha agreed in advance to present a pup from their den, so the sacrifice would be equal. Two men, Lancaster and Gordon, studied the pups for a week and then made the choice. Based on everything we found in the journals, your sire was proud you were chosen."

A cold breeze slid down Hawke's chest and settled until he felt nothing. He'd been picked like cattle being led to the slaughter. They had no idea of what he suffered at the hands of Lancaster. He'd been removed from the warmth of a dent to the cold, sterile walls of the castle. Day after day he'd been beaten, starved of food and affection, and cut off from all contact. For a pack animal the last had been what eventually broke him. To hear "good job" was better than the silence screaming in his mind.

"Proud?" he snorted his disgust. "It's just as well he did not live to see what I've become, he would see he received coal instead of a gift."

"He would be proud, Hawke, as I am to call you friend. In spite of everything you experienced you are smart, strong, a fighter with no equal, and you possess things they could never teach you. Loyalty, honor, empathy and dignity. No one can take those from you." Radoff touched Hawke's shoulder for a few seconds and then walked further into the room.

"He's right. Your sire would be proud. I am," Asia said and moved into his arms.

Hawke held her close, hoping the heat of her love would thaw the cold anger swelling in him. Memories from the past rose in a violent hiss, volleying back and forth, filling his mind. Images from his youth rolled across his vision on a constant loop. Hate, hot and putrid, suppressed for decades bubbled beneath the surface, cracking his control, his confidence, and his conscience.

Emotions locked for decades broke free from their confinement and took charge. "That Alpha gave me away like bartered goods and never came to visit. If he had come to check he would've known Lancaster's goal was to break my wolf not strengthen him. He would've seen me change into a monster with arms and legs of steel. If he had come once…. just once in thirty years he would know I had a fucking computer chip in my brain that controlled my actions to the point I crippled and destroyed the lives I'd been sent to save."

Jaw tight, he pulled away separating from his mate and clenched his fist. Blood and dirt covered his hands. He could see it now, him in the lab, destroying his brethren in the name of science. And for what? A super wolf? How did they fall for that? If his mate had not saved him, he would have turned on the pack and destroyed all of them without a smidgeon of conscience.

Radoff looked at him and then turned away. "In hindsight, I agree with you. And although I was not involved with the council, as an Alpha responsible for hundreds of lives I also understand what prompted them to try."

Hawke's gut churned. "And it was just one pup, right? Just one lucky pup who gave up his life for the pack? Is that it?" Hawke looked around the room as if talking to the ghosts of the Alphas who agreed to his enslavement. "Not much of a sacrifice to the whole pack, right? Who the fuck cares about one pup?" he yelled and kicked a chair across the room. It crashed into the wall and broke to pieces.

The immediate area darkened as the room shrank to that small airless room he remained in, chained to a wall for years in the castle. Footsteps approached his door, but hunger had stolen his energy and he couldn't see who entered to place the slop on the floor in front of him. The stench of the food burned his nostrils and he lashed out to get rid of it. He heard a crash in the distance, but remained locked in this nightmare. Harsh laughter mocked his attempts to break the chain. No matter how hard he pulled to break free he couldn't. Moving forward, he kicked everything from his path as he stretched and pulled to break the chains. The laughter grew louder. Lancaster pointed at him in the distance and then swung the cane across his back. The thwacking sound of the wood jolted him. He jerked and reached for the man, determined to stop the next swing.

"Hawke!" He fell backward and hit the ground with a loud thump. "*Hawke?*"

His chest expanded to take in more air to clear the darkness in his mind. The cold from the cobblestone floor seeped into his skin. Hawke blinked and squinted against the light above him.

"*Open your eyes now, dammit!*" Hands gripped his shirt and lifted his head from the floor. Her warm breath flowed across his face. "*Now, open your eyes,*" Asia yelled and shook him.

He opened his eyes. Even in another skin he saw the fear, concern and then relief in her gaze. "*You blocked me,*" she said in a cross tone.

"*Huh?*" He pushed against the floor and sat upright. "*What?*"

"*You blocked me, closed me out of our link. Why did you do that?*" her voice cracked.

"*I didn't. I mean I didn't try to block you.*" He thought back and couldn't recall anything other than the blinding rage that overtook him. "*It just hit me. After all these years, being in this place where I was sold into slavery... I didn't think. Just reacted.*" He pulled her close, heard the racing of her heart. Goddess, he must've scared her pretty bad for her to react this way.

A scraping sound across the room grabbed his attention. Radoff struggled to stand from beneath the crushed dais. "Radoff? What happened? Are you... Goddess, what did I do?"

The room looked as if a tornado had ripped through. Every chair and table lay smashed to pieces on the floor. Artwork hung in crooked angles. The dais was gone. The altar and podium destroyed and Radoff was half covered in the debris.

Hawke blinked a couple times to make sure he saw things correctly. How had this happened? He couldn't recall moving, not much anyway. Had he been angry long enough to cause this kind of damage?

"Hawke, look at me." Asia turned his face toward her with her fingertips. "*Look at me.*"

He met her gaze. "*What happened?*" Had he turned into the monster the Liege created? A beast operating without control, destroying everything in his path? Goddess, no!

"You blacked out."

That surprised him. *"What?"*

"Your eyes, they went black, I couldn't reach you. You were talking, and moving in a blur while destroying the room. I shifted to stop you because I wasn't sure how much the beams holding the basement could take." Her tongue ran across her lips and he wished she was in her female form. He wanted to feel her softness, needed her comfort, and needed her to tell him he wasn't a lost cause.

"For a few seconds, you were lost to me. I could not reach you at all. How can that happen between mates?"

Hawke had no idea. *"We're mated that's all I know. Something about this place got to me. It happened the first time we came down here, remember?"*

"You were on the floor in pain, I remember. No pain this time?"

He shook his head slowly. *"No, just red hot anger. It came out of nowhere, I exploded. Didn't think. I... I didn't hurt you, did I?"*

She released a long stream of air. *"No. Quite the opposite. The area I stood was never touched. Every place else, you tore apart. That's what makes it so strange, even though you lost control, you were in control enough to protect me. We'll ask Maheegan or Jacques if they ever heard of anything like this happening before."* She looked over her shoulder and placed a kiss on his lips, but it was too brief and set him aflame. He needed her and rolled his hips so she could get a better feel of his hard cock beneath her.

Asia turned and met his gaze. *"Not now. Later, I promise."* She pressed against him and stood. Hawke grabbed her hand, holding her in place.

"*You sure you're okay? You haven't changed your mind about us?*"

Her eyes softened and the tight coil in his belly relaxed. "*Never. You're stuck with me through eternity.*"

He released her hand and stood. "*I can live with that.*"

She grinned and turned toward Radoff who brushed dirt and wood chips off his pants. Torn skin healed and he glanced at them.

"I just found my mate, I'm not ready to meet the Goddess, thank you very much." He smiled and walked toward Hawke who stood a short distance from Asia. "Based on what you said I imagine you've held a lot of stuff in a long time. How're you feeling now that you've got it out?"

Hawke ran his hand through his hair and looked at the destruction he caused. "Better I guess. The air is lighter, not as foul. No pain, no headaches or darkness. Guess it worked kind'a like an exorcism. Sorry about this mess, I'll help clean it out."

Radoff waved down his comments. "Forget it, I was going to throw it all out anyway." He paused. "No one thought of what the exchange would do to you. I'm sorry it happened the way it did. But I have to say, watching you rip through this room while talking and making sense at that, was quite impressive. The only wolf I can imagine giving you any competition would be your mate, and La Patron."

Hawke stared at him. "What are you saying?"

Radoff crossed his arms and met Hawke's gaze. "The Liege created a super wolf, you. Their techniques were unorthodox and they never meant to lose control of you. By your own admission, your mate disabled the computer chip and set you free of them. My concern is this, if they duplicate you with other full-blood pups, we won't be able to stop them. Just now, your mate was the only person who could stop you. What if these pups in LOBO receive the same training you did and never break free of Liege control? What happens to our world? Will we be forced to serve the Liege to survive?"

Hawke hadn't thought that far, but what Radoff said made sense and struck a nerve. "I see your concern. The only thing I can say is stop the Liege, now before these pups are too far into the program. For those fully indoctrinated, we will meet them one at a time and either destroy them or help them as much as possible."

"How do we help them? Could we have helped you?" Asia asked, watching him and knowing the answer.

"No. No one but you could've helped or stopped me. Not after thirty years, but we can stop them. Lancaster is somewhere in the country, why not start with him?"

Chapter 19

Hawke, Asia and Radoff discussed different strategies to locate Lancaster and destroy him. The hybrids that traveled with the man would attract attention, which meant they were not in a crowded area. Ulric mentioned Lancaster arriving with one person, the smart ass on the side of the road seemed likely, they'd have Angus contact Ulric for more information to find Lancaster.

Afterward, they would track down and destroy every Liege Lord until LOBO fell apart. No more chasing down labs, or false leads. They'd wasted enough time. Radoff's questions and the lack of answers, lit the fire of urgency beneath them. Asia had no problems killing the weasel Lancaster, especially after hearing what he had done to Hawke. The man deserved to die a long, painful death which she volunteered to administer. The door at the top of the basement opened and they stopped talking mid-sentence.

Maheegan, followed by Granira and Niall walked down the stairs. "We found it, finally we—" Eyes widening, she looked at the room and then went to Radoff. "Were you attacked? Did the Liege find you down here?"

Granira and Niall walked around looking at the damages. "What the hell happened down here?" Granira asked, looking at Hawke and then Asia.

"What did you find?" Radoff asked Maheegan, turning her to face him.

After a moment she exhaled and explained. "Granira and I compared notes. And then it clicked. The Liege violated the agreement, but that alone does not break the power of the contract because it was sealed in blood making the covenant stronger."

Asia stared at Maheegan and then glanced at Hawke. *"Does this make any sense to you?"*

Hawke nodded. *"Yes. The way it starts is the way it ends. Problem is none of the Alphas still live. How can we break it without their blood?"*

"Good point. I think we need to follow through on the original plan, find Lancaster and kill him. He'll have hybrids, maybe a few bluebirds, but if we take a large enough group of men we can take them down faster as if we were in the forest."

Hawke nodded. *"Like a food hunt?"*

"Yes. You, me and Angus will run points and the rest of the pack will wear them down until we are in position to move in for the kill. Unless they've come out with something new, we can handle all the old stuff." She thought of the serum, and the tranquilizers that had been used on them before.

"Sounds good, let's fill La Patron and Angus in and head out. We can meet him on the way." Hawke turned to leave.

"Where are you going?" Radoff asked, sounding confused.

"To get started on our plans." Hawke looked at Radoff over his shoulder.

"But what about this? We cannot do this without you. It's the only way to stop them from accessing pack lands. Isn't that what we're trying to do?" Radoff took a step toward Hawke and Asia.

"Did I miss something?" Hawke asked, turning to meet him.

Asia stood next to him, realizing something big just happened.

"Did you hear Maheegan? The contract can be broken with the blood from those who sealed it."

"I heard that. But the Alphas are all dead." Hawke looked at Granira. Had she lied about that? The woman nodded and continued to watch Radoff.

"Yes, but their blood did not seal the contract. Yours did. The pup taken for training. All we need is a Liege member's blood along with yours to break the covenant. To break their power and hold over the wolves," Maheegan said in a quiet, authoritative voice.

Asia stared at Maheegan as if she spoke Latin. "They shed his blood?" she asked, trying to understand.

Maheegan nodded. "It sealed the covenant and created a tie of sorts. That has to be broken."

"What happens when it's broken?" Asia asked since her mate remained silent. She sensed his confusion and opened their link to monitor his thoughts. They couldn't afford for him to lose it again, not with so many people in the confined space.

"The Liege looses access to pack lands. They also lose their ability to heal and live longer. In theory they should become powerless to train the pups or the pups will not be subject to the training. Which is it Granira?" Maheegan asked.

Asia wanted to groan in despair. Granira could not be trusted to tell the truth.

"They should become powerless, but I am not sure how that plays out in reality." She hefted her bag on her shoulder and looked at them. "Since they broke the contract a long time ago, I would think they would be unable to train the pups yet they have continued to do so. Alpha Hiram discovered their deceit early on and tried to remove his pup without the aid of the other Alphas. But the Liege convinced them Hawke progressed according to the agreement. They refused to allow my Alpha to see his son, claimed it would set Hawke back to see or scent him. Then we heard the stories of mutilations at the castle and missing wolves. Over the years the Liege continued to lie and say they hadn't broken faith, but my Alpha knew they were lying. Guilt ate at him, he tried to find a way to release his pup. After many failures, ten years ago, he tried to storm Lancaster castle to rescue his pup. We never saw him again."

"*Hawke?*" Asia said, hoping this new information didn't set him off.

"*I am fine. Just taking a moment to let this settle. Do you believe her?*"

"Huh?" Asia looked at Granira and then at Maheegan.

"*Granira is a liar, how do we know she's telling the truth?*"

"*Why would she lie? What would she gain? We planned to kill Lancaster anyway, this just makes me want to do it faster.*"

He nodded. *"True. I am cautious to change my opinions of abandonment after all this time, that's all. I never knew my sire tried to find me or felt bad over his actions. Niall didn't mention this."*

"No, he didn't explain, other than say your sire died ten years ago. Perhaps it's too hard for him to discuss."

Hawke met Radoff's gaze and sensed his nervousness when he moved Maheegan behind him. "What do you need from me?"

Maheegan and Radoff exhaled. "There is one other thing. Until the contract is broken, the Liege Lords involved with the contract cannot be killed by pack. The covenant provided a safety net for Gordon and Lancaster since they were the two who originated the deal. I suppose they were afraid they'd be killed if anyone found out what they did to full-bloods."

"They cannot die?" Hawke asked.

"Yes, but not by pack."

"We must bring one of them in alive, take some of his blood to break the contract before killing him?" Asia asked for clarity.

Maheegan nodded slowly. "That's a graphic way of looking at it, but accurate."

Since she and Hawke were on their way to kill Lancaster she didn't think delivering the man alive a few moments longer would be a problem. Perhaps Hawke could chain him to a wall. The visual pleased her and she shared with her mate.

"We were making plans to handle that when you walked in," Radoff said watching Asia and Hawke.

"Really?" Maheegan asked, looking at the three of them. No one said more and she nodded. "I have more research to complete." She headed toward the stairs, stopped and looked at Granari. "Are you leaving now or will you be here for a bit?"

Granari lifted one of her bags, while Niall picked up the other. "I will return to assist you tomorrow after I check on my home. My Alpha has contacted me and requires a full accounting."

"Thank you, I will see you then. Oh, could you bring the original contract? I want to read through it before the ceremony," Maheegan asked.

"Yes of course."

Asia watched as Niall walked quietly behind the woman as they made their way down the long corridor. *"They have a weird relationship. I cannot figure it out."*

"Neither can I. Let's talk to La Patron and Angus. We need to grab a Liege Lord to bleed."

Chapter 20

Gordon watched the hybrid fly through the air and hit the mat in the mini gym Lancaster set up for practice in the new building they'd relocated to. Damian landed on top, pinning the huge warrior to the floor. Gordon's chest expanded with pride. Damian had exceeded their expectations and excelled in every test or challenge presented.

But he couldn't win against Hawke.

They all knew it. The idea of watching the light of life die in Damian's eyes sickened him. He prayed Hawke couldn't kill his seed, which was this last test and his hope. Sometimes living a long life was more a curse than a blessing. Down through the years he'd buried his wife and two sons before they reached twenty summers. Stephan had been his heir and Reginald his youngest. His wife died shortly after Reginald's birth with some type of pox.

Stephan died in the war, before his nineteenth summer, fighting in the Hungarian army. He had been

Gordon's' pride and joy, a perfect specimen of nobility. Burying his son had been one of the hardest things he had ever done.

Damian reminded him of Reginald, his youngest, who died of the fever in his fifteenth summer. Both were inquisitive with a thirst for knowledge and adventure. From the first time he met Damian in the dungeon of Lancaster castle, he'd been intrigued by the way the young pup adapted to change. Damian, and all the pups who qualified, had been sent to the LOBO camp in the states for training. Gordon and Lancaster ran the program but through the years, Damian had become his favorite. Gordon spent hours tutoring the boy in his studies and had been impressed by his sharp mind. There was no question he was indeed Hawke's seed.

Damian received surgeries to implant the steel rods in his arms and later his legs in his fourteenth year. Gordon remained at the lab until he was satisfied the surgery had been successful, leaving no permanent damage. The computer implant to help Damian control his limbs had been the last surgical procedure which created a problem. By bringing Damian on this trip without a tracker, or cam or kill chip, they had no way to control the young full-blood and could lose their entire investment. The board believed since Damian had been with the Liege all his life and knew nothing else he would remain loyal. At first, Gordon thought it dangerous to allow Damian contact with his sire without a cam or tracker. Now, he simply wanted the young pup to live through the meeting.

Gordon knew Damian looked at him as a father, and over the years he encouraged the connection, often times needing it more than the young pup. Often Gordon suffered from depression and Damian would help him through it by reading or talking or playing a board game.

And now those bastards intended to bring Hawke and Damian, biological father and son together in a test to see if they could destroy each other. Gordon didn't think they could, but no one listened to him. Instead, they planned to use his boy as bait to trap Hawke. The cup in Gordon's hand cracked and crumbled beneath the pressure of his clenched fist.

He turned and tossed it aside as Damian helped the hybrid stand and took his position again. There had to be a way to stop this. Verrick, that asshole, refused to assist him and took his pack to the mountains. It had been so long since he'd been in this cold wasteland, he had forgotten the names of their allies. He was certain Lancaster hadn't. Alpha Andrei dead by Angus' hands. The one councilman they could trust, dead as well. The European council, dethroned and ineffective.

Gordon looked over his shoulder and watched Damian punch the hybrid so hard it flew backward into the wall. In a few years, the young pup would be impossible to beat. Gordon intended to make sure Damian lived that long.

Lancaster strolled into the room, his thin face and pinched upturned nose on his long narrow face had made Boris the butt of jokes when they were youngsters. No one had been more surprised than Gordon, when he replaced his father in the Roundtable, and Boris sat across from him. The look of smug superiority in the bastard's eyes as his name had been called as a charter member made Gordon sick. But Lancaster's father had been Konstantin's game-keeper and rather than sit on the table with his master, the older man asked Konstantin to train Boris.

Neither spoke as they watched Damian train against another hybrid.

"Have you set things up for him to meet Hawke?"

Lancaster glanced at him and then grinned. "Yes… yes, I believe I have."

Gordon waited for him to explain further and when he did not, Gordon exhaled in slow degrees to keep his temper in check.

"Are you going to share?" He hated asking this man for anything, but he needed to know what plans were in the making.

"No. No, I do not believe I will. It will be a surprise."

Gordon's jaw clenched and he balled his fist. "I do not like surprises."

Lancaster chuckled and shook his head in a mocking gesture. "You shouldn't have grown so close to him. He's a wolf. An animal, a different species altogether and will never be your son."

Gordon's hand flew out before he could think to check his actions. The fight on the mat stopped. Hybrids and Damian watched as Lancaster spun from the force of the blow but did not fall. Instead, he licked the blood from the corner of his lips while watching Gordon with a narrowed gaze.

"You should never have done that."

Gordon silently agreed. Over the decades, he'd seen the man's cruelty and knew better than most how vindictive Lancaster could be. But the deed was done and he refused to apologize. The cut healed after leaking a few seconds and Lancaster straightened. If anger had a sound, Gordon would say Lancaster vibrated with it. The mark remained on his cheek as he looked toward Damian.

Gordon's chest constricted at the pointed gaze. Lancaster would destroy Damian to get back at him. "I apologize. I should never have done that." The words tasted like sawdust.

"No you should not have. It will cost you." Lancaster turned and left the small gym.

Gordon watched him leave with unease.

"Sir, are you alright? Do you require anything?" Damian asked, standing nearby watching him closely.

Without meeting his gaze, Gordon shook his head. What had he done? A sense of dread ran over him, leaving him cold. Lancaster would destroy Damian out of spite and there was little he could do about it. The other Lords complained about Boris behind closed doors, but none would go against him. Not even Roderick, their leader. For decades Boris had led the Liege down this path of lies and deceit, operating in the gray areas of their agreement with the old Alphas rather than the letter. Gordon no longer had the stomach for it. Despite being dual-natured, Damian's human side controlled his wolf and actions. He was a good boy, loyal and kind hearted. Damian deserved a chance. Gordon knew he wouldn't sit by and allow Lancaster to destroy the pup he loved as a son.

Chapter 21

Hawke and Asia headed toward their vehicle. There had been so many revelations in the past hour she needed a few moments alone with her mate to settle a few things in her mind. She had lost him. In the darkest moment of his rage, he blacked out and she couldn't reach him and that bothered her. "We need to get some answers right now," she said, opening the car door and sliding into the passenger seat.

"*Mistress?*" Asia opened the link for Hawke, tapped her finger along her leg and glanced out the window. Radoff and Maheegan walked at a clipped pace across the yard toward the main building. Had they learned more about the birthmark? So much had happened she hadn't asked.

"*Asia, how's it going?*"

Asia told Jasmine everything.

"*Silas, have you ever heard of a mate being kicked out like that?*" Jasmine asked.

"*He did not kick her out. His beast protected her. When the beast loses control to that extent, he will not allow his mate to be hurt by the emotional backlash. Believe me it could have caused you pain and discomfort. His wolf would cease to exist before he allowed that and could never be the direct cause."*

"So his beast closed me out to protect me?" Asia asked watching Hawke.

"He will always protect you first, he can do nothing else," Silas said with implacable resolve.

"Thank you for explaining, I did not know the answer when she asked," Hawke said.

"Understandable. The plan is to find Gordon or Lancaster and break the covenant?" Silas asked.

"Gordon? Is he here?" Asia remembered the dapper man she'd seen a few times over the years. Back then he wore a goatee with long sideburns and had thick bushy eyebrows over dark brown eyes, being one of the shorter Lords he always seemed to stand out.

"Yes. He arrived yesterday," Silas said. *"This one is different than Lancaster, not as slippery. He works directly with LOBO which I believe is in the states. Leon and Brix are searching possible locations right now. Gordon's old school aristocracy, blue blood. I don't have a lot on him, but I sent Angus a copy of a picture when he was a younger man."*

"Great," Asia said. *"How can we get in touch with Ulric? He mentioned to Angus that Lancaster arrived, hopefully he can give us some information that will point us in the right direction."*

"Why haven't you linked with Angus yet Hawke?" Silas asked.

"We just never got around to it. Things are moving fast," Hawke said. *"We need to tell Angus of our change of plans. He and Chacal were headed north this morning.*

Chacal wanted to check a place that they'd seen before. He thinks they missed something."

"He mentioned that. How large is Radoff's pack?" Silas asked.

"*I don't know. I've seen fifty in one place,*" she said thinking of the hotel where they first met the Alpha. "*There may be more.*"

"*You'll need to pull Ulric into this as well for backup. Understand, you two have lead on this, especially since the pack cannot kill Lancaster and Gordon until the contract is broken, it's important to keep them alive until then.*"

Asia frowned. "*I don't understand.*"

"*Imagine if you were human and had the advantage of the fountain of youth for decades. Your body healed, you lived well, made millions of dollars and your enemies could not kill you. Two men threatened all of that, what would you do?*" Silas asked.

"*Damn, they would eat their own. To keep that deal they'd try to kill Lancaster and Gordon.*" Asia looked at Hawke. "*We need to take a plastic bag and a cup of ice in case they're bleeding. They can send each other to their personal hells for all I care, but we will get the blood to break the covenant.*"

He nodded.

"*Asia, Hawke, watch your backs,*" Jasmine said. "*You are the other half necessary to break this thing. If they could destroy either of you, they're safe. Don't forget that.*"

Asia sobered recalling the tenacity of those men. "*Yes, Ma'am. I have his back.*"

"*I've got hers. This time will be different.*" Hawke paused and then cleared his throat. "*I killed my sire. He died ten years ago attempting to rescue me from Lancaster Castle. Ten years ago an enemy attacked and I pulled the switch to the roof, killing them all. It does not matter I had no idea who he was. I created and improved security at the castle. I am responsible for every failure my sire encountered trying to rescue me."* He exhaled and she held his hand, knowing he needed to say it. *"This time, there will be no failure. On my sire's honor, I will break this contract."*

No one spoke.

"How normal is it to seal a contract in blood?" Jasmine asked. That had sounded barbaric to Asia as well.

"Very common for that time period and given our nature and respect for blood, it signified the importance of the covenant. I suspect there is more involved. Maheegan is researching it and should know more when you return."

"Return? We are bringing one of the Lords here?" Asia asked looking at Hawke.

He shrugged.

"Yes, back to the place it began," Silas said.

"Understood." Asia looked out the window. Bringing either man all the way back here would require additional planning.

"We are in agreement then. The covenant will be broken through the shedding of blood, just as it was created," Silas said.

"Yes, Sir." Hawk and Asia said.

"What about Niall and Granira?" Jasmine asked. *"Maheegan contacted us about the contract you sent Hawke and she believes it's valid. But why would Granira have had a copy? Does Maheegan have copies of contracts for you, Silas?"*

"No, but I have Jacques. In smaller packs it may be customary to allow the historian to secure important documents."

"In that case we should be grateful she has a few missing pieces to the puzzle. Thanks to her help this should be over within the next few days," Jasmine said.

Asia nodded. *"Yes, Ma'am, that is the plan."*

"Good. Hawke when this is all over, I would like to meet you and your brother. Please extend an invitation on our behalf."

Asia sensed Hawke's surprise even though his outer appearance appeared calm.

"Yes, Ma'am." Hawke's eyes widen and then he shut them tight.

"Damn Silas that hurt," Angus said joining the conversation.

"You linked us?" Hawke said, opening his eyes and then looking at his mate.

"Yes. Time is short and you need to know what each other's doing," Silas said and then brought Angus current.

"I'll talk to Ulric and get that information. He's been waiting for something like this. We need to get Gordon or Lancaster out of the city, away from humans. Question, when you say we cannot kill them does that mean we cannot hurt them or they will not die from whatever we do to them? Because I cannot kill my litter mate, but we can fight," Angus asked.

"I believe it would be the same with Lancaster and Gordon," Silas said.

"Good to know because I plan to beat the shit out him over and over before the son of a bitch dies."

Asia laughed. *"We can have one of those lines we saw on the movies, Mistress."*

"Conga lines?" Jasmine said.

"Yes. Beat their ass, let them heal and then the next person can beat them to a pulp and then let them heal. It

could be a part of the celebration and a way to collect the blood," Asia said.

"*Sounds like a plan,"* Angus said. "*We need to find the slimy bastards first.*

Chapter 22

Angus and Chacal stepped through the doorway of the building they had visited two days before. Chacal wanted to check a room that had appeared suspicious the other day, but forgot about it after they saw the charred remains of the animals.

"There's been a change of plans Silas is sending us after the Liege Lords. Gordon and Lancaster are in the area," Angus said through his link with Chacal and then connected with Hawke. *"Ulric had a team watching their movements. Right now they are out of the city on a large farm with two large connected buildings. They've seen a couple blue birds and hybrids guarding the area. If we're going to take them it should be now while there aren't many humans around."*

"Give me the coordinates," Hawke said.

Angus gave them to him. *"Ulric contacted Radoff to coordinate security around the building in case the Liege tries to leave. He sent several of his pack members to help.*

Ulric and the rest of his pack will meet us at the farm, but won't engage until we give the word."

"*Have they prepared against the tranquilizer?"* Hawke asked.

"*Yes, they seem to like the nasty shit. We will be on the road in a few, just need to check out something.*" He followed Chacal down the hall.

"*See you later.*" Hawke disconnected.

The area smelled different than the section they'd been in before, something bitter to his senses hung in the air. He tapped Chacal's shoulder to get him to stop. Someone or something was in this building that was not here the other day or they hadn't picked up on them. Chacal sensed it as well and looked around.

Angus stepped to the side and inhaled. The pungent odor stung his throat; he wiped his nose and cleared his throat to rid it of the toxic smell. "*What do you think that is?*"

Chacal shook his head and turned back the way they had come. "*Too strong, my beast... he's not... too strong.*"

Angus agreed and followed, but glimpsed over his shoulder down the hall toward that door. He stopped. Something wasn't right. They needed to know whatever stood behind that door. He glanced at his chameleon bracelet, touched the wall to merge and inched backward. The wall vibrated as he drew closer to the door. Whatever hid behind these walls held an elusive scent, Angus couldn't determine if it were human, wolf or other. It was the "other" category that disturbed him.

By the time he reached the door a low grade hum filled the immediate area. Low rumbling sounds bled through the cracks. What the hell was in there?

"*Are you coming?*" Chacal asked through their link.

"In a bit, I need to check this out. Go ahead, I'll catch up with you."

"Go? Where? And leave you here with whatever that is? La Patron will have my head."

Angus didn't want to point out Chacal had already left him in the building, and remained quiet on that score.

The door shuddered as if something hard hit it from the opposite side trying to break free. Angus fell to the floor and returned to his natural form. That seemed to make it angry. Loud heavy thumps and thwacks like someone kicking on the door resumed with more fervor it seemed. Guttural, inhuman sounds made the hair stand on Angus' shoulders.

Another thump and the door creaked on the metal hinges. Another and a dent appeared in the middle of the metal door. Angus took a couple steps back, bulked to his hybrid and waited. Fist clenched, he wondered if he should alert Silas, but nixed the idea since he had no idea what was coming.

"You need me?" Chacal asked.

"No." Angus watched as another thump made popped the top hinge. He took another step back as another dent appeared in the door, with a loud sound. A few more hits and it would open.

Bending forward with one foot slightly back, arms and fingers loose, he watched as the door broke free from the hinges and slammed against the wall. Dust billowed from the room blinding him for a moment. The stench grew stronger and he jumped on instinct as something, ran out the room and hit the opposite wall. The room shook beneath the impact. Angus tried to see but the dust was too thick. The growling sounds persisted. He moved to the side and glanced into the room. A row of what appeared to be incubators lined a wall.

A snort was the only warning he had before the thing charged, barely missing him but hitting the back wall so hard a shelf of glass beakers and jars hit the floor, breaking on impact. A loud screeching sound filled the ear, so piercing Angus covered his ears as his knees buckled.

"*What the Goddess is that noise?*" Chacal asked

"*Don't know. Looks like they left something behind. I can't get a good glimpse of it yet, too much dust.*" He pushed away from the wall and watched the smoke waft toward the ceiling. "*The chemicals are burning it.*"

"*Can you save it?*"

"*Give me one reason why I should step into that room. It looks like an experiment gone bad. From where I'm standing whatever that thing is, it was left behind on purpose.*" The screams turned to mewling sounds and the movements slowed to an occasional arm swing. Angus leaned forward to get a better look in the room and stepped back when the thing growled. From where Angus stood, he could make out a row of razor sharp teeth in a long snout and little else.

The agonizing whine continued from the thing on the floor. Hearing footsteps, Angus looked over his shoulder at Chacal. He stopped level with Angus and watched the thing writhe on the floor, spreading more of the chemical on itself. The wretched smell diminished with the opening of the door.

Chacal stuck his head inside the room, looked around and stepped inside. The thing growled, but ended with a whimper as it tried to move toward Chacal and couldn't. Now that the dust settled, Angus noticed a thick, long tube filled with some type of powder on the ground near the door and realized the creature had used it to get out. He stepped into the room. The creature stopped. His eyes flicked toward Angus and their gazes clashed.

Blue speckles dotted the skin of the animal who was the size of a large Rottweiler with a malformed snout and odd shaped head. Angus looked closer, the chemical had burned through the animal's skin, down to the bone. Metal gleamed in one leg and bone in the others. The animal's eyes didn't blink, he continued to stare at Angus.

"What the hell did they do to you?" he murmured, looking at the padded feet of the, what dog? Miniature wolf? He had no idea what the thing was, it looked like a combination of things.

"Look at this," Chacal called from the corner of the room. He wore a heavy lab jacket, gloves and goggles. Angus looked around, grabbed similar gear and walked toward him.

"What you got?" he stared at the rod Chacal held.

"They were cross breeding, nasty stuff." Chacal put the rod down and walked to a large incubator with the sides broken out. "I think they left him here and took the others. There are six of these, all held something, we don't know what." Chacal toward the animal lying on the floor. "What do you think of it?"

Angus looked at each incubator, and the equipment surrounding it. Top notch, someone spent millions of dollars here. Why walk away and leave it? The equipment alone would be invaluable.

"It's smart, recognized someone was near and somehow used that tube to knock down the door."

"Impossible," Chacal said walking toward the door. "How'd he hold onto it? Plus that tube is heavy."

Angus moved closer, looked at the door, then the animal, and then the tube. "How'd he knock that door off the hinge?"

Chacal strode to the heavy metal door, bent down, looked at the dent marks and then at the animal struggling to breathe and then at the door again. "Body slammed into it. Probably stood on top of the tube once or twice but whatever it is knocked a solid steel door off the frame."

Both of them stared at the creature for a few minutes. This was more Hawke's area, Angus couldn't begin to guess what was going on with the creature. But he needed to move out and meet Hawke at the farm.

He pulled off the gear and dropped them across one of the tables. "Matt and Passen would have a field day in here."

"What?"

"The doc's back at the labs, this is the kind of thing they dream about. Pity we can't contain the area, now that the door is down. Someone is probably returning for this stuff." He looked around and then back at the animal on the floor who continued to stare at him.

"We gotta go." He turned and left the room with Chacal behind him. "See if you can pull up the layout from the records of the farm, it'll help knowing what's inside."

"This isn't the states where everything goes through planning and blueprints are followed exactly. Whatever I find, if anything, has probably been modified without going through proper channels."

"Got it. But anything you can find will help."

Chacal pulled out his laptop and got to work. They were driving down the long dirt road that led away from the abandoned lab when Angus noticed a small dust cloud coming up behind them. When he reached the main road, he stopped for oncoming traffic and heard a low growl near the driver's door.

"Don't tell me," Chacal said trying to see out the window. "I thought it died. What is it doing?"

Angus turned onto the highway and looked in the rear view mirror. "It's following us. But it didn't attack the truck. That's a good sign."

They drove the next few miles in silence, monitoring the beast. When Angus sped up, it did as well. It maintained an even pace and never dropped back. Impressed, Angus pulled into an abandoned petro station and opened the door. Curious, he watched what now appeared to be the ugliest breed of dog he had ever seen. The beast slowed from the trot and walked near but didn't come close as Angus stepped out. They stared at each other for a few moments and Angus searched for a link with the animal.

"I'm Angus, a wolf shifter. Can you understand me?"

The thing turned his head to the side, continued watching him, but moved a few steps closer. "Okay, no links, didn't think so, but I had to try." Angus reached forward to touch its head and pulled back when the animal growled.

"I just wanted to touch to get a reading with my bracelet, it won't hurt." "Why am I speaking through a link? Habit."

"And there is a chance he understands some things even if he cannot return communications with you. Keep trying it can't hurt," Chacal said from inside the car.

Angus moved slowly while murmuring through the link that he just wanted to touch, that's all. The tingling sensation from his link activated just as his fingertips brushed the blue speckled head of the animal. He listened for a computer chip and breathed a sigh of relief when he heard no mechanical devices. Good, the Liege wasn't using this animal. He stroked the beast's head a few times.

It purred and sat on its hind legs. Angus delved deeper and searched for information on the origins of the animal and learned nothing other than the beast was a part of the Canidae family. But so were foxes, wolves, coyote, jackals, and dogs. He scratched the animal's head and stood. The animal stood as well. The blue speckled plate wasn't as obvious on the back and sides as it was on the head. Thick muscular legs, short tail, wide and long snout made this beast the weirdest looking animal Angus had seen in his three hundred years.

"You need to make up your mind what you plan to do with it, we need to go meet Hawke."

"Yeah, I thought I'd be able to find out something, but that didn't work." He moved to the door and the beast jumped forward. Angus ducked and watched the animal hop into the back seat.

Chacal remained frozen in place and didn't move.

"You didn't stop it?" Angus looked at the animal who returned his stare and then settled into the back seat as if it were about to nap.

"No, I did not stop it. Not sure I could have either. That animal knocked down a solid steel door. He likes you, let's hope that lasts. I'd hate to be in its way if it decided to leave."

"*You going with me?*" Angus asked as he slid into the driver's seat. The animal's head lifted, he stared at Hawke and then rested against the seat. "*I'll take that as a yes. No chewing or biting anything. I'll get you something to eat later.*"

The animal made a purring sound and Angus smiled. "This could only happen to me on the way to take down the Liege. Talk about timing."

"I knew there was something at that lab, just didn't think it was… what is it?" Chacal glanced over his shoulder at the beast.

"I'm not sure. They mixed him up with some things, its got metal in one of its legs, and that blue metal on its body. No camera, no computer chips."

"What did they plan to do with it? How would they control it without the chip?"

"Don't know. Maybe they planned to come back for him and do that later. I don't think he's wolf though." Angus shrugged and pulled onto the road.

"Those teeth? Did you see them?" Chacal asked.

"Yes. But I think they're engineered or something. Can't be too sure. Don't want to get too close." Angus looked in the rear view mirror at the ugly beast and felt sorry for it.

"What are you going to do with it? Can't just let it loose." Chacal stared at him.

Angus looked at Chacal and smiled. "You need a guard dog, some companionship."

"No. I do not. Think of something to tell La Patron when you return stateside with this… thing. Customs ought to be interesting. Because if those chemicals that burned through its skin to the bone did not kill it, I don't know what will."

Angus hadn't thought about that. The thing had regenerative powers like a shifter.

Chapter 23

The miles seem to stretch forever as they made their way toward the rendezvous. Her blood sang in anticipation of coming face to face with the men who had made her life hell. Angus's idea of a prolonged kill suited her mood. She would return to the line more than once to beat either man down for the damage they'd done to her life and then for her mate and then for Gunnolf. Bastards ruined the lives of too many people in the name of greed.

Hawke's hand covered hers. "When we reach the farm do we drive up to the door?"

She hadn't thought much about their approach. "I assumed that's what the three of us would do and allow Ulric's men to surround the perimeter so no one leaves. Have Angus tell Ulric to search for an underground entry point. I'm sure there is one. Lancaster would never have just one exit. The man always had a lot of ways to leave without being caught. He's slick."

"We just need one of them to break the covenant and then we shoot the rest of the bastards, or blow them up. They won't survive without the covenant in force."

"I'd like to see the light die in Lancaster's eyes for what he did to you, but as long as he dies, and never touches another pup, I'll live without that visual."

Hawke squeezed her hand.

"Feels good, doesn't it? Finally going after them? Not their labs, or old buildings. After all this time we're going to kill another one of the bastards," Asia said.

"Why hadn't you gone after them before after your rebirth?"

"Too busy working with La Patron. Liege kept us on defense, and it took a while to enter the game. Now, we're on offense, going after them and it feels great."

"I can imagine. Time of reckoning."

She nodded, thinking of her years living in the Liege facilities, the missions she completed, the blood she shed, the surgeries. A shudder ripped through her when she recalled all the surgeries she endured. Gordon and Lancaster's throats should be ripped out for approving each time the doctors cut her open.

Hawke stroked her arm. "It's okay. We're going to close a chapter in the Liege's diary and shut down LOBO. No other pup will be taken and experimented on again. I promise we will shut this down."

Asia exhaled and looked at the greenish-brown landscape fly by. "I know. There is a part of me that feels this cannot be happening. I want to pinch myself. Understand, I've hated them for so long, they've always been there, in the background like cancer. Today, a part of that cancer dies."

"It's happening and you're front and center."

She kissed the back of his hand and continued to look out the window. "Ulric told Angus they have bluebirds and hybrids at the farm?"

He nodded.

"I was thinking..."

"What?"

"If we fight them, it will delay us which will give Gordon and Lancaster time to escape." She turned to face him. "But if we fight and get captured, they'll take us inside and then we can find them faster."

"Get captured? How? They know we can defeat the bluebirds and hybrids."

"They don't know the tranquilizer no longer works. Plus, it's just to get inside without wasting a lot of energy outside."

He nodded. "It could work. What if they try to kill us instead of taking us inside?"

"Then we'll need to destroy them. I'll fall first and if they don't take me then we'll know." She knew he didn't like that idea and waited for his objections.

"If they take you, I'm following." His voice deepened as his wolf rose to the surface.

"That is why they'll take me inside, they know you'll follow and Lancaster wants you. Remember what Greggor said?"

"No, he said a lot of stuff, not that it matters. If one of us goes down the other needs to run behind that one, maybe get shot as well. Links must be open at all times, I'm serious Asia. I won't be able to handle seeing you go down otherwise. Promise me you'll talk to me and my beast the entire time, especially if we get separated."

She stroked his hand. "I promise. This is the best way to get in quickly. Run it by Angus, see what he thinks."

A few moments later Hawke chuckled. "He said they have no reason not to kill him so he'll fight his way through and catch up with us inside. Plus, he wants to check the grounds for another exit. Chacal's checking to see if there is a floor plan of the building in public records, so far he hasn't found anything. Seems like we'll be going into this blind."

"Won't be the first time. I had no idea what to expect when I entered Lancaster's castle and went to the dorms. Pissed me off that I couldn't leave right away."

He kissed the back of her hand. "I'm glad you didn't."

She smiled in remembrance of the first time she saw him standing tall in the lab. Her wolf had done flips demanding she go to him right then. That hadn't changed. "Me too. So we go in cold, search for Lancaster or Gordon, grab them and drive back to Radoff's, is that the plan?"

Hawke frowned. "Not the best, too many opportunities for them to escape. Can Radoff come here?"

"La Patron said it had to be in the place all of this started. But you're right, grabbing them will be hard enough, transporting back to the basement... that's pushing it. Maybe we can take them by air, a helicopter? Ask Angus if Chacal has one we can use?"

"Good idea."

She watched him for a few moments going over the plan in her head. Strategizing was not her strength, she preferred to follow directions and get the job done. Jasmine seemed to think she could do it all so she would give it her best shot.

"Chacal has one and will have it ready in an hour, hour and a half at the most. He'll drop Angus off and go back to his place to fly it back."

"He flies helicopters?"

"According to Angus he flies everything, so we have an extraction plan in place. Angus wants to use the bracelet on the Liege to discover the location of LOBO in the states after we take his blood."

"No. Not unless I get a chance to spend five minutes alone with him first." Her heart raced at the idea of being cheated the opportunity to meet one or both of the men who enslaved her. "I want to look that bastard in the eye and then send him to hell."

"Asia."

"I'm serious. I need this for closure. They stole everything from me, I don't have a past. Don't know where I'm from or who my pack was. My mind was wiped to the point you can't see anything. They fucked me over and over, Hawke. I need to send that bastard to hell."

"I'll tell Angus. Isn't there a way to use the bracelet to get information without killing him?"

She nodded. "But to get it all you have to take over his body."

"We'll work something out, the important thing is to focus on taking them alive, meeting the copter, and breaking that damn contract. Agreed?"

"Agreed."

They turned off the main highway to the road leading to the location. They were five miles from the farm, Asia opened her senses and identified the hybrids ahead. She pointed to the right. "Hybrids in the tree line."

Hawke nodded and continued driving. "Two Bluebirds ahead. They haven't moved but we are on their radar. How close do we want to get to the building?"

Asia looked around, identified a couple more hybrids, four total. "Where is Ulric and his pack? I'm not picking up their scent. Maybe we should pull over and wait, go over everything with Angus." She turned in her seat, looked out the back window and saw nothing but trees and crops.

Hawke stopped the car in the middle of the road and looked at her. "Are you okay?"

Asia exhaled. "*I don't like planning on the run. Usually someone else has gone over the floor plan, can tell us what door to enter, where potential problems are and options to handle them. I keep feeling like I'm forgetting something important which will screw up this mission and that bothers me big time.*"

He took her hand, placed his finger beneath her chin and turned her to face him. "*I'll take your word for it on how things would go on a normal operation. But we don't have that this time and have to make the best of what we do have. Links open, merge completely with me. Feed me what you're seeing and I'll do the same. Instead of them dealing with one of us, they'll face both of us no matter where we are. Believe me when I say, I will destroy that building and everything in it before I allow anything to happen to you. At the end of the day seeing you walk out of there is the most important thing for me. They have an idea of what I can do and will try to shut me down. Mated, I am stronger. Merged, you'll sense their moves just as I will and we'll work together to keep each other strong. Remember, last time, we weren't merged, not like we are now.*" He brushed his lips against hers. "*We can do this. We have to do this.*"

Asia leaned into him and exhaled. "You're right." She sat up and looked behind her. A line of large trucks pulled onto the road. "Ulric's here. Find out how much longer before Angus arrives."

Hawke looked out the window and nodded. "Chacal pulled over and he got out the truck near the main road. He should be here any minute."

Asia released her breath as the tension unfurled in her chest. Angus would go over their plans and tell them if they'd work or not. She wouldn't be responsible. Leaning against the headrest, she rechecked the status of the hybrids.

"Hybrids over there moved in a few feet, if you look you can see them." She pointed toward the trees.

"Yeah. Bluebirds haven't moved, but as fast as they are, they don't have to."

She patted the hilt of her sword and silently agreed.

Angus slid into the back seat and then looked out the window. "Stay. I need to talk for a few minutes. Sit."

Asia leaned over Hawke to see what or who Angus was talking to.

"Where'd you find him?" Hawke asked in a somber tone that made Asia lean back and look at him.

"Who?" She asked.

"The TerraByte," Hawke said, looking out the window.

"Found him in that lab with the incinerator." He went on to explain what happened when he and Chacal returned to search the building. "He won't leave, if you can give me any information on him I'd appreciate it," Angus said.

"TerraByte or TB was Griffith's pet project. He had this weird thing about hunting dogs, and wanted to try the new technology with a few breeds. Problem is Griffith was the brilliant kind of crazy and kept breeding different species. Let's say he'd start with a Rottweiler and then breed it with another animal like a jackal-wolf hybrid. He kept breeding them until it's no telling what you have there. For the most part he handled his own experiments, did the surgeries and kept his notes close to his chest. Once Lancaster asked me to decipher a few of Griffith's papers, I could only make out half. The man wrote in a shorthand he created. Lancaster wanted to incorporate some of Griffith's techniques, but couldn't."

"You mentioned surgeries. This fella has metal in one of his legs."

Asia gasped. "What? That bastard. If I hadn't killed him already I'd kill him for what he did to that poor animal."

"That's not all, he has blue speckled metal on his body. That, whatever you call it, knocked down a steel door, has razor sharp retractable teeth and regenerative healing powers."

"And he chose you." Hawke glanced behind him and smiled at Angus.

Angus looked surprised by that announcement. "Yeah, he did. Not sure why, but he won't let me move too far without following."

"Well, from what I remember TB's are vicious predators that will protect you with their lives which is a good thing based on how hard he is to defeat. The downside is he won't leave you, even when you change your appearance. Your DNA is imprinted in his mind. Anyone who knows you will see him and it'll make it hard for you to work incognito. Your spying days as other people are over. One look at him and they'll know it's you because he is an original."

"Ugly you mean," Asia said when she got a look at the odd looking beast. "Are there a lot of those?"

"Not from what I heard, but like I said it wasn't my project. Rumor was they scrapped the project before Griffith's death because no one could control them. When they bonded with an owner it was for life. The Liege couldn't use or sell them because the TB's refused to leave their handlers from the labs. I thought they were all destroyed, possibly in that incinerator you found the other day. Don't know why they left that one."

"Well, damn," Angus said, shaking his head. "Lost a two hundred year career overnight. I guess it's time to retire in the mountains with my dog or whatever the mutt is." He chuckled not seeming the least bothered. "Can he understand what I'm saying? I tried to link to him and he looked at me, but that was all."

"Maybe, I don't know for sure. But he is intelligent and will protect you at all costs, which, given the fact the blue birds are stirring, isn't a bad thing." Hawke opened their link and briefed Angus on their plans. After a little fine tuning, Angus changed his appearance to a young, muscular, blonde male and stepped out the car.

Asia and Hawke stepped out as well. "You need to introduce us to him, let him know we are your friends. Kind of like open his circle of safe people for you to be around," Hawke said to Angus taking Asia's hand.

Angus knelt in front of the TerraByte and stroked the top of his head for a few seconds. The beast looked at her and then Hawke as if checking them out before returning his gaze to Angus. "Byte, that's his name," Angus said standing. "I told him to only attack the beasts I attack and no one else. Ulric would think I issued an Alpha challenge otherwise."

Asia unsheathed her sword, glanced at Byte who growled as he faced the building. "Appreciate that."

Angus took off, Byte followed in a burst of speed as the first bluebird reached them. Ulric and his pack fought the four hybrids and the other bluebird remained in place.

Byte leapt forward, grabbed the bluebird by the neck and tore off a chunk of skin, revealing flesh, bone and glints of metal. The bird dropped to the ground. Byte bit into the neck again ripping and tearing while the bird tried to dislodge him. His tough skin prevented the poisonous nails from penetrating and each tug from the bluebird made the tear worse. Asia stood fascinated by the long sharp teeth stained with blood in Byte's mouth. The bluebird tried several times to rise from the ground, its head lolled to the side with a gaping wound.

Angus sauntered over and cut off the head with a solid swing, sending it rolling a few feet. Byte jogged to the head, sniffed a few times and then bit into it. A few seconds later he tossed it aside and took off after Angus, who ran toward the building.

The whole fight lasted a few minutes. Asia couldn't believe how fast and strong Byte had been. Hawke squeezed her hand and took off. A few seconds later she caught up with him.

"I want one of those," She said as they passed Angus and Byte destroying another Bluebird.

Chapter 24

Boris sat in the chair in the lower chamber watching the battle outside. Hawke, his prized achievement, fought with the strength and cunning of ten hybrids. He sighed in regret. They could have gone far together, taken the world by storm. With Hawke's genius and his connections, there was little they couldn't eventually accomplished, even unlocking the secrets of the chameleon. He had been right, Hawke and Angus were mated. It was obvious in the way they fought as a team. Such a waste. Pity they chose to fight against him and his comrades instead of joining the winning team as many other full-bloods had.

"We are on the way, and it happened the way you suspected it would. Gordon attempted to leave with Damian and was stopped. What are your instructions?" a hybrid said through the intercom.

Lancaster touched his jaw with his fingertips reminding himself of the last confrontation with Gordon and continued watching the monitor. He laughed. Someone found Griffith's toy. The beast refused to die no matter how many times they tried to kill it after Griffith's death. No one knew what the former Lord had done to this animal since he worked on it alone. The man had created a monster they couldn't control. Boris leaned forward and watched the beast rip a chunk out the neck of the bluebird. *Impressive.* "Seems like the animal found a master," he murmured. Griffith had introduced the thin, metallic fiber that coated the bluebirds after testing it on his pets. They had never been able to recreate it to the degree of this beast's coat or re-engineer the retractable metal teeth. Griffith had been a pisser for sure, Boris didn't mourn his death, but in other ways the man had been brilliant.

"Show Lord Gordon to the conference room. I am sending Damian to meet our guests," Lancaster said, watching the beast race forward to the next bluebird.

"Yes, Sir."

Boris watched the screen a few moments longer. He had hoped to play with Hawke but the information he received meant he would need to wait a little longer. Thanks to that blasted busy-body Radoff, his timetable escalated and he had a ceremony to stop. Neither he nor Roderick were interested in losing the ability to heal and live longer like the wolves. That meant he and Gordon needed to leave right away. He sent the files he'd been working on to the clouds, turned off the monitor and headed toward the conference room. Gordon had better be grateful for Radoff' interference otherwise he'd be receiving a nasty surprise for his actions the other day. That too would wait. A hybrid followed behind him and stood outside the door when he entered.

Gordon turned to face him and pointed. "What the hell do you think you're doing having me returned to a room like I'm some babe? You are not in charge of me."

"True, I'm in charge of Damian and this assignment to destroy Hawke and his mate. You interfered with that."

Gordon stepped closer and leaned forward. "How. By walking in the tunnels to talk privately? By leaving the immediate area?"

Boris waved his arm. "You were trying to leave with Damian so he didn't have to fight Hawke. You don't give him enough credit, he might win." He smiled so that Gordon knew he didn't mean a word of what he'd just said.

"I don't want them to fight, he's not ready and you know it."

"Pity it's not your call. Roderick approved this. Damian is on his way to meet his sire now." Lancaster grinned at Gordon's red face and clenched jaw.

"If he's destroyed I will kill you." Gordon pointed at him and Boris knew the man well enough to know he meant it.

"That will have to wait because we need to leave now." He told Gordon about the contract and the move on Hawke and Alpha Radoff's part to break it. "We need to hurry, Damian will only be able to hold Hawke for so long, one of the others will slip in. We cannot be here." He moved to the door and looked over his shoulder. "Gordon, come on, we need to leave."

"I'll meet you below, I need a few seconds to say goodbye."

Lancaster rubbed his finger against the pouch where he kept his thin blades and looked at Gordon. "Say it on the way, he'll hear you. I'm not about to trust you to put the Liege first when it comes to that wolf." He waved toward the door. "Come on lets go."

Gordon crossed his arms and shook his head. "I have to say good-bye." He looked at Boris. "He and I have a bond, I refuse to just disappear from his life."

"I told Roderick not to allow you to come, this is a complication we don't need. Talk to him later when he returns to the hotel. I've instructed him to meet us there after he completes his assignment."

"Go ahead and leave, I'll meet you at the hotel with Damian."

Boris looked at the stubborn man and calculated his odds. Chances were Hawke could not kill his seed, but Angus could. Would he? Who knew? If Boris killed Gordon right now, Hawke would definitely come after him. From what his source told him they needed either him or Gordon and the only way to avoid being sacrificed was to be unavailable. He planned to do that and if Gordon stayed behind to save Hawke's pup, his blood would break the covenant. Boris couldn't allow that either. Most importantly, he was down to one blade until he returned stateside and couldn't risk using it on Gordon, not with Hawke after him.

"How are you going to get to the hotel?" He asked while searching the man's expression. Had Gordon out maneuvered him? Was there another player involved Boris hadn't accounted for?

"I'll meet you there. Go, save yourself first, that is what you do best," Gordon spat.

"This is not personal. If your blood is shed, the contract is broken and impacts all of us. Do you understand that?" Boris tried explaining again so that Gordon realized the danger.

"I'm not stupid. I'll be at the hotel in a little bit. Give us five more minutes."

Boris' eyes narrowed. In five minutes Hawke would be inside the building, it would take them a little while to find these hidden rooms, especially while fighting the hybrids. But he refused to take a chance of being caught in the cross-fire for anyone. "You're a pathetic ass, Gordon. Fortunately for you Roderick doesn't want me to kill you," he lied and removed his hand from the blades. He had complained about Gordon and Roderick blew him off with questions about Angus. "If you're not at the hotel, I'm leaving and you're on your own."

"Wouldn't expect anything else from you." The scorn infused words sent heat to Boris' face. He swung and connected with the other man's cheek knocking him back a bit. Gordon shook his head and charged, tackling Boris onto the floor and got in a series of punches before the hybrid pulled him off.

Boris' head and upper body throbbed and he couldn't see clearly at first. His chest hurt when he tried to breathe. After a few moments he looked across the room where the hybrid blocked Gordon from attacking him again. Boris pushed up from the floor, wiped the blood from his lip with the back of his hand, and spat in Gordon's direction. The man was dead to him. Turning, he left the room and headed toward the secure area to leave the building.

"Come with me," Boris said to another hybrid stationed near the secure area. Together they entered the chute to take them to the lower tunnel. When he reached the ground floor he headed into the control room, entered a series of codes, the chute would return to the lower level once more and then lock. He overrode all the other codes, making it impossible to enter or leave the underground area.

Once he was situated in the seat of the underwater pod he keyed in the co-ordinates for his pick-up and left the building. He placed a call on a secure line.

A few moments later, Roderick answered. "He refused to leave, and promised to meet me later."

"Damn that stubborn fool. Does he understand how important it is for him to leave that place? It's not just about him."

"Damian, he refused to leave the pup."

"I'm not surprised, we should've listened to you and not allowed anyone to bond with those beasts. Look where it got us. Did Angus show up?"

"He was with Hawke." Boris told him about the attack and the TerraByte.

"Any idea who the thing bonded with? It's important to know if there's a new player."

"Not yet. I spent a lot of time arguing with Gordon about leaving. Once I get situated, I'll look at the tape again. I'm leaving now."

"Yes, I heard you."

"No. I am on my way to the new meeting point, plan B is in effect. If they don't catch Gordon or if he dies, they will come after me. We cannot chance that."

"Hmmm, you make a good point. Did you tell Gordon?"

"Yes," he lied.

"Let me know how things progress."

Boris hung up and placed his hands beneath his head. In less than thirty minutes he would be in the air away from this area when the explosives in the underground tunnel detonated. It would take Hawke and the others much longer to get through all the rooms and bypass the traps he left specifically for Hawke in their private game of chess. He glanced at his watch and smiled at the small surprise for Gordon and his pet dog as well.

"Checkmate bitches."

Chapter 25

Asia wondered if Lancaster would allow them to simply ring the doorbell and invite them inside. She shifted into her hybrid and jumped aside as a group of hybrids rushed out the entrance. With a hard swing of her sword she took the head of the hybrid nearest her and swung to meet the next one. This one dropped low, she missed which caused her to spin and stumble. He tackled her to the ground. She managed to roll him over and tried the skewer him with her blade. He held her arms and a battle of strength ensued. Slowly, her metal right arm won and she pierced his eye socket, killing his chip. He screamed and bucked her off, sending her into the path of the fist from another hybrid. The punch to her jaw sent her flying. She landed with a thump, and shook it off. Another hybrid charged toward her as she stood. They always charged. Waiting for the last possible moment she stepped aside and hit him beneath his chin with her right fist, sending him flying backward.

Another hybrid took his place. Her sword lay across the field beneath a hybrid. It swung, the air of the missed hit brushed against her cheek. The hybrid's continued momentum left his side open. Asia plowed her right fist into his stomach stealing his breath and then clipped him beneath the chin sending him backward.

She ran toward her sword, grabbed it just in time to avoid being mowed down by a charging hybrid. He fell over another downed hybrid and Byte attacked him. The hybrid tried to dislodge the beast, but Byte's long claws and fangs sank deep. Seconds later Angus appeared and separated the head.

Asia looked around for Hawke and saw him battling the guy from the side of the road. She glanced over her shoulder, between Angus, Ulric and his remaining pack members the hybrids were losing this fight. There was something different about the one fighting Hawke.

"*He's good,*" she said through their link.

"*Maybe. Are you done playing with the hybrids?*"

"*Things seem to be under control. Are you playing with the pretty boy?*" Holding her sword loosely she watched the two battle. Since she had seen her mate fight many times, she recognized he wasn't trying to destroy his opponent which surprised her. They didn't have time for this, Gordon and Lancaster could be leaving while Hawke wasted time.

"*No. I'm hesitant to destroy him for some reason.*" He blocked a move and knocked the guy back a few feet into the building creating a loud booming sound. His opponent jumped up and came at Hawke again. Hawke sidestepped him, but the guy changed directions and hit Hawke in the stomach, causing him to stumble two steps.

"*Metal arms, legs. Probably got a chip and camera to record this.*" Hawke said as if dissecting an experiment.

"I'm going inside to find Lancaster or Gordon while you continue dancing with your toy." She sheathed her sword, pushed the hybrid filling the door on his ass and ran down the corridor. Opening her senses she tried to locate either man or both, but something dampened her senses. Damn it. She came to a point where the corridors split four ways and seem to go on forever. Inhaling, she searched for a human scent and found nothing. She started down the corridor to her right.

"Asia?!"

"I'm here." She stopped, looked over her shoulder and caught the tail of something flying down a different hall. Backtracking she ran toward the blur and saw Hawke in pursuit. Ulric and his pack ran down each hall, opening doors and taking anything of value. She had wondered what purpose the large trucks they'd arrived in served, now she knew.

"What's going on?" she asked Hawke.

"The guy took off after I stomped his chest, came inside. I'm following him. Hopefully he's headed toward one of the two men we need."

"Good thinking." She kept pace behind him and continued to scan the area, hoping to gather a clue where Lancaster hid. The doors in front of them opened. Hawke ran in first. She ducked as he flew back over her head and slammed into the wall.

A hybrid leapt forward with some type of long spear aimed at Hawke. Asia jumped forward, kicked it sideways intercepting the beast and sending it crashing into the opposite wall. She moved just as the black hair guy Hawke had played with outside attacked her.

After blocking his moves, she knocked him backward into the wall and leapt on top of him. Arm upraised, she punched him in the throat, listening for the snap of his bones. He pushed, but couldn't dislodge her. She punched him in the face and head repeatedly without allowing him to return a punch. As far as she was concerned, he was the same as any other hybrid. When his hands dropped to the side, his face a bloody mess and she saw bone, she grabbed her sword to take his head.

"*Wait*," Hawke said, drawing her attention.

She looked over her shoulder at him. "*We don't have time to wait, Lancaster and Gordon could be leaving and he's a delay tactic.*" She raised her sword and looked into the eyes of the hybrid beneath her. The skin on his face re-knitted, healing.

"*Don't... don't do that.*" Hawke said, walking to her.

Asia looked at the hybrid and then at Hawke. "*What's going on?*"

"*Just a strong feeling you shouldn't take his head. Talk to him, ask him his name or something?*"

"*What the fuck? I don't have time for this. You want to know his name, ask him yourself.*" She re-sheathed her sword, stepped over the hybrid and headed for the door. The hybrid grabbed her leg, tripping her and then twisted to break it. "*See, this is why you don't play with them or try to be nice. They're programmed to complete a damn job.*" She lifted her leg, along with his arm and rolled onto her back. Before he could move, Hawke grabbed him by the shirt and shook him several times before backhanding him leaving a mark on the hybrid's face.

"Never, ever touch my mate. I will destroy you if you do. What is your name?"

"Fuck you."

"No you won't." Hawke shook him again. "What is your name?"

"Fuck you."

Hawke threw him against the wall, causing his head to bounce and him to stand slowly. Hawke grabbed him. The hybrid kicked him in the chest. Hawke threw him against the wall again.

Asia watched the brutal beat-down for a few minutes and exhaled. *"We need to find the Liege."*

"This one will take us to one of them. Didn't you pick up the human scent on him?" Hawke punched they hybrid in the face, the sound of bones cracking filled the room.

She hadn't smelled the scent until he mentioned it. Now that she focused on the hybrid she noticed the difference. *"How can he lead us if he is beaten to a pulp?"*

"The human smell is strong on him, he will either go to him or he will find this one. We will follow, watch or wait. This hybrid is different from the others, more valuable. Someone is watching and will come for him."

"Or push the kill chip." She reminded him.

"Possibly." He threw the guy on the ground and stomped on one of his legs. The knee popped and the metal twisted for a moment before correcting. *"See, they have invested much in him."* Hawke placed his booted foot on the other leg. "What is your name?"

The hybrid gritted his teeth while holding the opposite leg as it healed. Asia had gone through several regeneration processes and knew the enormous amount of pain the hybrid suffered.

"Fuck you."

"Maybe his language is limited to those two words. He looks ignorant, why are you wasting time with the Liege's trash. They never spend a lot of time or energy on their toys, twist his head off like the rest and let's find Gordon and Lancaster," Asia said in a mocking tone.

"He tensed when you called the names. Say each one again to determine which is his master."

Asia went back over her sentence in her mind. "I'm going to track down Lancaster and take his head."

"Gordon. He blinked at Lancaster but no real response."

"That's a surprise. Given your history I thought it was Lancaster."

Hawke stepped on the hybrid's hand and ground his boot onto it. "Remember this while I snap Gordon's head from his body. I asked you nicely, but you want to fuck around."

The hybrid jerked and tried to get free, but couldn't dislodge Hawke, not with his legs healing and a smashed hand. But his efforts were those of a man possessed.

"Based on his actions, Gordon must still be here somewhere." Asia walked toward them and stood a few feet behind Hawke. "What's your name? Tell us your name and Gordon's death will be quick, he won't suffer."

"No. No. No." With a strong shove from his other hand, he moved Hawke's feet enough to free his hand, rolled to the side and stood. "You will not." He ran from the room. Hawke looked at Asia for a few seconds and then they followed his scent.

Hawke led the way out and stopped in the hall. He laughed. *"Seems he is running in circles to confuse us, not a bad strategy. Wait here for a few moments, and when he rescues Gordon we'll go after them. I'll check with Angus to see how things are going."*

"Just as you know his scent, he knows yours. He may not go to Gordon until he thinks it's safe."

"True, but we are not the only ones searching, he will know the place is flooded with pack and will need to

move his master." He paused. *"Angus took an elevator below and is searching. Someone left already by water, since Gordon is still here, my guess is Lancaster is on his way to the hotel or air strip. Ulric has men watching the hotel and the roads. No one thought to watch the river."*

"That's because it's long and winding through the damn country, without Lancaster's scent to track it would be impossible to locate him along the banks."

"But he is in some type of pod, Angus says. There is another one and he is following to see where it lands to see if he can catch Lancaster."

"Waste of time. Lancaster is gone. We need to concentrate on getting Gordon to Radoff to break the contract which will weaken Lancaster and the other Lords. They won't be able to heal and they will age and die."

"I agree. Angus does not have the code to make the elevator return to this level and will join us as soon as he can."

"Tell him to send Byte to search, I bet he can find anything," Asia said watching the corridor for hybrids.

"Told him. Let's go." Hawke took off down one of the corridors and ran through what seemed like a maze of hallways before stopping in front of a pair of steel sliding doors. *"They are in here."*

Asia stepped to the side and stared at the control panel. *"This is similar to the ones in Lancaster castle. At least they're consistent."* She typed in a few codes from her time in the castle, but wasn't surprised that none of them worked.

Hawke stared at the keypad. *"Lancaster would've keyed the pad for Lords only which means it would start with these two letters."* He tapped those keys. *"Hmm, let's try this one. He used it in the castle.*" Nothing happened. Hawke tried a series of combinations with no success.

"LOBO."

"Hmm?"

"Try LOBO," Asia said, thinking Lancaster would be ballsy enough to code his signature project.

Hawke typed it twice. The second time the doors slid open. *"Ego, gets him every time,"* Asia said while removing her sword and walking forward. Inhaling she picked up Gordon and the hybrid's scent.

The door closed behind them as they moved forward. *"I think we miscalculated,"* Hawke said through their link as they fell through the floor and hit the bottom of a metal container.

Asia's sword fell with a loud clank as she tried to get her bearings. "Miscalculated?" She ground out and kicked the side of the cage. "Is that what you call this… this bullshit?" She hit the side again.

"Yes."

There was barely enough room to move in her hybrid form, she morphed into her human form and slumped against the wall. Images of Gordon disappearing, the disappointment from Jasmine in her failing to break the covenant, the Liege continuing LOBO and stealing more pups, ran through her mind on a loop. Somehow they had to break that contract and stop the Liege.

"If you can stand in that corner, I'll get us out of here."

"Huh?" She looked up at Hawke. "What'd you say?"

"I need to morph and push out these walls. Can you kneel in that corner for a few minutes?"

She moved and knelt down while he morphed into his largest hybrid. The only other time she had seen him in this form had been during a fight against the bluebirds. The sound of bending metal hit a nerve and she covered her ears until she heard it pop. A large piece fell from the top, Hawke caught it and shoved it over the side. It took a few minutes before it hit the bottom. Wide-eyed, she looked at Hawke.

"Where are we? In an elevator chute or something?"

"I don't think so. Let me check this wall, cover your ears."

She replaced her palms over her ears.

He punched the side wall. It dented but nothing else. He punched each wall until his fist went through the metal. Using his long claws, he peeled the metal back until she saw a sliding door in front of it. She stood slowly as he reached forward and opened the doors revealing a dark hallway. Hawke shrank to his hybrid, glanced over his shoulder at her and winked as he leapt forward.

She shook her head at the cocky gesture and took his hand, allowing him to pull her into the hall.

"You shouldn't doubt your mate." He took her hand as they moved through the corridors seeking Gordon.

"I will remember that next time."

Chapter 26

Hawke and Asia walked through every corridor, searching for Damian and Gordon. Find one, the other would be nearby, especially with the hybrids defeated and Ulric's pack taking everything of value from the building.

Voices. Full-bloods always used their links in situations like this, being human Gordon would need to speak. Even if he whispered, the full-bloods would hear and close in on them.

Turning, Hawke and Asia walked down the corridor to his left, and stopped. Not this way. He waved in the other direction, and followed her. The voices grew stronger.

"Not on this floor. Either below or above us," Asia said, looking up and then down.

Hawke pointed up. Asia nodded and they headed toward the emergency stairs and ran up two flights before easing the door open.

"Damn asshole. He locked the code on the lift. I knew he'd try something. Son of a bitch. We need to get down to the tunnel."

Hawke glanced at Asia. *"How much you want to bet Gordon's talking about Lancaster?"*

"Nothing. Lancaster would sell the Pope and screw the devil to stay safe. Which way?"

Hawke waved her forward. They walked down a few halls and saw the black haired hybrid standing outside an elevator. No doubt Gordon was inside.

"Why can't I kill him?" Asia asked as she bulked to her hybrid.

"Don't know. Killing him just seems wrong to me. But if he tries to kill you, rip him apart."

"Gee, thanks."

They walked forward. The hybrid charged. Asia stepped in front of Hawke and took the hybrid down. He bucked up, dislodging her. She jumped up and charged him before he reached Hawke, who headed for the elevator.

He twisted and tried to break her grip, but she had a tight hold on him and pounded his head and face with her right fist. He pushed her off with his legs, sending her backward a bit and tried to go after Hawke. She leapt forward, grabbed his ankles and pulled. He hit the ground hard. Asia dragged him back toward her as the elevator door opened. He kicked out, stood and tried to run.

She grabbed his shoulder, spun him around, punched him in the stomach and then beneath his chin. He flew backward. Moving forward, she grabbed his shirt and slammed her fist into his face in rapid succession until she saw bone.

"Stop," Gordon yelled.

Asia dragged the hybrid forward and slammed him face down onto the floor. She lifted her sword and raised it above the hybrid. *"Negotiate with him now or I'm taking this head,"* she told Hawke.

"Stop, you can't kill him," Gordon yelled and tried to go to the hybrid.

"Why not?" Hawke asked, holding Gordon's arm. Something wasn't right. The man vibrated with sorrow and fear for the hybrid.

Gordon turned and shook his head. "He's your son, Hawke. Your first born. Haven't you looked at him? Why don't you look at him?"

Hawke stared at Gordon processing his words. "Son? I don't... no one told me... what?" He looked at the hybrid struggling to stand and then at Asia. *"He said that is my seed. They took a pup from me and raised it?"*

"Hawke..." Asia said, looking at the male on the ground.

"What do you mean he is my son? I have no son." He met Gordon's disturbed gaze.

"He's your seed. One of the first bitches you mated birthed him twenty years past. You cannot kill him." It was the demand in Gordon's voice that pissed Hawke off, he no longer took orders from any Liege.

"Perhaps not, but my mate can." Hawke placed his foot on Damian's shoulder while Asia placed her foot on his back. "What is his name?" Hawke continued staring at Gordon rather than the pup on the ground. A son... he couldn't process that right now.

"Damian."

"A life for a life," Hawke said, pressing harder when Damian tried to move.

"No... no," Damian said.

Gordon looked at Asia and then at Damian.

Hawke sensed Ulric's pack was nearby. "Never mind. The pack is here. Just pin him to the wall and they'll rip him apart." Hawke pushed Gordon to Asia, who caught the Liege Lord and shoved him roughly out of the way. Hawke bulked to his largest size, picked a struggling Damian up and met his gaze. Was he supposed to feel something for this pup? Hawke waited a few seconds, there was nothing. Damian's face resembled Niall more than him.

"Stop. Hawke put him down. A… A life for a life. Take him with us, keep him safe from the other full-bloods. I'll go with you," Gordon said, looking at Damian.

"Noooo," Damian screamed and tried to break free from Hawke.

Hawke tucked Damian beneath his arm and carried him out the room. Asia walked behind Gordon, who moved with a slow, dejected air. Hawke contacted Angus. *"I have Gordon we are on our way out, is Chacal here?"*

"Not yet, but he's on his way. Lancaster's a slimeball. The bastard set explosives beneath the walls down here. Byte just sniffed them out. Damn it to hell. I would love to wrap my hands around, the bastard."

"Time? How much time left?" Hawke wasn't surprised about the explosives, the Liege used them often. He picked up speed and took the stairs rather than trust the elevator.

"Don't know, yet. He just found it while searching for another exit. We'll board the pod as soon as I find out an answer. Ulric and his pack are leaving now. We'll meet at Radoff's. Son of a bitch."

"What?" Hawke took off at a slow jog down the corridors, getting lost at times and turning around.

"Fifteen minutes. Damn. Can you make it out?"

"If I can find the main hall, yeah."

"I just updated Chacal, he'll wait as long as he can. Follow the scent of the bluebirds, they are outside. Maybe that will help."

"Good idea." Hawke told Asia what was going on and inhaled. It took a few seconds, but he finally identified the bluebirds and did a three sixty turn. They had been headed in the wrong direction. With the scent locked in, he tightened his hold on a squirming Damian and moved at a faster pace. Asia picked up Gordon as they ran toward the exit.

Moments later they hit the front entrance and heard the copter. Hawke morphed to his smaller hybrid, knowing he couldn't enter the copter in any other form than human, but he needed the extra strength to hold onto Damian.

He veered right, ran past Ulric and headed toward Chacal. The whirring of the copter blades must have motivated Damian because he used both his legs and pushed free, falling on the ground. Hawke turned, reached for him just as he leapt and knocked Asia down. Damian morphed as he grabbed Gordon and took off running in the opposite direction.

"I don't have time for this shit," Hawke murmured as he took off behind the two morphing to his larger form. In a blur of speed he caught them and pushed Damian from behind, sending him rolling on the ground dropping Gordon in the process. Hawke growled at the hybrid, picked up Gordon and ran back towards the copter. Once he reached the copter, he returned to his human size and all but tossed the older man inside. Asia caught Gordon and placed him behind her as Chacal lifted off.

"Here he comes," Asia murmured.

Hawke watched Damian run toward them and jump. The first leap fell short. The next leap Damian grabbed hold of one of the skids on the bottom. His weight jolted them for a few moments but Chacal leveled out and they continued toward Radoff.

"*You okay?*" Asia asked.

"*Not sure. I reproduced and no one ever told me. Is he the only one? Over the years, I... there were a lot of bitches.*" He met her gaze. "*He told me nothing came of it, that I wasn't good for that.*"

"*When I worked at the castle one of the workers said something about your breeding, but with everything going on, it slipped my mind. I think there is one more, but I'm not sure.*" She paused. "*You didn't know you were breeding for them?*"

He scrubbed his face with his fist. "*Not directly. Sex, that's all it was, scratching an itch. I never thought beyond that. Damn.*" He looked behind her at Gordon and wanted to rip the man's heart out. "Damian has been with the Liege since birth? He knows nothing other than the bullshit you fed him?"

Gordon's face reddened and he straightened as much as he could in the confined space. "Yes, he was born in Lancaster's castle and taken for training once we decided he would fit. He has an exemplary education, and has been enhanced as you were. Damian is the best in his class, in a few years he will rise to the top."

Hawke's brow rose. "Top of what?"

"Our program leaders, you, Asia and Damian. The best we've produced so far." Gordon looked at Asia. "Roderick believes your mate uses a chameleon bracelet to hide his identity. Is that true?"

Hawke shook his head. "No."

"Not that you would tell me anyway, but he believes Angus hides behind the bracelet." Gordon watched him and Hawke smiled. *"They think you are Angus, I must tell him."*

Asia looked away. *"He will love that. Poor thing, he'll need to take one for the team."*

"You say Damian is enhanced. Arms, legs and computer chip, I picked up on those. What else?" Hawke glanced outside and saw the pup continued to hold on.

"Why should I tell you anything? You'll probably kill him after you get what you need from me anyway."

Hawke couldn't kill Damian but Radoff, Ulric, hell, even Asia could, so the man wasn't too far off. "I'm curious. You say he's my seed, but I feel nothing for him, shouldn't there be some recognition?"

Gordon stared at him for a few seconds and then sighed. "I hoped so, but it's the same with him. He denies the connection which creates a problem."

Hawke frowned. "Problem?"

"Yes, if I die, he will attempt to destroy you and yours. Which will set the stage for his destruction; I understand how mates work but he does not. Although he cannot win against you now, Damian is talented and damn good. He will not make a good enemy."

"Are there any good enemies?" Hawke asked.

Gordon shrugged and looked away. "It does not need to be that way."

Hawke gazed at the man's side profile. For years he'd been held beneath their thumb, doing whatever they demanded without question. In his mind they'd been gods. This was no god sitting next to him, just a man. They were all men with huge egos and a contract that allowed them privileges they had abused.

"*Hawke, calm, please. We are in a small container in the air. There will be time for you to express your anger later, after the covenant is broken.*" Her hand covered his and he noticed his long curved fingernails and felt the sting of his extended incisors.

Nodding, he turned from Gordon and looked at Asia, his port in the emotional storm. "*Thank you.*"

She nodded and looked out the small window. The ground grew closer. He exhaled. They were almost there.

"*Sir?*" he contacted Silas.

"*Hawke.*"

"*We are landing with Gordon. There has been a small complication.*" He told Silas about Damian and the relationship with Gordon.

"*Damn. It's always something. Why couldn't this be cut and dry? What do you think? Will Damian go rogue or will the Liege use him the same way they used Asia?*"

"*He is good. And in a few years will be better. Asia and I wrote the training plans they use for the hybrids, so his fighting skills weren't that difficult for us to win against. That won't be the case with other full-bloods. With metal in his limbs, he will be a real threat.*"

"*How do you feel about destroying him?*"

Hawke glanced at Asia. "*He attacked my mate, if I could kill him, he would be dead.*"

"*Understood. Should I have him terminated? Is there any way to rehabilitate him?*"

"*I don't know. Have Angus bring him to you. Asia told me how you handled her when she was infected with the computerized chip, deal with him the same and see what you can learn. If there are more like him, that will be a problem. Like I said, he is good and Asia and I cannot be everywhere to destroy them.*"

"Thanks, I'll discuss it with my mate and we will inform Angus what we decide. Let me know when the covenant is broken."

"Yes, Sir." Hawke gazed out the window as Chacal sat the copter down. Radoff's pack surrounded Damian, who stared into the copter, waiting.

Chapter 27

Hawke watched Damian for a few seconds. *"Angus?"*

"I'm on my way, the explosion pushed me ahead and I thought I saw Lancaster, but can't be sure. When we got out the water, I sent Byte to search for signs, but he came up empty. Just grabbed a ride and heading your way now. Chacal says you have your hands full with your seed."

"Yeah. Gordon's inside, Maheegan should get what she needs first and then I'll lock him and Gordon together in the cage while we have the ceremony."

"Sounds like a plan. On my way, Ulric's not far behind me."

Hawke glanced at Asia. *"I'll contain him and then you take Gordon inside to Maheegan."* He didn't wait for her to agree or disagree, his turbulent emotions needed an outlet and Damian would be the recipient. Like Niall, Damian represented another person or relationship the Liege stole from him. Emotionally he wasn't sure what he felt for what Asia called his family, but he refused to allow Damian to stand between him and a successful mission for Asia. Chacal turned off the copter, Hawke stepped out.

"Back the fuck up," Hawke growled to Damian, who had morphed to his hybrid form.

"Fuck you," Damian said, rubbing Hawke the wrong way. He stepped away from the blades, morphed and tackled Damian to the ground.

"Get back." He heard Radoff say in the background as he and Damian fought. Gordon had been right, the pup was good, but not good enough. Hawke punched him in the face and the placed his hand over Damian's face, allowing his curved nails to penetrate his flesh. Next he pushed Damian's head into the ground.

"Go ahead Asia. Lock Gordon in a cage. Have Maheegan take whatever blood she needs and watch over him until Angus gets here to help you. I've got to deal with this."

"Hawke... be careful." Asia picked Gordon up and carried him across the area while Damian tried to buck Hawke off him. Instead of moving Hawke applied more pressure, burying the bottom of his head into the ground. He leaned close to Damian's ear. "You attacked my mate, that's a death penalty."

"Mate?"

Hawke froze, closed his eyes and ignored the tingling in his mind where Damian spoke to him through a link. If he answered they would be irrevocably linked and he might have the pup killed in the end. It was up to Silas.

"My mate, the one holding Gordon."

"Gordon?"

"He is a Liege Lord, who has done terrible things to my people. Your people."

"*No. No.*" Damian pushed, but couldn't move Hawke.

Hawke glanced at Radoff who stood a short distance and nodded. "I've got this. I'll explain later."

Radoff nodded and walked off. Chacal stood a distance, watching and then headed toward the basement. "If you don't want anything bad to happen to Gordon right now, remain still."

Damian stopped moving. Hawke exhaled and looked toward the building. "*Has Maheegan taken his blood?*" He asked Asia.

"*Not yet, there's a special way it has to be done or something.* She's working on it." She paused. "*How are you holding up? Make any progress with him?*"

"*He spoke to me through a link.*"

"*Shit. Did you answer?*"

"*No. Silas may decide to terminate him rather than meet him on the battlefield later. I don't want that connection.*"

"*I'm sorry you have to make a choice like that.*"

He glanced at the hybrid created from his genes and shook his head. "*What would you do?*"

"*What?*"

"*If they'd done this to you, and you met... you're... him? What would you do? Let him go? Have him killed? What?*"

"*That could have happened and I may not know. With all the surgeries I've had and all the time I've been out of it... who knows what they've done. But you cannot kill him, the Goddess made sure of that. The rest, I don't know. Whatever you decide, I'm behind you, okay. Just remember that.*"

"Thank you." He released his breath and pushed up, bringing Damian with him. After they stood, placed his other hand around Damian's neck and released his face. The skin healed over his nail marks and Hawke looked down into the pup's face.

"Do you want Gordon to die?"

Damian's face tightened, his jaw clenched. He spoke through tight lips. "No."

Curious, Hawke moved closer. "Why? Is he your sire?"

"No."

"Why do you care if he dies or lives?"

Damian's lips tightened.

Hawke shook him. *"Answer me or you know what'll happen."*

"He is my master."

"You're wolf. He's human."

Damian frowned. *"Wolf?"*

Hawke frowned and looked into eyes that mirrored his own. "Have you never shifted?"

"Impossible." He shook his head and Hawke wondered if he were aware he spoke to Hawke through a link.

Hawke looked across the compound and called one of Radoff's men over. "He does not believe we shift."

The male looked surprised and the next moment he stood on his paws looking up at them. The next second he stood on two feet and then he returned to wolf form, looked at Hawke and then ran off.

Hawke sensed Damian's surprise and wondered what type of training the Liege employed. The instructions for behavioral modification he had written took the temperament of the dual natured man into account. Based on Damian's response the Liege did not teach the two sides must walk in harmony to be whole.

"That is impossible," Damian said. "I cannot do that." He looked at Hawke with a question in his eyes. "Master says you are my sire, do you also become wolf?"

"Yes. It is my nature and the nature of everyone else here except Gordon."

Damian's eyes widened and then narrowed. "Will they hurt my master?"

"It depends on how you behave out here."

"How will they know?"

"I speak to them like this," Hawke said through their link.

Damian jumped and struggled to break free from Hawke's grip. Hawke squeezed his neck tighter, closing off oxygen until his movements slowed.

"Get out of my mind," Damian said in a hard voice that might have been the equivalent of a scream if he could speak.

"Believe me, I hate to be here, but since I am…" Hawke invaded his thoughts and marveled at the ability to do so. *"Your computer is different, not as hostile. It only controls your limbs not your actions, no tracking. Did they never expect you to meet your kind?"*

"Get out," Damian said, trying to move Hawke back but failing.

The computer chip lacked the kill mechanism, and camera. What had the pup used the other day? The fight on the side of the road had been recorded for Lancaster and the Liege, Hawke would bet money on that. The pup wore sunglasses, the camera must have been loaded near the lens.

"Calm down, has anyone ever linked with you before?"

Damian stopped moving and met Hawke's gaze. "Linked? What is that?"

"*Mind speak, wolves speak mind to mind and no one else can hear you or knows what we are saying. Humans cannot.*"

Damian blinked a few times. "But I am not a wolf."

"Technically you are a full-blood, which is a dual-natured person." He paused. "Like me." Hawke admitted the connection and continued searching through Damian's memories. Gordon played a predominant role in Damian's upbringing, their relationship more personal than master and slave. Gordon treated Damian as a son and had taken on the Liege for Damian.

"Lies, all lies." Damian pushed against Hawke and punched him on the shoulder.

Hawke tightened his grip around his neck and continued looking through the memory bank of Damian's life. The pup excelled early and lived in a decent environment, nothing like the cell Hawke had endured. It took a moment before he realized Damian had entered his mind. Hawke shut down the area leading to Asia, but allowed Damian to see the brutality he suffered at the hands of the Liege.

Damian's eyes widened and then narrowed as if he suspected some sort of trick.

Hawke chuckled and didn't pull back.

"Black wolf."

Hawke's brow rose at the two words.

"They are the top of the line." He frowned. "That is what we were taught."

"How many were in your class?"

"Three started. I alone finished."

"Are there more classes behind yours?"

"Yes. Why are you in chains?" He looked at Hawke with a perplexed look. "Why is Master Lancaster standing over you while you are chained?"

"That was my training with the Liege, different from what I saw you went through." Hawke heard a vehicle approach and turned aside to see Angus pull to a stop.

"Angus is here, are we about ready to start?" he asked Asia.

"Yes, she just took his blood and secured it in an ice pouch. How does it feel being linked to your son?"

Hawke should have known she would sense the connection. *"Gordon treated him more of a son than I have. He has had a decent life so far. Is Gordon caged?"*

"Yes. You can bring Damian inside. I'm not sure the cage will hold him if he morphs, it wouldn't hold me."

"Okay."

Angus and Byte approached. "So this is your seed? I see the resemblance. It's time, let's do this."

Hawke loosened his grip slightly and they walked toward the building housing the basement. "Byte and I will take him in. You go ahead and prepare," Angus said, moving into position to contain the young pup.

Hawke looked down at Byte and then at Damian. "If you try and run or move too fast the TerraByte will catch you, he took down a bluebird, I doubt he'll have a hard time with you." He removed his hand and walked inside.

"Don't move," Angus said to Damian when he turned to follow. Byte growled.

Hawke looked over his shoulder at Damian, who stared at him. *"Don't kill him, please."*

"It's not my decision," Hawke said as he walked inside and met Asia at the bottom of the stairs, took her hand and walked over to Maheegan. The woman offered him a

small smile, removed the needle and while murmuring what sounded like a chant took a few vials of his blood. When done, she stored the vials in what appeared to be a cooler, removed another and locked the chest. Radoff removed the box and took it somewhere. Seemed like a lot of extra work, but as long as the contract was broken, Asia didn't care. She wondered what they would do next.

Radoff stood on the dais and Maheegan stood next to him holding the two vials.

"We will begin," Radoff said as he looked down at a page of paper on the podium. Hawke watched as Radoff's beta brought a bowl of water for him to cleanse his hands and then dried them.

"What's that?" Hawke asked Asia.

"Hmm? What?"

"I thought I heard something." He listened hard. *"Never mind."*

"Angus isn't coming?" Asia asked.

"La Patron has him doing something right now, he'll be down when he is done."

A few minutes into the ceremony Hawke's eyes watered and his vision dimmed as Radoff continued reading the paper. He cleared his throat and wiped his nose. *"You okay?"* he asked Asia who leaned into him.

"No. Tired." He caught her as she fell forward.

"Asia?" He called through their link even though his mind seemed fuzzy and his vision blurred. He went to his knees, holding her and looked over his shoulder. Everyone lay on the ground as if sleeping. Struggling to remain awake, he glanced at the dais, Maheegan and Radoff had fallen to the ground, the blood spilled and ran across the wood hitting the floor.

In his mind he called out to Angus but wasn't sure if his call was heard before he fell forward and hit the floor. In the distance he heard footsteps and tried to open his eyes but couldn't. He recognized the voice.

"I told you he could do it, see the blood hasn't been used," Granari said in a low tone. "Everyone overlooks him because of his size, but he slew Goliath as promised. That one is not Angus, I told you that." She paused. "We kept our end of the deal."

"Yes, you have. Chemical engineer, indeed, potent stuff, no sound or smell. Verrick, give her the case and then bring Gordon and these two. I'm curious to discover just who is his mate," Boris Lancaster said.

"*Angus, its Lancaster and Granari.*" Hawke delivered the message and passed out.

Chapter 28

"So you're Hawke's pup?" Angus asked as he walked around Damian, whose gaze flicked between him and Byte.

Angus wasn't surprised Damian didn't respond, he doubted he would have either. Byte was the only reason the pup didn't take off behind Hawke to rescue Gordon. Damian vibrated with indecision.

"Have you arrived?" Silas asked.

"Yes, I'm outside with Hawke's pup while he prepares for the ceremony. Shouldn't be that much longer."

"The pup? Let me take a look at him."

Angus moved to stand in front of Damian and sensed when Silas entered. *"Something's wrong with his beast."*

"What do you mean?" Angus moved closer to the pup, looking for signs of his wolf.

Damian straightened and braced his legs.

Byte grumbled his displeasure at the movement and stood as if daring the pup to move again.

"Not sure, but it's weak, not like the Detective's but he was much older. Wonder if he's ever shifted?"

"Want me to ask?"

"No. Hold steady, I'm going to pull his wolf."

One second Damian stood in front of Angus the next a lone black wolf lay wild-eyed panting on the ground.

"Based on his response, I'd say this is his first shift."

Like a skittish colt, Damian tried to stand without success on his first two attempts. And then he stood, wobbling for a few seconds.

"Take him for a walk or run in the woods," Silas said.

Angus shifted, looked at Damian and walked in the opposite direction from the building. Damian followed, slowly at first and then at a trot. Pleased with the pup's progress, he picked up speed. Soon they were running in the woods at the base of the mountain which belonged to Alpha Radoff.

Byte took up the rear behind Damian but stopped every once in a while to explore. They came to a stream. Angus stepped into the cool water and lapped a drink. He watched Damian take small steps looking at his image before he drank. When he finished Damian took off running in the wrong direction which would take him off pack lands.

Angus chased and slammed into him before he got too far. Damian rolled on the ground and tried to rise. Angus stood over him snarling and baring his teeth. The pup didn't move. When Angus felt he had made his point, he turned and ran back into the wooded area.

Once again Damian followed, they ran through the entire forest until Angus sensed Damian had connected with his wolf. Angus stalked a deer and along with Byte brought it down. Damian was hesitant at first, but after minutes of watching Byte rip into the meat and Angus eating his fill, he took a few nibbles. Pretty soon they were all sated and sat beneath a shade tree.

"*Angus, its Lancaster and Granari,*" Hawke said in a weird voice interrupting the impromptu training session.

"*What?*" Nothing. Hawke didn't respond.

"*Silas I got a weird message from Hawke –*"

"*I cannot reach him or Maheegan. Jasmine cannot contact Asia and is concerned. Go check things out,*" Silas said.

"*On it.*" Angus jumped up and ran toward Radoff's, Damian and Byte were fast behind him. They made good time in wolf form. He slowed as they broke through the trees. Granari, Niall, and a few other scents he wasn't familiar with had been there.

Angus morphed into his human form and strode to the building where the ceremony took place. Someone locked the outer door. He morphed to his hybrid and kicked until it crashed open. Angus ran inside, pushed the locked door leading down to the basement aside and peeked in. From his vantage point everyone lay on the ground as if they were at a large sleep-over. Steady heartbeats and even breathing filled the room. Inhaling, he picked up Asia, Hawke, Granari and Niall's scents. Verrick, that bastard, he'd been there as well.

He took the stairs two at a time searching for Hawke and Asia. Chacal lay on the floor in the corner, Maheegan and Radoff were on the dais, blood stained the floor, but Hawke and Asia were missing.

"*Don't see them. Everyone's asleep, I don't smell or taste anything in the air. Whatever they used, it's new.*" He started down the corridor searching for Niall or Granira's bodies but came up empty. That sucked. "*Niall and Granari were here. Gordon's gone.*" The woman had been too accommodating, he should have guessed she was up to something. But why? Why challenge him and Silas like this? Was it her or her Alpha? Why involve Niall? She had to know Hawke wouldn't allow anyone to mess with his mate. He looked down the long corridor and sent Byte ahead to check for surprises.

"Damian's with you?"

"Yeah." He looked over his shoulder at the pup who remained in wolf form. *"Might need to help him shift."*

"No, let him become accustomed to this form and track Gordon. Find them, Angus."

"Will do." He looked at Damian, who walked slightly behind him. "Someone took Hawke, his mate and Gordon. Do you know who? Are any of the scents familiar?"

Damian's body shook as he ran back toward the cell and then caught up with Angus who followed Byte. Damian ran ahead, stopped at the corner of another tunnel and watched Angus.

"They went that way? Okay." Angus ran to catch up as both Byte and Damian took off. After many twists and turns Damian stood in front of what appeared to be a solid wall making noises.

Byte growled and watched the wall as if expecting someone or something to walk through at any moment. Angus slid his palms and fingers along the seams of the walls searching for a control mechanism. A click, a whirring sound and then the panel slid aside revealing a stairwell. Byte took off, followed by Damian and then Angus. They emerged on the outskirts of a small town and remained in the tree line to get an idea where they were.

Angus snapped his fingers. *"Byte stay by my side."* The animal turned, walked to him and sat on his haunches watching Angus. "A blue dog and a wolf," he murmured wondering how to get where they needed to be without being shot or attacked.

He pulled them back into the woods and stooped low. "We need to find Gordon and Hawke but we cannot allow the people to see us." He looked at Damian and then Byte. "We cannot be seen by people, not these people anyway. Chances are whoever took Hawke had a car or truck waiting out here."

Angus looked around wondering if he could rent a car. If Damian were in human form they could run without raising an alarm. There wasn't much he could do about Byte, his new pet would always draw attention.

"Stay here. I am going to find transportation and then we'll find them." He waited until the pup lay down with his head on his front paws. Angus stood. "*Stay here, watch. Protect the wolf. I will be back,*" he told Byte and headed out the woods.

After securing a small vehicle he returned to pick up Byte and Damian. "*Silas I need Damian to give directions, I had to rent a car.*"

Damian lifted his head as Angus approached, the next moment he stood in human form with a look of wonder on his face. His mouth opened and closed. He looked at his body and then at Angus. "That… that was unbelievable. Comfortable. Different." He frowned. "My thoughts were linear, uncomplicated, simple."

Angus snapped his fingers toward Byte, turned and headed toward the small SUV. "Can you lock onto Gordon's scent?"

"What? Yes, although not as easy now. Before was a lot stronger. In fact, everything was amplified. Vision, hearing, taste, everything." He followed Angus and slid into the front seat talking the entire time.

"Yep, you're Hawke's boy."

"What?"

"Curious, like Hawke. The man's a genius, dissects everything. When we find them, have him teach you how to shift. You can do it anytime, it's not difficult."

"Then why didn't you teach me?"

"Had other things on my mind. Where's Gordon? Which way do I go?" They were at an intersection with cars behind them.

Damian pointed. "That way."

Angus made the turn.

"Back in the tunnel, the other scent, it was Master Lancaster. He left with Master Gordon."

Angus was surprised. "Thought he skipped town, must've grown a conscience."

"Why didn't you teach me to shift?"

"Didn't have time."

"The wolf affects my limbs, my computer went silent. Everything on the inside stopped when I became wolf."

"You are wolf and human. Both. Is your computer on now?"

Damian hesitated. "It's running an assessment on my legs. Turn right."

Angus glanced at Byte on the back seat. The animal lifted his head and met his stare. Angus chuckled. Three hundred years, no mate, but he got a mutt. Where was the justice in that? At least this one was loyal, followed directions and covered his back. When Byte attacked the bluebird and brought it down, Angus had been surprised at the ease and confidence of his pet. There had been nothing left for him to do except swing his blade and remove the head. Whoever created Byte had definitely been on to something, the beast would make the ultimate weapon.

The road led them out of town into the rural areas.

"I would like to return to the wolf."

Angus glanced at Damian and then the road. "I need you to give me directions. Can't do that in wolf form."

Damian cleared his throat. "Hawke, my sire, he talked to me... in my mind. He said it is how people like him communicate. Can that happen while I am wolf?"

Angus hid his surprise. Hawke linked with the pup, he hoped Asia's secrets were protected. "Yes, it can happen. Can you contact him now? Find out if he is alright? If he knows where they are?" Angus had been reaching out through their link and had no luck. But this would be good for the pup to build a connection with Hawke.

Damian frowned. "How do I contact him?"

"Think about him and start talking in your mind, he'll hear you.... If he can. Otherwise, it'll be quiet, a different kind of quiet though."

Angus continued down the road, but glanced at Damian from time to time. If this young pup was the final product the Liege produced, he was impressed. Damian drank knowledge with determination and excitement.

"Nothing," Damian said, looking disappointed.

Angus nodded. "Tell me about the place you grew up. How many were in your classes? What did you do during the day and at night?" He asked the young pup a barrage of questions to get a better understanding of the program and the cost to the wolf nation. One thing for certain, over the decades, hundreds of pups were taken, Angus prayed they hadn't all been destroyed in experiments or trying to escape.

Chapter 29

Granira watched as Lancaster's minions carried Hawke, his mate and Gordon down the long corridor with an equal measure of pleasure and trepidation. Verrick nodded at her with a smug smirk and followed. She wanted to kick him. He was no better than her, using the Liege to get what she wanted. Niall wanted that Alpha spot and now they had the means to challenge that interloper Muzik.

Holding the box Lancaster had given her close to her chest, she waved to Niall to hurry before Angus or La Patron discovered what happened. Angus made a horrible enemy, but it was a chance she and Niall decided to take for this lifetime opportunity.

Once they cleared the main corridor, they increased their speed toward the area leading to their pack lands. Excitement coursed through her veins as they crossed into their border and headed for her home.

"Did you see that?" Niall asked, his eyes wide. "All of them, knocked out on the ground. The mist worked. One day we will look back on the day the Farkas pack rose through the ranks, not by flexing our muscles but by using our minds."

She smiled but kept her thoughts to herself. Wolves would always rule with muscle, that was their nature and the reason she made a deal with that devil, Lancaster. "Let's see how this works." She moved into her inner room and locked the door behind him. "Sit here." While he moved to the chair she opened the box and took out the instructions. He booted the laptop to access the codes to start the transformation.

"What does it say?" He asked, taking the paper when she handed it to him. "Seems pretty straightforward. Do you trust him?"

"No. Not at all, that's why I have something extra." She pulled the metal necklace from the box and placed it on the table. Niall picked it up and inspected the three symmetrical rings that created the band.

"Lancaster said the device was a modified version of what they used on the Hybrids, something they marketed to militia groups." She chanted for the spirits of the Black Wolf to guide their next steps.

When done, the neck brace was warm. She waited a few seconds and touched it again. Taking the cooled brace, she returned to Niall. "Ready?"

"To avenge my brother, my Alpha? Yes." He straightened in the chair so she could clasp it on his neck. Once in place he keyed in the codes to activate it.

Granira stood to the side with a prayer in her throat. This had to work, otherwise they were dead, literally. Angus and Hawke would not forgive easily. Niall needed to be Alpha in order to find a way to survive their wrath for betraying them.

Niall had gained a new appreciation for pack life and politics while living in the city working for a large pharmaceutical company. Perhaps the disappearance of pups or the downward spiral of the quality of life of his pack-mates set the nostalgia in motion. He could not pinpoint the exact catalyst that caused him to return home to plot and make changes.

Alpha Muzik had been suspicious of his motives when he crossed pack lands because the seed of Alpha Nikolas was destined to always rule the Farkas pack. It had taken some side-stepping to avoid having his throat ripped out, but he played the role of omega and moved to the outskirts of pack land with Granira where they plotted Muzik's downfall.

She had heard about the Hybrids and he had researched the technology. The merging of technology and human flesh fascinated him. They recognized he needed more strength and cunning to challenge Muzik. Adding an extra hybrid would be the way to go if it could be done safely with him retaining control.

Planning had taken almost a year and Hawke's liberation happened at a perfect time. Muzik constantly worried Hawke would return and unseat him. Although Niall never would have allowed that to happen, Hawke's genuine disinterest made life easier. After months of hacking into databases to insure the device worked, Niall initiated this plan.

With her love of power and prestige, Granira was the perfect accomplice and would serve well as the pack historian again. Muzik had not seen the value in having someone who knew more than him in his ear and dismissed Granira as soon as he came to power, shaming the older woman. Niall understood her motives for helping him were not just about him, but also to settle a score with Muzik and a few pack members who rejoiced at her dismissal.

Niall stiffened as jolts of energy shot through his body. At first the pain wasn't too bad, but given he had never had a high threshold for discomfort, after a few seconds he tried to remove the damn thing. It wouldn't come off. He glanced at the laptop, watched the irrevocable download and tried to turn off the laptop.

"Don't fight it. The instructions say once initiated it cannot be stopped, it's coming from someplace that only uses the computer to start, not to finish. The entire process is five minutes," Granira said, standing to the side holding the instructions.

Five minutes. He'd be dead by then. No way could he last that long with this fire running through his veins. His stomach rebelled, his throat tightened. There wasn't a part of him that did not hurt and wish for death. In the recesses of his mind, his wolf howled its displeasure over the intrusion. Niall sunk into his beast, seeking comfort and found a measure of peace, not enough to negate the debilitating distress that made him curl into a fetal position on the floor, but enough to stop from crying like a pup for his mam.

Cool hands rubbed his forehead and stroked his back as his body shook like a twig beneath the force of the transformation. Sweat soaked his shirt and jeans, his head throbbed and his eyes had a gritty feel as the pain ebbed. Had Hawke gone through this? His mate? Or was this something completely different?

"Drink this." Granira placed a cup next to his lips. He sipped at first and then drank it all appreciating the cool beverage running down his throat.

"Thanks. I think that's the worst of it." He pushed up from the floor and looked around. "That hurt worse than fire.

She smiled and cleaned the floor from where he soiled himself.

"I can do that," he protested, embarrassed.

"No. You must rest for an hour or more to complete the transformation. While you take care of that I will find out where Muzik is hiding so that you can make a formal challenge."

Niall nodded and stood on shaky legs. Grabbing his laptop, he moved to the long sofa and lay down. Now that the necklace was activated he needed to make a few changes so that no one could access it again, that included Granira and Hawke. A file appeared on screen, when clicked a series of codes and information raced across the screen that he was able to decode and accept. Defensive strategies, offensive maneuvers, healing herbs and techniques to keep his new Hybrid form in tip-top condition. With so much information being fed directly into his mind via the device, Niall wondered what the street value of the necklace was. There was a sense of empowerment he'd never had before.

Intuitively he knew he could win the Alpha challenge against Muzik and set the pack on a different course of safety and prosperity. When the last file downloaded, Niall accepted the mantle of Alpha and refused to allow anyone to stand in his way, including Hawke.

Granira left the house and he slid off the couch and shifted to his wolf form. No matter what happened, he needed peace with his beast. While in this form he rested, allowing his beast to experience the changes in his body and accept them. He remained on the floor in that position until Granira returned. The smile she wore didn't bear well for Muzik. The fool must have done or said something to piss her off which was never a good thing.

She sat on the floor next to him and stroked his fur. He purred beneath her hand. "He boasts that he has changed history and that one of his seed shall always be Alpha. Fools, all of them. No one can change that which was spoken. They listened and applauded his words as if he were the Goddess spouting truth."

He looked at her and purred.

Granira met his gaze and smiled, a real one filled with warmth. "How are you feeling? I was gone longer than I thought. Are you hungry?"

Niall hadn't thought about it, but he could eat. He morphed into his human form and helped her stand. "I'll get us both something," he said, heading toward the kitchen.

She followed. "You're Alpha. Alpha's don't cook." She took the steak from his hand and pushed him aside.

"This Alpha cooks and takes care of his space. Until I meet my mate, I will handle those things myself. I refuse to lose myself, who I am at my core." He met her gaze. "Do you understand that? I'm a geek at heart and will use force when necessary without delay, but I will always try to make life better for the pack using my mind first. That's who I am." He hoped she understood, but if not, she would come around or leave.

She patted his cheek and placed a kiss on the back of his hand. "And that is why you are the only Alpha for our pack."

He smiled and they prepared a quick meal for the upcoming battle. "I will run into the woods to see how this thing works before the challenge. Despite how the low hum of energy running through me, I need to be sure I can handle it."

She nodded and sat in front of him. "Finally, after all this time we will have our Alpha. The right Alpha. One who cares for everyone, not just a few favorites. I can go with you or wait here, whatever you want."

Pleased, she offered a choice it made his answer easier. "No, this first time I will go alone, iron out the kinks and make sure I am sure footed. When I return we will find Muzik and I will challenge him."

She nodded and he could tell she was relieved. Granira had aged well, but she tired easily and the past week had presented a strain.

"Okay, I will rest and wait for your return."

Niall nodded, left the house and headed toward the mountains at an easy pace in case someone watched. Despite Granira's opinion, Muzik wasn't dumb. The Alpha understood as long as he and Hawke lived his position was in jeopardy. It wouldn't surprise Niall if someone followed him and Granira and made reports to Muzik. Within moments he hit the tree line on the mountain. Inhaling and sensing no one nearby, he took off at a faster pace, impressed by the increased speed.

He headed for a cave where he hid as a boy when no one had time for him. It had become his private place to dream and hope. Today, it seemed the proper place to practice before reaching the culmination of his dreams.

 # Chapter 30

"*Hawke? Hawke? Wake up.*" Asia's called again as she had been doing for the past ten minutes. She lay on a gurney in a lab where a technician had taken her blood and had her lined up in a long metal tube for x-rays. Pretty soon, Lancaster would recognize the metal in her legs and arm and know her identity.

"*Mistress?*"

"*Asia? Where are you?*"

"*I don't know where but Lancaster is running tests on me and will know who I am soon. I cannot wake Hawke.*"

"*Not again,*" Jasmine murmured. "*Angus is tracking you guys. The door was locked and he had to enter another way. He and that animal took down a couple of hybrids and saved Maheegan and her mate. But you were gone by then.*"

"*Does he know what happened?*"

"*Hawke told him it was Granira and Lancaster.*"

"*What? That bitch. I will personally kill her when I get out of here.*"

"Let's work on getting you out first. I'll have Silas work on Hawke while I help you."

Asia tensed and then forced herself to relax. Her Mistress wasn't very good at this yet, but anything she could do to help would be appreciated. The motor started and she moved slowly toward the tube. Many times in the past she had been in this same position, helpless. After all she had been through, her death, rebirth, mating and falling in love, it seemed impossible that she'd be subjected to all of this again.

Her wolf growled.

Not again. Her wolf howled in agreement. If Lancaster was anywhere in this building the man would die by her hands today. Earlier, she and Hawke planned to allow themselves to be captured to be close to their prey, well this wasn't how they imagined things would work out. But it would have to do. She sought her link with Hawke, he was still unresponsive, but his energy burned bright.

"Mistress, I have an idea, let me try it and if it doesn't work I'll let you know."

"Okay."

Asia touched his energy, it coiled around her like a lost lover. She warmed and then burned hot as the two of them linked. While in the container she lifted her hands popping the security bands and threw energy toward the controls causing them to burn and short out.

The technician re-entered the room as Asia inched forward. Their gazes met. The woman pulled out what looked like a small tranq gun and fired just as Asia jumped aside. The needle fell to the table. The tech fired again and again missing until Asia reached and backhanded her, knocking her to the ground.

"I'm off the table."

"Good. Silas is still working on Hawke."

"Tell him, I know how to wake him and I'm on my way." She dragged the tech to the door, ran the ID card through the slot and placed her thumb on the pad. The door opened. Two hybrids met her in the hall. Asia inhaled searching for her mate as she jumped up, pushed the charging hybrid into the lab just as the door closed behind him and turned to face the other. He charged and she dropped low, gut punched him and then kicked him beneath his chin sending him flying down the hall. He dented the wall, causing dust to float around him. Good, they hadn't reinforced this building for hybrids.

Locked on Hawke's scent she headed in his direction. On the way she broke the glass and pulled an ax from an emergency exit box. Since no one opposed her on the way she suspected a nice welcome from Lancaster and Gordon.

"Hawke," she called when she reached the door to the room where he was located.

"Asia?"

She breathed and sent energy to clear the cobwebs from his mind.

"What the fuck? How'd I get back here again? Damn it."

"Doesn't matter. We'll deal with that later. Right now plan B is in effect."

"Plan B? Refresh my memory."

"We allow ourselves to be caught to get close to the Liege. They die today, Hawke."

"Yes… I agree. Is that you at the door?"

"Yep, just waiting for an invitation."

His chuckle filled their link. *"I'm blindfolded and suspended over something, don't let that distract you from our mission. I'm really hard to destroy."*

She swallowed hard. *"You first always."*

He didn't respond right away. She sensed her words impacted him the same way his always hit her. *"Understood. By the way, come on in."*

"I need to borrow a little of your energy, hold tight, this won't hurt a bit." She wrapped his essence around her and shifted. Once in her hybrid form she kicked the door. It flew off the hinges into the room like a torpedo.

"Nice. I felt the wind as it passed."

There was a small room higher up with human heartbeats, she counted two and one full blood. She wondered who had betrayed the wolf nation and promised to make that bitch suffer.

"Welcome Asia. It has been a long time since we've seen you. Blood doesn't lie and yours was a perfect match," Lancaster said through an intercom. "Please come in, I'd love for you to join us, after all this party is for you."

"Mistress, where is Angus?"

"His pet is tracking you, I don't know where he is exactly. Why?"

"I need a little help." She told Jasmine what she learned so far.

"Sounds like Hawke will need the help."

"I plan to kill all of them, but I need to make sure my mate is safe. I don't want to look at him, instead I want to focus on that room."

"I see. Good plan. I'll tell Silas, he and Hawke will work out whatever he's going through and I'll help you." She paused. *"I've been practicing Asia. I can direct an energy bolt into that room and start a fire if you look at it long enough. Promise I won't hurt you."*

"I wonder if I can redirect Hawke's energy and do that?"

"Try it and if it does not work, I'll help."

"Yes, Ma'am." Asia prayed to the Goddess and stepped inside. Her plan of not looking at Hawke failed the moment she entered since he was suspended in front of the small glass pane where Lancaster, Gordon and Alpha Verrick stood.

Testing the weight of the ax, she moved further into the room, and threw the ax into the glass causing it to web but not shatter. Next, she picked up the lone chair in the room and sent it flying into the glass, this time it broke in several places. Running, she leapt and fell short of the window.

"You bitch," Lancaster said, holding the side of his head as blood ran down and then stopped. "You just killed your mate."

Trusting Silas to keep her mate safe, she focused on that small upper room. She tapped into Hawke's energy, allowed it to burn and merge with hers. Running she leapt for the room and landed inside. It was much larger than she thought.

Lancaster screamed as she backhanded him so hard he flew into the wall and slid down. Gordon backed against the wall, inching for the door.

"Kill her," Lancaster screamed at Verrick who caught the brunt of the shattered glass. His face re-knitted as he bulked to a hybrid.

"So you accepted the poison," she mocked.

Verrick shrugged and walked toward her. Asia grabbed the chair and slammed it into the control panel jamming the door.

"No! No," Lancaster yelled and ran toward the door.

Verrick tried to grab her around the waist. At the last moment she jumped and kicked him in the chest, sending him flying backward. He hit the wall, shook his head and fell backward.

Asia backed up, looked at Gordon and grabbed him by the throat while Lancaster punched the destroyed control panel trying to open the door. She squeezed and then threw Gordon at Verrick when the Alpha ran at her. Both hit the floor. Turning, she grabbed Lancaster by his shirt and shook him like a leaf. All the lives this bastard ruined. She put her hand around his neck, prepared to snap it when Verrick knocked her back into the wall. Lancaster rolled to the side holding his neck trying to breathe.

She blocked Verrick's punches and kicked him in the gut, sending him backward knocking Gordon down in the process. "They didn't warn you, about these did they?" she asked, pointing to her legs before going after Lancaster again.

"Mistress, I can't kill them until the covenant is broken, have Maheegan break the contract."

She backhanded Lancaster again. He spun and hit the floor. "That was for chaining my mate to the wall when he was a pup." He tried to crawl away. But she grabbed him by the back of his shirt and punched him in the gut. "That was for taking his pup without telling him."

"Stop... stop," Lancaster cried, covering his face as she picked him up again.

"This is for Gunnolf." She hit him in the face again.

"What about Gordon... he did it too," Lancaster cried, pointing at Gordon who stood behind Verrick.

"All of you'll die for what you've done to full-bloods but you... you are a slimy bastard who abused my mate. I promised to kill you myself."

"They are working on it Asia. It's going to take a few minutes," Jasmine said.

"Hawke?"

"He'll be okay." It was the hesitancy in her Mistress' voice that concerned Asia. Her mate wasn't dead, she would know, but he'd blocked her, which could mean a lot of things. She had to have faith that he would be okay. Otherwise all of this would be meaningless.

"You sniveling asshole," Gordon growled at Lancaster.

"I saved your ass." Lancaster tried to crawl toward Verrick but Asia blocked and dragged him back to the opposite side and pinned him against the wall by his throat. Damn, she wished she could squeeze the breath out of him right now.

Footsteps. She looked at the door before the knock came.

Hybrids.

Lancaster's eyes widened with what she identified as hope. "The door is jammed on –" she increased the pressure on his neck cutting off his words.

Verrick stood, dusted off his pants and met her gaze. "Either kill him or let him go."

She laughed and slammed Lancaster so hard against the wall, his eyes rolled to the back of his head as he slid down the wall.

"Make me," she challenged Verrick as she stepped in front of Lancaster. Verrick she could eliminate.

Verrick's gaze slid to Lancaster and then back up at her. The next moment he was airborne, she dropped to the floor missing his outstretched arms as he hit the wall and landed on top of Lancaster. She moved quickly, grabbed his head and twisted hard until it snapped.

The pounding on the door increased and then someone kicked on it. Asia looked out the broken window, grabbed a struggling Gordon, and pulled Lancaster from beneath Verrick and tossed them out the window. Seconds later she jumped and landed near Gordon, who moved slowly. Lancaster remained limp on the ground. She looked around the space.

"Where is Hawke?" She asked Gordon.

His face tightened and he looked away.

She grabbed him by the shirt and shook him like Raggedy Ann. "Where is Hawke?"

He pointed down and she looked over her shoulder at the smooth floor. "It opens?"

He nodded.

"Hawke?"

"Almost done. I'll meet you in a bit."

Happy to hear his voice she didn't ask any questions. Instead, she lifted Lancaster and Gordon and ran out the room.

Chapter 31

In the hall Asia tightened her hold on Lancaster and pulled Gordon along. They needed a secure place where she could knock both men out while waiting to kill them or until either Angus or Hawke arrived.

After turning down two short halls, she stopped and looked at Gordon. "Open it." The surprised expression on his confirmed her suspicions. This section was a private area, although none of the rooms were marked or had door handles.

He placed his palm on the wall and it moved. Rather than wait for her instructions, he stepped inside with her right behind him. The small room held a table barely large enough for two people and one chair.

"What kind of room is this?"

"Holding." He took the seat and leaned back in the chair watching her. "Is Damian okay? He wasn't there when I woke up and I'm wondering where he is."

Asia released Lancaster, allowing him to buckle to the floor, but kept her palm on his shoulder to rifle through his mind to find out locations, names, dates, traitors and anything about LOBO.

The man's mind was littered with so many failed ideas, hopes and challenges that it took a few minutes to unlock the area with Liege information and read through it. She sat on the floor next to Lancaster, moved her hand down his arm and held his wrist. "As far as I know, he is fine and on his way here. That should make both of you happy."

Gordon's brow rose at her actions, but smiled, nodded and then closed his eyes with the information on Damian.

LOBO was located in the mountains of Colorado, she didn't see a name for a close town, but the facility looked like a college campus. She'd have Hawke research abandoned schools or permits for new ones along with the landmarks. Over the years they had many pups enter, but later discovered few pups could handle the surgeries. There were so many faces she wanted to cry over the destroyed lives in the name of science and progress.

Next she searched for information regarding current projects, their client base and products. Whereas the names of projects were in his mind, in-depth information was missing unlike LOBO, his personal project. She continued opening his mental doors and searching for information that would help La Patron, Hawke and anything regarding her true identity. One thing that didn't surprise her was his alternate plans in case he needed to ditch the Liege. Seems like he took the reversal of the covenant serious and made arrangements for his disappearance.

After securing information on the Liege operation, she searched for data on Hawke and was surprised by the level of pride and affection the old bastard had for her mate. There was a love and hate battle going on in Lancaster's mind with Hawke.

Lancaster had encouraged Greggor's feelings for Hawke, even told his disturbed nephew that Hawke returned his interest. Later he installed a corrupt neck brace on Greggor knowing either the brace or Hawke would kill the young man. She paid close attention to the neck brace information finding it interesting that under certain circumstances the effects could be reversed.

Asia watched Gordon and continued taking information from Lancaster. He was no doctor, but understood the mechanics of their enhancements. After a few minutes longer, she gave up, there had been no mention of her other than her surgeries, assignments, progress and disappointment that she escaped. Lancaster didn't really believe she and Hawke were mated. He clung to the notion of Hawke and Angus.

The project underway to duplicate the power of the chameleon disturbed her. The Liege had secured natural crystals and rare herbs from all over the globe to recreate Angus' work. She would inform him and her Mistress of this new threat. The idea of a Liege Lord in high positions of power sent shivers of distaste through her.

Standing, she searched the area for Angus or Hawke. *"Where are you?"* she asked her mate.

"When I fell through the floor I hit a caged ball which rolled out the building and landed into the Nistru River. I'm headed back in your direction, but look for me on the side of the road, I'm quite a distance away."

She told him everything that happened since she saw him last. Hawke laughed. *"Pity you couldn't kill him. They never expected you to focus on them rather than try to save me.*"

"*You didn't need saving.*"

He chuckled. "*Angus, Damian and Byte are in the building searching for you. Angus took information from Damian as well.*" He paused. "*La Patron pulled Damian's wolf and had Angus train him in the woods. That's where they were during the ceremony.*"

"*Are you okay with that?*" He sounded put off for some reason.

"*Yes. No. Well, I'm not sure, but I think I would have enjoyed seeing him as a wolf his first time and giving him instructions. But I'm not sure that's what I'm feeling. It's all new. Does that make sense?*"

Asia had no point of reference and tried to imagine if she ran across a pup from her loins, how would she feel? Would she want to train the pup? Teach him how to survive? Possibly.

"*Yes, the confusion and uncertainty makes perfect sense to me. Hopefully you will have time to run with him in the forest and answer questions I'm sure he has.*" Encouraging him to further bond with his son seemed the right thing to say and do. At least for now.

"*You said there is another?*"

"*In the lab one of the workers said you had two. I'll ask Gordon, he's waiting for Damian. I don't think he likes Lancaster much, you should have seen them.*"

"*Thanks, I'm curious if there are more, even though I'm not sure what we should do about it.*"

Neither was she, but she could hear her Mistress saying it was all about family. "*We'll work it out.*"

She leaned against the wall next to the table where Gordon sat and looked down at him. The man sat slumped in the chair with his head down. "Is Damian the only pup from Hawke's seed?"

Gordon's head rose, in slow increments until he met her gaze. "No. There is one more. A female, two, no three, I think. Extremely smart, cute, definitely Alpha material. Strong willed from the beginning, she will need to temper that in order to survive the training."

Asia swallowed hard at the sorrow in his gaze. "You'll kill her if she doesn't... what? Obey? If she has a mind of her own?"

He nodded. "Behavioral optimization. She is too young for any of the surgeries, so she is punished in a traditional manner." He chuckled. "Doesn't work though. As smart as she is, we cannot keep her if she does not bend. So yes, she will be terminated if she does not change. I'm telling you this because she is Damian's... sister, I suppose and Hawke's seed. If I survive and return to my duties, she will undergo a series of tests, her future is dependent on how well she does."

"Can't you just release her?"

"No. I don't work alone in a vacuum." He glanced at Lancaster on the floor. "Do you think he would ever release someone who could one day return and destroy him or the Liege? None of us would do that."

"Why doesn't Damian have the same computer chip as Hawke?"

Gordon released a long sigh. "Meant to, but things kept coming up, labs destroyed, merchandise lost, lost staff and things like that. Takes time and resources to find and train doctors. Since he was born in-house and the expense of the surgery, plus finding the right personnel, we put it off until later. That asshole brought him out before we put a tracking device in Damian. He wasn't ready in more ways than one." He shook his head.

"What about his wolf, did he ever shift?"

"No and we didn't give him drugs to suppress it either. I think it had something to do with him not wanting his beast. He wasn't the only one. Some shift at puberty, others never do. We haven't figured out why yet. Do you know?"

"No. All pups shift, it's unusual not to."

"If they are around full-bloods and see it as a normal occurrence, but when it's not... I'm not sure."

Since she had no idea, she'd ask Matt in a Patron's laboratory how that played out long term for the health of the full-blood. "What about Asia, did she have any pups?" She had searched Lancaster's memories and found nothing.

Gordon glanced at her and snorted. "I wish, that would be the icing on the cake, but as far as I know she didn't." He closed his eyes as if savoring the idea. "Now that would be something." He looked at her. "Asia is still our top enhanced work. Never understood what it was about her biology, it was different from the others. Her body accepted each additional enhancement, her arm and legs when she fell from the plane and crushed her original set. Once she was in Japan on an assignment, lost an eye, we were able to replace it with an improved version."

Asia had forgotten the incident when she fell onto the mountains. The pain had been excruciating. Hours passed before the extraction team found her. When she woke up one of the doctors told her of the surgery.

Gordon's account of the situation made it seem as if they'd done her a favor and that their actions had been benevolent when that wasn't true. Too bad she couldn't tell him what she thought of their treatments.

"Hawke is amazing as well. Even without the computer chip he has excellent utilization of his limbs. One day we hope to create the right balance with the metal so that no chips are needed."

"So Damian has something?"

"No. Hawke's behavior needed optimizing, he thought like a wolf with a pack mentality and refused to respond to Lancaster as his Alpha. His chip overruled his wolf and controlled his limbs. But the chip no longer works, I don't think it's still embedded. How did that happen?"

Asia shrugged and scented the air. Angus was nearby. "Mates. It cancels out everything."

Gordon nodded as there was a knock on the door.

"That's Damian."

Gordon brightened and opened the door. Byte entered first causing Gordon to back up and return to his seat. The animal looked at her, sniffed Lancaster and then settled beneath the table.

Damian entered and headed toward Gordon. Angus stepped inside as the door closed behind him. "You good?" he asked her.

She nodded.

"Let's go then."

Before she could turn, Lancaster jumped up, placed his palm on the wall behind him, which opened. He dove into the small opening and lashed out his hand. The wall closed and he was gone. It all happened within seconds.

Asia placed her palm all over the wall trying to find the trigger. "Bring Gordon to open this," she said over her shoulder.

"*It's done,*" Jasmine said. "*Maheegan completed the ceremony five minutes ago. Sorry for the delay, I had a few things to clear out. You still have them?*"

"Thank you, Mistress." Now that she could kill Lancaster she wanted to go after him. *"Lancaster just jumped through a hidden compartment, but I still have Gordon."*

"I am so sorry. If I had told you when it happened, he would be one less problem."

Although Asia agreed she refrained from saying so. Instead, she focused on how to find the man and surfed through his memories. Nothing. She slapped the panel.

"Gordon I need you to open this panel." Turning, she noticed Damian kneeling beside Gordon on the ground. "What happened?" She took a step for a better look.

"Lancaster threw a blade, I think he aimed at you and missed. It hit Gordon in the chest, sank deep," Angus said, kneeling and placing his palm on the man's forehead.

Damian stared at the blade. "Why is it bleeding? It should've stopped by now." His gaze whipped around and met hers. "Can you help him?"

"I don't think so. The covenant is broken, nature will take its course." She took a step back, contacted Hawke and told him what happened.

"I'll keep an eye out for the slippery bastard, chances are he's on his way off the continent. Can't believe he killed the man, wonder if there are cameras in that room."

She looked around, didn't see any and then shut out all the sounds to isolate on the hum of a camera. There was one. If there was any justice, Lancaster would be kicked out of the Liege for murdering Gordon, but she doubted it.

Damian rested his forehead on Gordon's thigh. The man placed his hand on the back of Damian's head and stroked his hair while looking at her. "You allowed me time with my boy and I thank you for that."

He lifted Damian's hand and kissed the back of it. "Here is something you need to know. Lancaster, the bastard, didn't play fair with Niall. He gave him a neck brace that would make the man a puppet for the Liege and told him it was one we sell on the open market. It's not. He modified this one so that Niall would attack Hawke and his mate whenever he sees him. And he fixed it so that Niall will be driven to seek Hawke out. I warned Granira to let it go, but she wanted to avenge her Alpha and felt they could make it work."

Asia hid her surprise over Niall and Granira taking a hybrid neck brace. She had seen what those things did to full-bloods and wondered why Hawke's litter-mate would take on that risk. It didn't make sense, but she passed on the warning to Hawke and Jasmine. If he came after Hawke, she would kill him and Granira without hesitation.

Gordon looked down at Damian. "I need you to do something for me."

Damian nodded without lifting his head.

"Pull the blade out. I refuse to have anything of Boris Lancaster's in my body a second longer." His breaths became shorter as he struggled to talk.

Damian lifted his head, placed his hand on the top of the blade and stared at it. Gordon covered his hand, causing Damian to look at him. "After you pull this out, there will be blood. A lot of it. In the end I will stop breathing and will rest with my sons. Remember I told you about them?"

Damian nodded.

"I want you to go with Hawke and his mate. They are going to find your sister before Lancaster destroys her. You can help them."

Asia hid her surprise when Angus looked at her.

"I don't want to go with them. I will stay with this one. He is teaching me how to be a wolf," Damian said glancing at Angus.

"Good, you have discovered your wolf. I am happy. The others voted against me when I said the pups should have a relationship with their beasts." He paused, coughed. "But, this one is not your sire and cannot teach you all you need to know. Promise me you will go with Hawke to find your sister, she is special like you."

After a few moments, Damian nodded. Asia wasn't sure why, but she exhaled in relief when he agreed. Her mate had two pups. It boggled her mind what she should do about that. But they would deal with it later, right now she wanted to leave this place and find her mate.

"Thank you," Gordon whispered and removed his hand.

Damian pulled out the blade and stood as blood pumped out the wound. He refused to leave until Gordon breathed his last labored breath.

Chapter 32

Niall entered the mouth of the cave and moved with purpose to the middle area deeper into the mountain. Stretching and jumping in place to warm up fired the blood in his body, releasing endorphins and something else he couldn't identify. The space around him wavered. A deep pounding started in the back of his head. He shook his head to clear his vision and inhaled before releasing his breath in slow degrees.

"Okay, okay… easy now." Closing his eyes, he exhaled and shifted into his beast. When he opened his eyes, he marveled at how intense the colors around him became. He noticed everything that moved and sensed prey on the other side of the mountain. Smiling, he envisioned a night of hunting with his pack and bringing down large game. After padding around the area for a few minutes he morphed seamlessly into his normal hybrid. It was smaller than most of his pack members and the main reason for the collar. But his senses were still enhanced, which was an added bonus.

"Good, feeling good." He ran in a circle, stretching his arms and hitting an imaginary punching bag. Laughing at how good he felt, he completed a few roundhouse kicks that he had seen Hawke's mate use during the fight against Verrick's men.

He thought bigger, his muscles burned for a few seconds as he morphed into his larger hybrid. Blood rushed through to his head, his vision blurred. The neck brace burned into his flesh as he held his head to stop the sharp pain that shot through him. His knees buckled as he fell to the ground. No one mentioned this debilitating part of usage and hoped it was a one-time thing.

Minutes passed and he remained on his knees until it ebbed. His body was three times its normal size and for him that was monumental. Standing, he stretched, kicked and practiced both defensive and offensive moves. Hours later, sweat dripping from his body, he was ready to challenge Muzik. Niall had morphed through all his forms repeatedly until they flowed easily without pain.

He stepped out the cave, jogged back to Granira's place, showered and changed before waking her.

"I'm ready," he said, knocking on her bedroom door. Now that he'd sold his litter-mate out for his personal gain, he wanted this part over. Taking the Alpha position which belonged to him, at least in his mind, would validate his actions and make things right. As Alpha he could assist Hawke in his mission as well as preserve their heritage. The more he thought about it, the less guilty he felt over the betrayal. The ends would justify the means in this instance. First, he needed to win the Alpha challenge.

Granira stepped out her room, eyed him and smiled. "You are wearing Lorenzo's necklace and Jirek's shirt. I have something of your father's if you'd like."

Niall's father hadn't paid him any attention while growing up and many times said, within Niall's presence, he had three sons and one of them was Lancaster's prisoner. The old man never approved of him and didn't bother hiding his disdain of his bookish son. When he heard of the old man's death, he'd been relieved and did all he could to help Lorenzo. Lorenzo had been all about war and didn't live much longer after becoming Alpha. Jirek had been Niall's favorite because of his level-headedness and unswerving loyalty to his litter-mate. No one messed with Niall whenever Jirek was nearby and Niall followed his brother everywhere. When Muzik challenged Jirek after that last battle, Niall had been away at the University. The news of his litter-mate cut deep and he did not return for years. But his hatred for Muzik continued to grow along with the need to avenge Jirek. Today would be that day and he wanted no memory of his sire to spoil it.

"No, I'm good. You ready?" he headed toward the door.

"Yes, let's do this." She followed him out the door, they shifted to their beasts and headed toward the Alpha house. Someone must have alerted Muzik they were on their way because he, his beta and a few members of the pack stood outside in a semi-circle as though waiting.

"I see you were telling the truth, in this at least," Muzik said looking at Granira. The older woman's face reddened, her jaw clenched, but she remained quiet. Niall had no idea what Muzik referred to but figured Muzik would tell him soon enough.

"So she finally talked you into challenging me? I wondered when you'd have the balls to step from behind her skirts and speak for yourself."

Niall glanced at Granira. *"What did you tell him?"*

"We will talk of it later, watch out for his beta, the man is sneaky."

Rather than argue the point, Niall faced an all too confident Muzik. "I don't know what you have been told, but I am challenging you for my birthright as the seed of Alpha Nikolas."

"So you have finally decided to show your true colors? I knew you spoke false when you returned to the pack, but allowed you to remain out of respect for Alpha Hiram, your sire." He turned and looked at those in the circle. "You are my witnesses that I have been challenged by the runt of Alpha Hiram's litter, his death is not on my conscience." He looked at Niall. "This will be to the death, do you recant your challenge?"

"It's not the way I would choose, but if you insist, I agree."

Muzik and the others laughed. "Oh, I insist. I would not go through this again. Tell me, is Hawke next? Will he challenge me as well?"

"Hawke has no interest in you or the pack. He serves La Patron."

Muzik's smile slipped as he nodded. "He refuses to return? What of his heritage? He is in Nikolas' line as well."

Niall shrugged. "Maybe he will return later after he finishes his assignment for his Alpha."

Muzik stared at him for a second. "What has happened? You seem different, has the witch given you a dampener for your fear?"

"No. This conversation is not for you, but for the pack. You will never see Hawke or anyone else after the challenge." His words were delivered so matter-of-factly it took Muzik a second to react.

The Alpha shifted to his hybrid, and Niall shifted to his large hybrid, stepped aside and punched him in the belly sending him flying backward. Before Muzik could move, Niall jumped on his back, twisted his head until it snapped and then stood facing the beta and the rest of the pack who had assembled.

"Are you next, Kendall?" he asked the beta in a calm voice in contrast to hum of blood singing in his veins. No one moved or spoke. Niall took a step to the beta who had bullied him all his life. The urge to snap the man's neck rode him hard. "I asked you a question." His fist opened and then closed.

Kendall knelt in front of him. "No, Alpha." The rest of the pack, including Granira who wore a serene smile, knelt as well.

Niall howled and called the entire pack to him. When they were all assembled he had the beta tell the others what happened.

"Do you accept me as your Alpha?" Niall asked, watching the faces closely.

"Yes!" They shouted and howled their approval.

"Take his body and burn it in the middle of the square." He watched the beta swallow hard before motioning to another pack member. They dragged Muzik to the middle of the clearing and set a bonfire. Moments later Niall morphed to his beast and sat watching the blaze. One by one, the pack all shifted. When the fire died, he howled as Alpha. Yes, the ends definitely justified the means. Now to prepare to defeat Hawke.

Chapter 33

Hawke waved down the vehicle carrying his mate and stepped inside. The somber atmosphere surprised him. With the death of another Liege Lord, their "to-do" list grew one shorter.

"Everybody okay?" he asked watching Asia.

She nodded and glanced at Damian who sat in the front seat looking out the window. "Yes. I talked to Mistress, gave her the location of LOBO and a few other places I got from Lancaster. Did you talk to La Patron?" she asked Hawke.

"Yes, a few minutes ago, he told me you'd pick me up around here and we need to get back to Radoff's. They found something he wants us to look at." Hawke met Angus' gaze in the mirror. "You gave him the information on the Liege?"

Angus nodded. "He's sending teams out now. Not sure what Radoff and Maheegan found, but I'm ready to go home."

Hawke wasn't sure what to say about that. His home was with his mate, wherever that took them. From what Asia told him, La Patron would be rescuing the pups from the LOBO compound, and that included the other pup he sired. According to his mate, her Mistress was big on family connections and she believed Damian would get along with La Patron's two older sons and godson. All three were mated and Damian might find a mate in the states.

Hawke still couldn't wrap his mind around the concept of a family. Mating Asia had been the best thing to ever happen to him and he thanked the Goddess every moment of the day. But pups? That took things to another level he wasn't sure how to handle.

Asia placed her hand over his and smiled. *"We will figure this out. Once we get to Radoff's and finish whatever we need to do there, we should be done with this assignment. Like Angus I'm ready to go home."*

He kissed the back of her hand. *"Okay. Will we stay with La Patron or will we need to purchase a home?"*

"No. As personal security, we stay in the compound. A place will be provided, no worries on that score. The place is huge, three or four times the castle above ground. Underground is huge, with tight security. You've never seen anything like it."

Impressed with her high praise he settled back and watched the scenery pass by. "How will you get Byte into the country?" He glanced at the beast who lifted his head at the mention of its name.

"Non-commercial, private jet landing on La Patron's land, can't leave him behind. Something tells me we're going to grow old together."

"La Patron wants to see and study him?" Asia said with a hint of laughter in her voice.

Angus frowned and then shrugged. "Yeah, that too."

"I thought there were pups in his den," Hawke said, confused that the beast would be allowed anywhere near the compound.

"They are, why?" Angus looked at him in the rear view mirror, all laughter gone. "Is there a problem with TerraByte's being near pups? Is it unsafe?"

Hawke glanced at the beast and then at Angus. The man couldn't be serious. Byte took down a bluebird and slammed open a metal door. "Not sure because nothing is known on his biological makeup, his triggers, and what makes him tick. I'd move with caution."

Angus agreed. "Silas will meet me and we'll decide if I can return to the compound or if he'll move me to another area." They turned onto the road leading to Radoff's. Hawke looked at Damian, who hadn't spoken since he'd been in the vehicle.

"Are you okay?"

Damian didn't respond.

"How soon do you think before we leave the country?" Hawke asked Asia.

"I don't know, Mistress hasn't said anything. But we have completed our assignment and stopped the Liege from accessing pack lands in secret. Now, the Alphas will have their scents and can track them down. Unless there is more for us to do, we will return home with Angus." She paused. "Are you taking Damian with us?"

Hawke glanced at the silent pup and shrugged. "What choices do we have? Lancaster is out there, and the rest of the Liege. If they re-take him I will meet him across the battlefield one day, unable to kill him. If La Patron can use him, it would be better for everyone."

She squeezed his hand. "Okay."

"I would like to shift and run as the wolf," Damian said surprising Hawke.

"You have met your wolf? Made peace with him?"

"Yes. Earlier Angus took us into the woods to run and hunt. The feeling is liberating and I would experience it again."

The buildings came into view, they would be at Radoff's in a few minutes. "Okay, after I see what Alpha Radoff needs to show me, we will take off into the woods." He'd invite Asia as well, they hadn't ran on four legs in over a month and he missed it.

"Thank you," Damian said in a controlled voice as if the words pained him.

Hawke smiled and told Asia. "That sounds good, count me in."

The car stopped in the outer bailey. They spilled out and headed toward the main building where they sensed Radoff's presence. Before they reached the main entrance, Radoff, Maheegan and a few other pack members met them on the porch.

Maheegan embraced Asia and held her hand, which struck Hawke odd. "Come we have a lot to tell you." Hawke walked on Asia's other side holding her hand as they headed toward the smaller building where the ceremony took place.

"La Patron told you the covenant is broken. When the mixed blood ran across the pages and the words were spoken the paper burned," Maheegan said as they entered the building. "The building shook, we thought there was some type of seismic activity going on until it stopped and we saw the door."

"Door?" Angus asked, moving ahead to open the door leading below.

"Yes. It seems Konstantin was indeed smarter than the Liege gave him credit for," Radoff said following Asia and Hawke. "Keep this door closed until I tell you to open it," he said to one of his pack members and then met the others on the ground floor.

"Konstantin, the Hungarian Lord, who started the Liege?" Asia asked for clarity.

"Yes," Maheegan said, taking Asia's hand again before following Radoff down the corridor.

"This is how Niall and Lancaster entered to take us before?" Hawke pointed down the long hallway.

"Yes, there are doors that open in various regions on pack lands, I've temporarily locked them all. This is too important for anyone to stumble across," Radoff said.

"Really?" Hawke asked, intrigued.

"When do we run as wolves?" Damian asked from above ground. Radoff hadn't extended an invitation to the pup and Hawke didn't blame him. For now, the pup was a wild card with unknown allegiance. Lancaster killed Gordon, but did that mean Damian would go against all the Liege or just Lancaster or would he allow it to pass? Hawke didn't know and until he knew with some measure of certainty which side of the fence the pup stood, he'd keep him close.

"After I am done down here. Make yourself useful and offer to assist in the cleanup."

"I'll wait by the car."

Radoff stopped in front of an old door filled with symbols. Hawke looked around certain he had passed the area before. "I don't remember seeing anything like that, where'd it come from?"

"After the ground shook, we did a quick search to make sure the underground was still safe and came across this door. It took a while to read and understand the writing on the door, but once Maheegan figured it out, she opened it and then contacted La Patron. He wanted you to see it because it had been warded for so long."

Asia released Maheegan's hand and stepped closer with Hawke by her side.

"*Familiar?*" Hawke asked.

"*In a weird way. My stomach clenched when I first saw it.*" She looked over her shoulder at Maheegan. "Can we open it?"

"How long do you think this has been here?" Hawke asked as his fingertips stroked the wood and markings.

"Yes, you can open it and go inside. Hawke I'd say it's been here since the 1800's. Some of the meaning of the symbols is older than that, but the wood, I'd say mid-century," Maheegan said even though she went no further.

Hawke pushed the door and stepped inside. A light flickered on and then another and then another until the room was bathed in a soft warm glow. Asia followed and then Angus. The three of them stopped and stared at the large portrait on the wall.

Two men sat on each side of a beautiful woman who reclined between them holding a small child. They were in this room or one similar. One male had black hair, green eyes, and muscular, long legs and wore an air of superiority.

"That must be Alpha Nikolas," Angus said, pointing to the green eyed man. Hawke agreed, even after all these years the man oozed authority.

"And that's probably Konstantin." He pointed to the other male with pale skin and light brown eyes who stared down at the woman. So far Hawke hadn't come across much information describing the long-time benefactor, but the way he looked at the woman connected with Hawke. She was beautiful, like his mate.

"But who is that?" Angus asked, pointing to the female.

Hawke hadn't been able to take his eyes off the woman with the coffee colored complexion, long, thick black hair, and well-toned body. Asia's increased pressure on his hand meant she had been similarly stricken by the portrait. The woman's whisky colored eyes looked down at the babe in her arms with warmth and affection.

"Maheegan, who is the woman and what is the purpose of this room?" Angus asked.

Asia's belly quivered as she dragged her gaze from the picture to look around. A large metal chest stood in the corner and there were several volumes of texts similar to the ones Hawke interpreted earlier. A bed lay in the back against the wall and smaller pictures and statues were all over the place. This seemed like someone's personal resting space. Like a magnet, her gaze returned to the woman, flicked over the men and then rested on the female again. The warmth in the woman's eyes touched her.

"Does she look familiar to you?" Maheegan asked Angus, who turned and stared at the portrait again.

"Wow," he said softly and turned toward Asia. She met his gaze and leaned into Hawke. One moment she was the white male everyone saw as his mate and then next she was in her true form, staring at the woman who could be her twin.

"Bless the Goddess," Radoff said in a reverent tone. "You said they were kin, but this is my first time seeing her like this and you are right." He kissed Maheegan on the cheek.

Angus walked to her and smiled. "For years you have searched for answers, I believe you'll find some in this room." He squeezed her shoulder and headed toward the door where Byte stood guard.

"Wait," Maheegan said before Angus left. "One other thing La Patron wanted you three to see." She took a small locket from her pocket and handed it to Asia. "We found this on that dresser when we entered the room earlier."

Asia looked at the intricately carved piece and opened it. Her breath caught and she met Maheegan's gaze. "What?"

"I don't know what it means, but at least we have a place to start our search for a better understanding. Mistress is adamant that all of this ties together somehow and believes the Goddess set this in motion. She wants you and Hawke to learn everything you can from the notes, books and artifacts in this room. Then maybe you can explain it to us."

Asia's eye watered as she continued to stare at the picture of the woman with the birthmark, which Asia had seen on the pups, on her arm. Hawke's hold tightened as he looked at the picture.

No one questioned Asia's relation to this woman, the resemblance was almost a perfect match. She glanced at the babe in the picture, the cloth covering its lower area prevented an immediate identification but Asia sensed a connection. She handed the piece to Angus. He stared at it for a long time and then nodded.

"We need answers. I will take your pup for a run Hawke, you have more important matters to deal with. There is something in this room, my head aches, does yours?" He looked at Asia and then Hawke.

Surprised, she met Angus' gaze. "No. It feels fine." She looked up at Hawke. "You okay?"

"I'm good." They both looked at Angus who shrugged.

"Figures, just means you belong here." Angus pointed at Maheegan and Radoff who remained on the outside. "It bothered you to be in there?"

"Yes, after a while we both started feeling woozy," Maheegan said with a smile. You're right, she belongs in that room. I hope she finds answers and peace. No one will disturb you two, take all the time you need."

Asia walked around the room, it was much larger than she originally thought. Hawke picked up a journal, opened it and took a seat. "What about Damian?" she asked, remembering the run.

"I told him to go with Angus." He settled back into the chair and read.

Her mind filled with questions as she continued to stare at the woman in the locket. They were related, but how? Mother? Sister? Cousin? Aunt? Why was she with the Hungarian and the Alpha? Who were they to her? And where did the birthmark come from and why did it show up on the pups a continent away?

"Her name is Amynta. Not a native, but from someplace else which may be in another book. Seems she was some type of warrior or princess or both, not sure yet. This book deals with her pregnancy and wishes for her unborn child. Seems her father would be furious if he ever discovered she'd had a child and she was afraid."

Asia watched Hawke turn the pages. Amynta, the name meant nothing to her other than defender in Greek. She turned and sat on the bed, surprised at the firmness of the mattress after all this time. There was some dust, but not much, no cobwebs, or insects, nothing.

Is this where she hid from her father? Why was it revealed with the breaking of the covenant? Was that related in some way? Asia gazed into the locket for answers.

"Doesn't say who the father is, it may have been one of those two but I don't think so. Seems they were her closest friends or allies against her father. They protected her and offered her refuge. From the tone of her words, it seems she didn't know the father of the child or she was taken by force. Most of her writings in this journal tells her unborn child to rise above the circumstances of her birth, to become the light on a moonless night, to not venture off course, destined for greatness, that type thing. I can read it to you if you'd like."

Asia didn't want the message without knowing the messenger. "No, you can either read that to me later or translated it on the laptop and I'll read it myself. Right now I want to know who she... is to me. I need to know that first to put everything in context."

Chapter 34

Angus, Byte and Damian ran through the forest chasing rabbits and small game for sport. His mind kept returning to the portrait on the wall, the woman looked familiar, so did Alpha Nikolas. They came to a stream and stopped to drink and rest a bit. Damian wanted to play and Byte indulged him in a game of hide and seek while Angus gathered his thoughts.

Nikolas looked like the Black Wolf from his dreams, the original Black Alpha. But that didn't make sense. By the 1800's that Alpha was dead, although rumor had it the Alpha returned every year and impregnated women. Angus shook his head. Those tales happened in the new country, America, not here.

In the portrait, Konstantin looked like a man smitten while Nikolas appeared pleased by something. Angus wondered what had been going on in the man's mind at the time and who painted the blasted thing? One question led into another, and he knew Silas well enough to know answers were required.

Perhaps Hawke would be able to meet that requirement after reading all the books or diaries scattered around the room. Angus sighed with the realization that he wouldn't be going home until the mystery of the birthmark was solved.

Byte growled and yipped in the distance. Angus hopped up, ran toward the sound and saw Byte running back and forth at the top of a ravine. He moved closer to the edge to look over. Damian lay struggling on the bottom with something protruding through his leg.

"Damian is hurt," Hawke said.

"He fell into a dry bed, looks like he's pinned down. I'm on my way to get him,"

"I'm on my way," Hawke said in a tight voice.

Angus shifted to his hybrid and jumped, his feet sank into the soft sand and it took a few minutes and shifting to his human form to break free. Damian lay panting on the ground a few feet from him trying to break the branch off.

"Let me do that otherwise it might heal with the wood in your leg and you don't want that." Damian stopped moving, but it was obvious by the grimace on his face the pain was intense.

A sound from behind him caused him to turn but not before four or five tranq darts lodged in his arms and legs. "Byte come." A growl and then Byte hit the ground in front of him. His body vibrated with anger and Angus knew he wanted to charge after whoever attacked them. The scents were unfamiliar to Angus, he tried to break the wood in Damian's leg but the excess doses of the drug in his system slowed him down. He went down on one knee next to

Damian while Byte jumped and blocked every dart that came at them.

"*Someone is shooting tranq's at us, I've got five and Damian has one. Can't see them, be careful,*" he told Hawke and sat on the ground fighting the drug.

"*Almost there, I've got Damian's scent. And the other scent is familiar, it's Niall with a dampener but those don't work against litter-mates. What the hell is he doing?*"

"*Don't know. Is Asia with you?*"

"*Yes. Why?*"

"*Because you can't kill the bastard, she can.*"

"*We're here. I see you.*"

The next moment Asia, dressed as an older white male, dropped next to Angus and gave him a piece of the root Hawke had instructed them to eat. As nasty as the root tasted in the past with each bite, it diluted the toxins of the poisons in his system. She held Damian's head up and dribbled the juice from the root into his mouth. When he coughed and opened his eyes, she handed him a piece of the root and told him to chew it.

Angus stood slowly and then sat back down. His head spun, it would take a little longer to stabilize.

Asia moved to Damian's leg, broke off the stick from the bottom and then pulled it out. Next she poured water from a canteen she took from around her neck over and through the wound.

"Shift," she told him.

After a few seconds, Damian morphed into his beast and lay next to her on the ground. She ran her hands through his fur while watching the forest. A loud smacking sound rent the woods. Asia covered Damian and Angus bent his head as bodies landed in the sand near them. Angus counted ten before Hawke and a super-sized Niall crashed through the gully.

Asia checked Damian's wound, it was healing and should be fine soon. She watched Hawke fight Niall, felt his anger and sorrow that it had come to this. His litter-mate betrayed him and used Damian as bait to trap him. Touching the hilt of her sword she prepared to be the sword arm of her Alpha.

Niall fought hard and against someone else might have had a chance of winning, but Hawke knew his moves before he executed them and had him pinned to the ground gasping for air as his injuries healed.

"What are you doing?" Niall asked. "We cannot kill each other."

"Nevertheless, you attacked me and caused my mate to be taken by the Liege," Hawke said.

"I needed to avenge my brother, since no one else would."

"At the risk of my mate and my pup?" Hawke squeezed his neck harder. Damian raised his head and watched.

"I had to help Lancaster rescue Gordon so he'd give me the neck brace to defeat Muzik."

"Not my problem, involving my mate, my pup... that's what caused your death." He nodded to Asia who unsheathed her sword and shifted.

Niall's eyes widened when he saw Asia, he struggled and tried to free himself. "Wait, wait, after all these years of being on the bottom, I rise to the top and you take it from me. Have you no idea what my life has been like? Living in the shadow of brothers who couldn't think their way out of a paper bag, and serving Alphas who allowed the pack to die from starvation because the only thing they think about is fighting?" he yelled.

He inhaled and closed his eyes. "I admit I went about it the wrong way, I could've talked to you, but I didn't know who to trust. And then you said you had no interest in the pack so I didn't bother."

"You helped Lancaster, the man who enslaved me for years and killed our sire?"

"You killed our sire," Niall screamed pointing at Hawke. "His love for you and no one else, killed him and destroyed mam. Consumed by guilt, he never allowed us to mention your name, he hated the other Alphas because they wouldn't help him get you back. Soon our pack became ostracized, they laughed at him because he couldn't keep it together. No one came to our aid when we were attacked and lost more of our land. We lost the respect of the other clans and I lost my brothers who defended a pack that had lost its honor."

Hawke tossed Niall away. "You blame me? As if I had choices in this bullshit? I did not," Hawke yelled, moving closer to Niall as the other man backed away. "Everything was taken from me."

"Not everything. You left Lancaster's smarter and tougher than you went in, yet you have no ties with the pack, no interest in righting the wrongs we've endured while you were away. Do you truly believe you were the only one who suffered?" Niall laughed, it was a dry, mocking sound as he pointed to the bodies on the ground.

"Ask some of these how many meals they've gone without, or the pups they've lost or mates. We live on a sliver of our former land because we lack the strength to defend it. Our numbers shrunk because of sickness, poverty and the inability of our females to breed. We. Are. Dying," he yelled and shook his head. "And you don't give a damn. No one does. So... yeah. I betrayed you after you made it damn clear you wouldn't help. I sold you out for a neck brace that allowed me to kill the former Alpha in a challenge. He killed my brother, an Alpha who did give a damn about the pack." Niall lifted his arms and morphed to human. "There you have it."

"Why attack now if you've already avenged Jirek?" Asia asked in a somber tone.

Niall opened his mouth and then closed it. "I'm not sure. We were hunting game for the pack and..." He looked confused. "I don't know."

"Gordon said Lancaster tricked him with a faulty neck brace, remember?" Angus said standing slowly.

She nodded. "Lancaster set it so you'd come after Hawke and his pup. I think there is a way to change that. If you mean what you say about helping your clan, then give Hawke your computer information and he'll send you the code to remove that command. It won't impact the brace, but it will save your life because you will never get another chance like this again," Asia promised.

"Understood, thank you." Niall turned to Hawke. "I apologize for betraying you, but did what I felt I needed. I had to protect the pack." He extended his hand. "If you ever need me, my right arm is yours." It took Hawke a moment to accept the gesture, but in the end he accepted the apology and hoped he never needed Niall.

Niall turned and looked at Angus. "My apologies."

Angus nodded, but didn't speak.

Niall took a step toward Damian, Byte growled a warning and he stopped. "Damian, I am your sire's litter-mate and apologize to you as well."

Damian morphed to human and stood. "You took Master Gordon from the basement?"

Niall shook his head. "No, Boris Lancaster did that."

"But you helped?"

"In a way, yes. Lancaster said he needed to rescue Gordon from the cage they put him in."

Damian nodded. "That is right, I remember. Lancaster killed Master Gordon."

Niall's mouth dropped open before he snapped it shut. "I didn't know that."

"Yes, he will be missed." Damian turned toward Hawke. "Can we return to the woods to hunt?"

"Yes." Hawke turned to Niall. "My mate gave you a second chance, do not squander it, send me the link as soon as you return to your pack lands so the code can be corrected."

"Yes and thank you." Niall went to each person on the ground and assisted them to their feet.

Asia turned and followed Angus and Damian up a path with Hawke bringing up the rear. "Tonight you will tell me what you read in Amynta's journal that caused your face to turn red."

"What?" Hawke asked, trying to sound innocent and failing.

"Right before Damian called out to you for help, your face was apple red and your jaw was tight. What did you read?"

"I believe she was your mother or your aunt, although I'm leaning to your mam. Her manner of blatant speech and thought reminds me of you. There is a passage of her complaining over her lovers... um, uh... performance."

Asia laughed, feeling free and hopeful for the first time in years. A door to her past opened with answers to her questions and she would soon know more than tidbits of her history.

"Well, I don't have any complaints, so in that regards I am not like her."

He swatted her on the backside and took her hand. "Glad to hear it. La Patron wants a report later, so after we run a bit we need to get back to the books."

"Okay." She morphed into her beast and took off behind Angus.

Chapter 35

Two days later, Hawke closed the last journal and looked over his shoulder at his mate who lay on the bed her mam used many years ago. Amynta's writings of her tortured past with her family broke his heart, and he marveled at the strong women in her line. How could he tell his mate, she was the product of a horrible rape engineered by her grandfather the Alpha of his pack and leader of their country.

Asia came from royal stock, her mam had been a princess from a small country bordering Lyrill that no longer existed. For many years the two countries had been at war until her mam's country fell and was taken over by Lyrill.

Konstantin and Nikolas found Amynta in the countryside along the lake near death, and brought her into the tunnel for safety. At that time there had been a price on her life. Hawke shook his head at the similarities between mother and daughter.

"What's wrong?" Asia asked, sitting and wiping sleep from her eyes. "You look like something's bothering you."

"I just finished the last journal, these books don't tell everything, but there is enough to give you an idea of your beginnings."

She rose and sat on his lap. Cupping his face in her palms, she stared into his eyes. "It's okay. Whatever you need to tell me, it'll be okay because I have you to share it with. Who was Amynta?"

"Your mam. I'm fairly certain that's you in the portrait."

She nodded and glanced over her shoulder at the picture. "Okay, she seemed happy with me, so that's a good thing." Asia faced him. "Any mention of my sire?"

"Lord Barticus, he was from another pack, but there were a lot of suspicions about his origins. Your mam didn't want anything to do with him, he scared her. But her father beat her and… Barticus raped her."

Asia's eyes widened and she dropped her forehead to his as he repeated the tale of her mam's ordeal. When he mentioned Lyrill, her head snapped up.

"I've been there, met the princess and her father the Prime Minister. There was no king, at least I don't think so. Damn, I can't remember." She shook her head. "Raped? Does Barticus still live? Or his kin?"

The gleam in her eyes said she'd like to pay them a visit and somehow return the favor. His bitch never failed to surprise him with her ability to bounce back.

"Don't know, we can check now that we have names. One thing confuses me…"

"What?"

"Why did she leave here? Where did she go? How did you wind up with the Liege? Is she dead?" He paused and released a breath. "That's more than one, but this isn't adding up. She was safe here. This room was hidden and somehow tied to the covenant, what did that have to do with her? Or you? Konstantin knew you, at least when you were a babe, did he make special arrangements or did he die before that?"

"Good questions. Was she involved with, them? Nikolas or Konastantin or both?" She asked.

"There is little mention of the two men other than they took her in and helped her survive. She sounds grateful not like a woman in love."

Neither of them spoke.

Asia gazed at her mam's portrait and then looked at him. "I don't know if we will ever find the answers about her and these two men, but we can find answers about my mam and sire. Someone remembers her and the feud between Lyrill and her homeland." She ran her fingertip across his lip. "Just as you know the truth about your sire, I would like to know mine."

He nipped her fingertip and then sucked it in his mouth for a second. "Understood. What will we do with Damian? Does he go with us or do we send him to La Patron with Angus?"

"The holidays are coming. I'm not sure what Mistress has planned so we should take him with us, but we'll discuss it with Mistress and La Patron. What about your second pup, Gordon thought Lancaster will try and kill her."

Hawke's palm ran up and down her back in a soothing motion. "True, we will discuss that with La Patron as well. It may be that we go rescue her and return here or he may send someone to her rescue."

Asia nodded and sunk against his chest.

Hawke waited for her to say what bothered her.

"Her father beat her and gave her away, how old was she?"

He closed his eyes and swallowed, hoping she wouldn't ask. "According to her journal, Barticus took her when she was ten and four, just after... well she could, you know."

Asia stiffened. "Took her? You mean she lived with him and he just... took her whenever he wanted?"

Hearing his mate's horrified whisper made it worse for him. Barticus should be hung out to dry for what he'd done to Amynta, but that behavior was common during those times. Rather than give the answer a voice, he nodded.

"Goddess, what kind of sire does that to his daughters? I cannot imagine Renee or Jackie being given away or raped by anyone. La Patron would kill anyone who thought such a thing, so would Mistress, or Rese, or Rone, or Cam, or Angus or–"

"Or you," Hawke said, placing a kiss on her forehead. "That is not something done often today. But if her father was at war with the king of Lyrill and needed allies, then he would do whatever he thought was necessary to save his pack. Alpha's think pack first, den second."

"Not La Patron."

He smiled at the certainty in her voice. "No, but he has a special relationship with the Goddess, not all Alphas have that."

"Even without, he wouldn't give up his pups. When you know him better you'll see how he protects his den. They may not always appreciate it, but keeping his pup safe is his number one priority, all sires should feel that way."

Thinking of his sire and everything that happened, Hawke agreed.

Asia couldn't believe she had the name of her mam and sire. She offered a prayer of thanksgiving to the Goddess and peeked at the portrait again. Amynta's simple beauty was masterfully captured on the canvas, she couldn't believe their resemblance. One day soon she would read all of the journals after Hawke placed the translations in the computer and hear her mam's thoughts on life and family. Just knowing a little of her history, despite the violent beginnings, settled her.

"Mistress?"

"Asia, how are you? I've been worried, so much is happening so fast, are you okay?"

"Yes, Ma'am. Hawke finished the translations, and even though I haven't read them yet he has told me quite a bit of my history."

"Oh, Asia I am so happy for you. Tell me about it, do I need Silas?"

"It would be easier to tell you both, it's not all pretty, but that's how life falls." She then whispered to Hawke. "Listen in on this link while I talk to Mistress and La Patron."

He nodded, tightened his hold on her waist and entered the link.

"Silas is here. Go ahead," Jasmine said.

Asia and Hawke explained what they'd found and her plans to seek out more information on her mam and sire.

"I understand and you have my blessings," Jasmine spoke first and Asia smiled. No doubt La Patron wouldn't have given her a blank check to go on a personal mission now that they were in offense mode against the Liege. With the covenant broken these men would eventually die out

unless they came up with new tricks. At least they no longer had access to pack lands and wouldn't be able to take pups from dens.

"*Yes, I agree,*" La Patron said slower. "*As for your pup, I have already sent men to every location you and Angus told me about from Gordon and Lancaster. We are seeing results and have rescued some pups, not as many as I hoped but we have them on the run. The equipment we've taken and the personnel that have been arrested will set them back financially for a while. Unfortunately, I haven't gotten any of the Lords, but they've gotten the message to leave this continent, I've been very clear.*"

Asia wished she could be a part of the cleaning crew at some of those raids, but she understood the Alpha of the state would handle those jobs personally.

"*Once we find her, I'll contact you and then she can stay with us until you come home,*" Jasmine said.

Touched, Asia met Hawke's surprised gaze and smiled. "*Thank you, Mistress. I am not sure how all of this will work out. Damian is so much older and she is a small child, but I believe the Goddess is aware of everything, we will take it one day at a time.*"

"*Of course, that is the best way to look at it. When will you leave for Lyrill?*"

Asia looked at Hawke. He shrugged.

"*Within the next day or so. There is no reason to delay things. We will search the internet first, and then map our course. I want to know as much as possible about both of them before we begin.*"

"*That's good. Have you made peace with your brother, Hawke?*" Jasmine asked.

"*Yes, I sent him the code to correct his neck brace and he seems to be okay.*"

"Good."

"Any sign of Lancaster?" Asia asked.

"Not yet. I don't think he returned to the States, I have people looking for him," La Patron said. *"Angus will be returning for the holidays unless you need him."*

Asia's heart sunk a little. She would miss his counsel and presence, but she had Damian. *"We should be fine, thank you, Sir. He has a pet that is fearless."*

"Ugly you mean?" La Patron asked and then chuckled. *"He sent a picture of the thing so I would understand why he needed a private jet. After taking a look at the thing, I agreed. Alpha Radoff and Ulric assured me they would handle any remaining Liege sympathizers and are searching for Lancaster as well."*

"They are reconstructing a legitimate council again. My brother has been asked to be a charter member," Hawke said.

"So I heard and I wish them the best of luck," La Patron said. *"Asia find your answers and come home. We all miss you and want you to settle for a while."*

His kind remarks stole her voice. Surprised, she nodded and then squeaked. *"Thank you, Sir. I will."*

Hawke hugged her tight as they disconnected. Asia gazed at the happy smile on her mam's face as she looked down at the babe in her arms. Soon the gaps in her mind would be filled and complete. She'd know her history and the meaning of the birthmark that was stamped in every journal.

"Tomorrow we will search for the pearls of my past."

Sword of Justice is the next exciting book in the Sword series. Here's a peek:

Chapter 1

"This is it," Hawke said, looking at the thick copse of trees. The temperature dropped the further they traveled deeper into the Romanian forest near the Ukrainian border. Long dark shadows prevented them from seeing any signs of a town or castle or bailey. No one knew what they would find beyond this row of trees.

The air sat heavy on their shoulders, as if it carried a load. A light odor, not foul, but one he noticed and cataloged as out of the ordinary. The hair on the back of his neck rose and his skin prickled.

His wolf didn't like this place.

If it were up to him, they would leave and continue to seek concrete information about the decimated pack elsewhere. But each day they didn't find information on Amynta, Asia's mother, his mate grew more distant, despondent. She remained in her chameleon-generated male disguise twenty-four hours a day, much to his dismay, in preparation to follow new information on a moment's notice. Nothing he said made any difference, so he stopped offering suggestions and accompanied her anywhere, no matter how unlikely the results.

"The directions say this is Albuslupos, land of the White Wolf Clan, your mam's pack." He looked at the overgrown tree stumps and grass, and then at her. "Asia?" he called out to gain her attention.

She dragged her gaze from the thick foliage to meet his. "No bugs. No noise. Nothing."

Hawke looked at the brownish tint on the leaves of the trees in front of them, not quite dead, but a discernible difference to the green leaves hanging on trees behind him. Damian stood on the other side of her, nodding.

"I'm not sensing anything," Angus, littermate of Silas Knight, La Patron, said. "There's no life along this perimeter. Nothing's lived here in a long time. Even Byte's not moving toward those trees." He reached down and rubbed the blue speckled head of his new pet. Byte barked a few times and then made a purring sound while rolling on his back. "Is it possible Jacques sent us the wrong directions?" he asked Hawke.

"Anything's possible, but –"

"No." Asia said, holding her hand up. "This is it. But there's…" She moved forward. Hawke stepped up beside her. They had discussed strategy at the hotel in town. This journey would be taken together, she promised not to go roaming off on her own and he planned to hold her to it.

When she remained silent, he looked over his shoulder at Angus. The older man shrugged and stuffed his hands in his pockets while looking around. Damian had moved back, and looked up at the tall trees that blocked the sun. Shadows lengthened as if a hidden hand drew a curtain at the end of a performance.

They all looked up as the area darkened. "The only thing missing is the dreary music," Hawke said, trying to lighten the mood.

Damian and Angus chuckled.

Asia continued staring forward as if she saw something none of them did. He tapped into their link and realized she was scanning the area. Angus' declaration had been correct, but there was something… something he hadn't noticed until he piggy-backed on her scan.

Old buildings which proved the pack had lived here before. Someone went to a lot of trouble to keep that information hidden. "So this is it," he said, taking her hand.

She tightened her hold on him and stepped forward.

"Are we going in there?" Damian asked, sounding younger than his twenty years.

"Yes," Hawke said as they moved further into the dark, gloomy woods. "We saw some buildings." The air pressed against his skin, creating resistance as if he swam upstream. Each step forward became a struggle. Asia appeared immune. His grip tightened on her hand, deepening their connection.

"This place is warded," Angus said as a tingly sensation flew across Hawke's skin. He stumbled but remained standing.

"*Where'd you go?*" Angus asked him through their link.

Hawke turned and looked behind him. "*In the village, where are you?*" He and Asia retraced their steps and stopped at the edge of the forest.

"*We can't come through. Can you come back?*" Angus asked.

"*Let's try,*" Asia said when he gave her Angus' request. They returned the way they'd entered. Byte's growls grew louder as they moved through the woods.

Relieved they could leave at will, Hawke told Angus and Damian the little he'd seen. "We'll go back and search. There's a reason this is hidden, maybe we can find some answers." He tried to remain positive even though the entire place smelled like death.

"Here you'll need these." Damian handed him the satchel with the camera and video equipment. Hawke and Asia took the bags. "We'll wait for you here."

Surprised, Hawke met Damian's gaze. The past two weeks they'd had made an effort to know one another better and he thought things were going well. "Thanks. Keep your links open. I didn't sense any life in there, but you never know."

Damian nodded and watched as Hawke and Asia turned back toward the village. When she went ahead of him, he couldn't enter alone.

"*I think we have to be connected for me to go inside,*" he said through their link.

"*Oh, maybe I can bring the others in, too.*" She returned, grabbed his hand, and pulled him inside. "Let me try with Damian first. Tell them what happened and that I'm returning for them. It's better if we don't split up," she said, walking off.

Hawke agreed and explained the matter to the men.

"*It's not working,*" Asia said. "*I can't bring him across.*"

Hawke heard Damian's moan of pain through their link, and headed in the direction Asia had taken.

"I'm so sorry, Damian," Asia said, releasing his hand. "We thought since it worked for Hawke, it'd also work with you guys.

Byte barked at the trees and ran in circles while Angus looked at Damian's arm. "It's warded for those in the pack I suppose. Since this was your mom's pack, it recognizes you. And you and Hawke are one." He helped Damian sit on the ground. "Go ahead, we'll be fine. If something comes up we'll contact Hawke. Don't stay too late, I'd prefer not to be in these woods at night. We don't know who owns this land, and Silas wants us to be mindful of other packs. We can return at first light every day until you're satisfied," he said with a stern look.

The guilt in her chest eased and she nodded, anxious to explore her mother's homeland. She turned and met Hawke on the other side.

"Damian okay?" he asked, concerned.

"Yes. Angus is sitting with him as his skin heals. Have you looked around?" She waved toward the pathways and buildings beyond.

"No. Waited for you. Doing this together works both ways." He took her hand. They stepped onto a worn path and walked toward the first building. When they reached it, she noticed several others scattered about.

"Why isn't it dark in here?" she asked, looking around for the light source.

"Why isn't it overgrown with grass and vines? These buildings should've fallen down by now, but they look like they haven't aged. Are we in some kind of protective bubble?" Hawke searched for clues but didn't find any logical reason for the well-preserved condition of the village. Time seemed to have stopped, leaving everything the same as the day it was sealed.

"Look at this," Asia said, standing in the middle of what might have been a courtyard.

As he approached a large circle, possibly the center of the town, he saw two skeletal remains. One adult, the other a child.

"I wonder who they were," she said. Bending down, she looked at a chain on the child's remains. "Think this will give us a clue?" Before Hawke answered she lifted the chain and stared at the symbol of a white wolf on the locket. Asia stared at the majestic beast for a few moments and then shoved the chain into one of her pant pockets. Standing quickly, she brushed off her pants. "Let's look around. Angus wants to leave before dark. We can get an idea how big the place is and come back in the morning to keep looking."

He nodded.

She appreciated his support. Lately she hadn't been the most wifely mate, but she wanted answers and the delays wore on her nerves. Rather than lash out, she reined in her tattered emotions and kept quiet, keeping her thoughts to herself.

"Which one do you want to start in?" He waved at the single level crude stone dwellings. She looked at all the buildings, some had wood doors, a few had openings in the exterior walls that may have served as windows, giving them a homey feel.

There were several outdoor cooking areas, a water well, and drainage system. She reasoned the alpha would have lived in the largest house and continued her search. Starting in the place where her mother had lived appealed to her.

One stood further back and overlooked the other buildings. It had two windows and an image of a wolf carved into the large wooden door. She pointed. "That one." They headed toward the large stone building. Asia counted ten other structures before they reached their destination. The large door opened easily. She tapped down her excitement at hopefully learning more of her past, well, her family's roots. Not some made up story from the Liege, but real facts about her mam. How and where she'd lived. Asia breathed deeply and then coughed. The musty interior was darker than the outside. Hawke pulled a halogen lamp from his bag and set it in the middle of the room.

"This was the Alpha's house," she said softly, thinking of the man who'd beat his daughter and then gave her to

Lord Barticus, Asia's sire. The stone walls were cold and uninviting. The large fireplace doubled as a stove, heavy cast iron pots hung in the hearth.

"Ahh, now this is nice." Hawke stood beneath a large tapestry of a group of white wolves. Ruby red blood dripped from the teeth of the largest wolf, giving insight about the pack. "Would you like to take that?"

She continued staring, wondering what kind of man Alpha Bertoff had been. Although Hawke had explained the mindset of men in that era, plus the responsibility of the entire pack, and she could understand times had been hard. But not hard enough to give away your kid to some sex-starved pervert. She wouldn't ever grasp that.

"No." She turned and walked through each room, taking a journey through time. What a difference a century and a half made. In every room, she wondered if her mam had spent time in there or maybe in the one across the hall. None of the rooms looked inviting for a young girl. There were no female clothes or toiletries, nothing that suggested Amynta had roamed these halls.

Frowning, Asia stood in the great room and looked around. For some inexplicable reason she knew her mother had not spent much time in this house, it lacked warmth. But where then? They explored three more buildings before finding an old book half-buried in the ground with her mother's name written on it. The building was small. Three mats lay next to each other on the ground. There were old, ragged dresses hanging on pegs in the wall near the mats.

"This looks like the servants' quarters," Asia said, touching the material reverently. Hawke flipped through pages of the book and then handed it to her.

"She doesn't say much in this book. Someone may have given it to her and she never got a chance to write anything."

Asia's fingertip traced the leather cover and then the gold inlaid letters of her mother's name. Her throat tightened with the sure knowledge she had found her roots. Good or bad, she now knew where she came from, which made a world of difference. Now she could begin coloring inside the lines of her history.

"White Wolf Clan."

"What?" Hawke said from the other side of the room. The construction of the buildings and how well they'd been preserved fascinated him. Someone had warded the area to keep out intruders, but they didn't understand why.

"That's the name of my mother's clan." Her voice held a ring of pride.

"Yes, it is." He moved toward her and stopped. "Shit, we've got to move."

Asia stared at him and didn't like the sharp furrowing of his brow. "What?"

Jaw clenched, he looked at her. "Angus and Damian were arrested for trespassing and are headed to Lyrill."

Hello,

Thank you for taking the time to read the second book in the La Patron's Sword series. I love paranormal books and characters in general and shifter stories in particular. Throw in the romantic element, strong Alpha characters who bend beneath the power of love and I'm over the moon. Sighs…

In her quest to learn her past, Asia bumps into her future. The Liege is stealing black wolf pups for research. Silas Knight, La Patron, has four black pups in his den and is determined to stop the Liege before they attempt to take his pups. Asia and Hawke are chosen to discover the Liege's plans and shut it down. First Asia must learn to t978-1-937334-65-9rust someone other than Jasmine. Next she must merge with Hawke as a cohesive unit to infiltrate and take down the Lancaster Castle which belongs to the Liege. The Liege refuses to go down without a fight. They have been operating for centuries and have no intention of stopping, even if two of their most prized products are the ones gunning for them.

You're invited to journey with me through all the books in this series. If you like fast paced action, suspense and great love connections like me, you won't be disappointed. Feel free to drop me a line, SydneyAddae@msn.com or join my Facebook group, La Patron's Den, where discussions regarding Silas and the Wolf nation abound. Also you can find me at my website, SydneyAddae.com.

Knight Chronicles is a newsletter for my Readers Group from the characters of the series to keep you informed of what's going on in the Wolf Nation. Each issue has a personal message from Silas Knight, La Patron, or his mate, Jasmine. Character profiles with in-depth interviews and thoughts you won't find anywhere else. Also works in progress, new releases and special give-aways in every issue. If you would like to receive **Knight Chronicles** click this sign up link! Thank you. (http://eepurl.com/bb3csz)

La Patron, the Alpha's Alpha is my first paranormal series and I'd like to ask a favor. When you finish reading, **please leave a review**, whatever your opinion, I assure you I appreciate it.

The following books are in the La Patron Series, enjoy!

Thanks again

BirthRight
BirthControl
BirthMark
BirthStone
BirthDate
BirthSign
Sword of Inquest
Sword of Mercy
Sword of Justice
La Patron's Christmas
La Patron's 2nd Christmas
KnightForce 1
KnightForce Deuces
KnightForce Tres'
KnightForce – Damian
KnightForce - Ethan

Booksets
La Patron Series Books 1-6
La Patron Series Books 4-6